HOW
TO
SPIN
GOLD

HOW TO
SPIN GOLD

A Novel

Elizabeth Cunningham

Epigraph
A Division of Monkfish Book Publishing Company
Rhinebeck, New York

Contact the publisher for information:
Epigraph Books
A Division of Monkfish Book Publishing Company
27 Lamoree Road
Rhinebeck, N.Y. 12572

Printed in The United States of America.
Cover illustration is adapted from a Walter Crane illustration of Rumpelstilkin
Cover & text design and author photograph by Georgia Dent

Library of Congress Cataloging-in-publication Data (previous edition)
Cunningham, Elizabeth, 1953-
      How to spin gold : a woman's tale / Elizabeth Cunningham.
        p.   cm.
      ISBN-978-0-9824530-2-5
      I. Title.
PS3553.U473H69 1997
813".54---dc21   96-51167
                                                          CIP

Bulk purchase discounts for educational or promotional purposes are available.

For my son and my daughter
Julian and Marina
for their inspiration and astute reading
of this story

Take the dung and make it flower,
Take the pain and make it power,
Let your own fear make you bold,
Take the straw and spin, spin, spin the gold.

The Story of The Story

IN LATE APRIL, 1983, almost nine months pregnant with my first child, I put was on bed rest for high blood pressure. A late spring snow and ice storm knocked out the electricity and flattened daffodils and early tulips, which my husband brought inside before he had to go away for the weekend. I can still hear the silence of the house. I can feel the heaviness of my belly, resting in the trough of the foldout couch. I can see the brilliant red and yellow of the flowers. In my memory, I still watch them, translucent with the snow light shining through the window, slowly tracking the movement of the sun.

I wrote a poem about that day, long since lost. But it was because of that day and the poem, gold spun out of the dross of bed rest, discomfort, and inconvenience, that I ditched a novel that wasn't going anywhere and began to write *How to Spin Gold*. First I thought I was writing a short poem, and then a short story. Soon the story evolved into a novel-length fairytale, albeit the shortest novel I have written—perhaps because it was written during my childbearing years. Three weeks after I began writing, my son was born. I completed the novel in the autumn of 1986, six months after my daughter was born.

(When they were older, I read *How to Spin Gold* aloud to them in manuscript, and they asked me to re-name two of the characters for them, which I happily did. Trust me: their names are an improvement over the originals.)

In preparing this new edition, I re-read *How to Spin Gold* for the first time in many years. I was struck by the intensity and detail of the birth scenes. I owe a huge debt of gratitude to my midwife, Angela Colclough, who supported me through both my pregnancies and who generously shared her expertise and wisdom as I wrote this book.

I am pleased to note that I seem to have done a great deal of research on life in feudal times. For the herbal lore, I remember consulting the books of John Lust. Cindy Thayer of Darthia Farms in Gouldsboro, Maine, a fiber artist and novelist, was an invaluable source of information on the arts of spinning, dyeing and weaving.

As for the realm of fairytale, from which I never stray too far in any of my novels, I thank my late mother, Emily Meeker Cunningham, for reading aloud to us fairytales and works inspired by fairytales.

For those who are interested in chronology, *How to Spin Gold* is the third novel I wrote, following *The Wild Mother* and a second novel that was never published. Not long after I finished it, I began to write *The Return of the Goddess, A Divine Comedy*. Although *How to Spin Gold* features a wise woman, I had no knowledge at that time of a revival of interest in feminine divinity or archetypes—though during the writing I began to notice my proclivities in that direction.

How to Spin Gold was my first foray into the use of the first person narrative voice. It is a fairytale voice from another time, unlike Maeve's deliberately anachronistic voice in THE MAEVE CHRONICLES. I like both voices, and I believe there is connection between them. This voice had to be heard before Maeve's could emerge.

Enough said. Now let the one who has told her name to no one, not even me, spin her own tale.

BOOK ONE

THE GIRL
with the
SILVER EYE

CHAPTER ONE

I HAVE TOLD MY NAME TO NO ONE: no, not even uttered it in some exultant frenzy. That part of the tale is a lie. Once there was one who knew my name: she who named me. Now there is no one; nor will there be anyone until I so choose. For my name is my secret, my wealth, my power.

Another lie they told, she told: that I am a man, despised, misshapen. Like that name, so hideous I cannot bear to write it. I am a woman. Like her. Not like her. For I have nothing, and she has all: a fair face that, with my help, has brought her fame and fortune, not that I care for those. It is what she has stolen that maddens me: my love, my child, and now, it seems, she means to rob me of the valor of my one great deed. I never minded that the miracle should remain unknown. I never sought the world's acclaim. But that she should publish abroad this thrice-cursed ballad, this mangled tale that makes a mockery of my name, my person, my virtue, my very life.

I am resolved to write the truth on such parchment as I may find, though few hereabouts can read, and fewer still will care. What other recourse have I? She is the highest lady in the land, while I, though reputed to have powers I know I do not possess, have always been an outcast. Perhaps, though my words be neither Holy Writ nor philosophy, I might employ some monk or scribe to make a fair copy of my story. Then I will send it forth throughout the land. But first I must spin the tale from its bitter beginning to whatever bitter end awaits.

I WAS YET ANOTHER DAUGHTER in a house of daughters, though you could scarcely call our leaky hovel that hovered at the village edge a house. My mother and father were cotters, like their parents before them and theirs before them. Having no land to till, we lived on sufferance mostly, though there were ways to earn the pennies my father spent on drink—mole catching, water carrying, and the like. Our grain we got from gleaning, and at various times of the year, there were wild foods to forage: roots, mushrooms, nuts, the latter forbidden, being reserved for swine and for the wild boar, a royal quarry. Nor were common folk allowed to fish or trap, though nearly everyone did. Our family had not even the status of villains, but my sisters and I did join in the common employments of village children, such as chasing pigeons at seed-sowing time, raking and turning the new-mown hay, thus earning a crust of bread or a bowl of stew from time to time.

But I make no complaint of poverty; it was the common lot. In truth our village was more prosperous than some, for it was the market town. The King himself was our overlord, and though he imposed heavy taxes and fines to support the wars he was fond of waging, we had many tradesmen who enjoyed royal patronage. Thus, our village had more free-flowing coin than most. We even had a money-lender, though he was near as despised as I.

Yes, despised. I might well have lived and bred and died without much ado save that I was born with certain features of face and limb that set me apart from birth: a mark the color of dried blood in the shape of the crescent moon on my left cheek, a left leg that was shriveled, though serviceable. I could walk well enough for all that I limped, and I needed no crutch. Deformity was common enough among the poor, and I might have been looked upon as one of God's afflicted had it not been for the third of my remarkable features. My left eye does not match my right, an ordinary brown. Instead it is silver—or so folk called it. It was the nearest they could come to describing a quality more like that of water, without any color, yet able to reflect all colors.

This sinister trinity—left cheek, left leg, left eye—combined to convince folk that I was in high favor with the Fiend, who was known to be left-handed, even as I was. The village priest, for all his ample girth, was morally a slender reed who bent to the strongest wind. He did nothing to dispel popular superstition; nor did he argue with my parents when, disgusted at having yet another undowered daughter and a grotesque one at that, they refused to choose a name for me. Thus I went on the parish rolls as "girl, daughter of Sim, molecatcher and wife, Joan."

Namelessness merely increased suspicion of me. Many believed that, without a name, my cursory baptism could not have had the desired effect. Perhaps they were right. My bodily peculiarities seemed natural enough to me, and in time I learned to use the power they gave me. But to have no name filled me with a shame and misery I could never for a moment forget. More than anything it was the taunt of namelessness that taught me to hate.

I must, in honesty, record that, except for their great cruelty in denying me a name, my parents treated me indifferently. Indeed, I must credit them for feeding and sheltering me when many, I later learned, counseled them to turn me loose as a beggar. Nor were my sisters either kind or unkind. No one beat me. I believe they were too afraid to touch me. When there was food to be had, no one withheld it from me.

As I grew beyond infancy, my sisters discovered that I could be useful; for I had clever fingers and a cleverer eye—my silver one no doubt. I could take the plainest work-a-day shift and, with a tuck here and a gather there, change its shape. Then I would take thread idly spun in odd moments, not just from flax or wool but from anything I might find: thistledown, milkweed, the golden hairs from the manes and tails of the King's horses that birds used to line their nests. With these I would embroider birds and beasts and flowers to rival any found in the margins of monkish scrolls. Mock jewelry I made, too, from feathers, seeds, and nutshells, which I tied around my sisters' necks or waists or wove into their hair.

Yet all that I made was so subtly wrought that no one noticed anything unusual in my sisters' apparel. Indeed, the wonder of my work was that it drew the eye not to itself but to the one it adorned. My sisters were pretty girls, but in a placid, undistinguished way, one not much different from another nor from any of the local maids. I had the knack of seeing what each one might have been had something stirred her sluggish soul. When I trimmed a gown, I called forth that hidden being. All my sisters married well and above their station, one the smith's son, another the carpenter's. Several married sons of the more prosperous villains, and one even married a freeman. No one guessed that it was I who dowered them with brief, uncommon beauty.

I was content enough in such solitary pursuits, and when I could escape the round of common work, I delighted in roaming beyond the village walls, wandering through field and hedgerow and along the edge of the great Western Wood. No one, not the swineherd nor yet the boldest poacher, ventured too deep into the forest unless he had dire need. For all that it was the King's Wood, the common folk for miles about knew full well that it was the dwelling place of the one called Wise Woman or Mother to her face; behind her back or in stories round the fire of an evening: Witch.

She alone of all the folk I knew, old or young, did I fear. I was not afraid, as other children were, that she might turn me into a toad or bake me into a pie or suck the marrow of my bones while I slept. No, I feared the way she looked at me, as though she knew me, as though we shared some secret. I had seen her often enough on market days when she came from the Wood to sell her wares. But unlike the other children, who played a game of dares to see who could come closest and escape unscathed, I always kept my distance. I wanted no kinship with a witch.

It was on my forays into countryside and woodland that I gathered the materials for my handiwork as well as other things that pleased me: evergreen cones, abandoned birds' eggs, and pebbles from the shallows of the river that rushed past our village, turning the mill wheel, then meandering more leisurely through the fields and finally out of sight into the Wood. Some of these pebbles I tried to pass off to the other children as gold in a vain attempt to buy friendship. But their fear of the evil spells with which my proffered treasures must be riddled overcame both curiosity and greed. I must confess that when my gestures of goodwill were scorned, I often flew in anger and incanted mock maledictions that sounded real enough, even to me.

I early learned that my surest revenge on my fellow creatures was to command the fear and revulsion I seemed to inspire whether I willed it or not. Nor did I stop at words. I had a habit of hiding in hedges at the twilight hour, when weary folk wended their way home from the fields, and strewing snakes in their path. Once, carefully gloving my own hands, I got some stinging nettles and concealed them beneath my apron. Then I put myself in the way of a crowd of children—they were always bolder in numbers—and when they dutifully began to taunt and menace me, I thrashed their bare arms and legs with the nettles, taking great satisfaction in the boils and welts I raised.

Yet I found no lasting ease in these acts of petty vengeance. Solitude was my balm and my refuge, and so I often sought it, but I truly I believe I am not a solitary by nature. Despite repeated rebuffs, I longed to be companionable and was eaten up with envy at the sight of other children and their games.

Of these, the May revels were the maddest and the gayest. It was on a May Day that yet shimmers in my memory, though by now it should be dull as tarnished silver, that I first saw her—or rather that she first saw me. Let me say her name and be done with it, though it is bitter to me now as it was sweet then. Aurelie. Aurelie, the miller's daughter. But I must do more than remember. Let me live that moment, as I lived it then, with no foreknowledge of what was to come.

Aurelie was of about my own years, maybe a season or two older. But where I was yet a child with a body no different from a boy's, she had crossed that mysterious boundary and entered the lush country of womanhood. She had never played much with the other children, for her father, though a villain like the rest, was prosperous and had an overweening pride in his only child. Aurelie's mother had died with her babe in her second childbirth, and her father had never taken another wife. The more charitable of his neighbors claimed that he yet grieved for Aurelie's mother, but it was common knowledge that his daughter had always been his one great passion.

Her father had allowed her, that day, to be crowned Queen of the May. No doubt he deemed it just that she should be thus honored. So did everyone else. None of the usual rivalries ensued. It was plain to all that God and nature had set her apart. Her reign merely began that day. Throughout her maidenhood, she was always May Queen, Queen of Midsummer, of Harvest, of Twelfth Night. Let me see her as she appeared then: tall and straight and slender, like ripe wheat, her hair red-geld as befitted one named for the dawn, her head wreathed with violets and myrtle that, with her gown blue as the Virgin's mantle, made her grey eyes look deep and dark as the heavens on a clear night.

She had just finished leading us in the great dance round the May pole. Yes, even I was among the dancers. For a moment, she stood still in the midst of a crowd milling with May madness, her cheeks becomingly flushed. I do not know if, in truth, she was taller than all the rest. To me she towered, a goddess. I could see nothing and no one else, nor ever wished to. Before then a fair face had no meaning to me, save that by fortune's whimsy it was not mine. But here was no mere passing prettiness. Before me stood Beauty, perfection that made Aurelie different from all others, just as I was different in distortion. Here was not just another person, but my eternal opposite, a magic glass that gave me back myself transformed.

Or so I felt that day as I moved through the crowd, drawn by irresistible force. I did not know what I would do or say, only that I must go to her. My hands in my pockets, working in feverish excitement, encountered the latest treasure I had secreted there. I knew, with joy, that here was a worthy gift. The outside curve of this wondrous object was a rough grey-white, but the inner curve shone, smooth, shimmering, aglow with all colors, like water in certain lights, like my left eye.

To a child who lived by the sea, what I know now to be a shell might not have seemed so rare a gift. But the hills and valleys through which our river ran were a long journey from that vast body of water. I do not know how the shell came to lie in the fallow field where I found it. Perhaps it was carried there by some storm-blown bird. Then I did not even know the name of the thing I clutched in my sweating palm, only that it was the finest thing I had ever possessed and that I must offer it, the gift of my unnamed self.

I cut a swath through the crowd—as I have remarked, folk feared my touch.

Then I stood before her, wordless, my hand outstretched, the shell quivering like some strange live thing. Had Aurelie refused me at that moment, I would have ceased to exist. She did not.

She turned her gaze on me, and I looked into eyes that showed nothing of fear, nor of distaste, nor yet of pity. I read her look, rightly or wrongly, as one of recognition. Ah, she knows me, sang my pounding heart. Hope sprang from nothing into full, wild flower. Now, now she will speak my name! But she said nothing, only looked down at the shell in my hand. I had no need to explain. She understood the gesture at once and received the shell calmly as homage due her.

Yet I did not go unrewarded. I watched her as she examined the shell, and I saw her smile. I like to think she smiled with sheer delight, forgetting for a moment her high station. Then, slipping the shell into her pocket, she bestowed that smile upon me. I knew a moment's bewildering joy, such as the blind must know when restored to sudden sight or the lame when they rise to take that first brave step. The world I knew fell away, and I found myself in some strange and dazzling place. Then someone beckoned her, and she turned away from me that fiery head, those seeing eyes, and I knew once more where I was.

Save that now my small world had a center.

CHAPTER TWO   ·

I NEVER CAME SO CLOSE TO AURELIE AGAIN, not while we were maidens in our native village. Indeed, I made no attempt. For what if, another time, she failed to know me or worse outright scorned me. I would not risk it. Though the memory of that look, that smile remained chief among my treasures, making my material hoardings paltry by comparison, time diminished the first intensity of fascination. Nor could observation of her life, which despite her extraordinary beauty would doubtless follow the time-worn course of marriage and child-bearing, ease my growing restlessness and discontent.

What life was there for me? Undowered and deformed, I could hardly hope for marriage. In our village, save for widows, unmarried women above a certain age or without a hearth mate (for not all bothered with the Church's rites) were unheard of.

It was my parents who pressed the matter and forced me to take action when they announced they were giving up the lease to their cottage and moving into the household of one of my married sisters. There was no question of my keeping the lease, for it had already been given over to the bee-keeper, who thought the location of our cottage more propitious for his trade. Thus, my hope that I might bide there, setting myself up as a needle woman, had to be discarded. My parents scoffed at the very idea. Who, they argued, would allow the clothing that covered her body to be touched by me? Should I manage to get some trade, I would be blamed for every miscarriage, every outbreak of wart or ague. My parents did not seem overly concerned for my fate, feeling they had more than done their duty by me, and they had nothing to suggest but that I seek out some sister and beg sustenance in exchange for servitude.

I lay awake that night listening to my parents snore and watching moonbeams probe the chinks in our roof. It came to me that I might as well cast my lot with the wanderers of the earth and beg my bread if I be not allowed to earn it. Or better yet I would subsist on wild foods, beholden to none but nature. It was then full summer, and though I knew I might not survive the winter, the knowledge lacked potency. At that moment, not hungry and in health, I deemed myself not so attached to life that I would seek to prolong it in service to some grudging sister. I was not wholly impractical. Before I set forth, I packed such food as I could find and took the stoutest cloak.

Thus fortified, I slipped away, heading for a certain tree in the old orchard that could be relied upon to give me a lift over the wall. Then I found the river, having no other plan than to follow where it might lead. By the moon's light, without so much as a backward glance, I left all that I knew: my parents, my village, my childhood. So gossamer was my tie to all that was now past, I scarcely felt the break.

Why should I? Only Aurelie, of all those I dwelt among for so long, had ever known the unnamed me. Her memory I carried within me; I no longer needed to attach it to her person. I was done with my own kind, I told myself. Like Job of the Holy Writ, whose tale was sometimes enacted by traveling players, I would be sister to dragons, companion to owls.

Well before daybreak, I had followed the river into the Wood, not without some trepidation, but I was reassured to find the river shared my qualms and ran close to the Wood's edge. On climbing the steep slope that rose from the river's bank, I could see clear of the trees to the fields that lay like a vast dry lake in the moonlight surrounding the Castle—for so I guessed the massive darkness that loomed atop the highest hill to be. It looked like a star-swallowing monster with blazing eyes and nostrils, though these I reckoned to be the torches of the Watch. Tomorrow, I vowed, I would put the Castle, too, behind me. I returned to the stream and drank deeply, resolving not to break my bread until hunger drove me to. Then I curled up beneath the cloak on the driest leaves I could find and went to sleep.

I cannot have been sleeping long when a rumbling sound disturbed me.

Though I was new to life in the open, already animal instinct stirred, and I was instantly alert to danger. Listening intently, I discerned hoofbeats, the baying of hounds, the blast of a horn all confirming the likelihood of a hunt nearby, but not so near as to give me cause for immediate concern. Indeed, as I waited in the disrupted dawn, the sound of the hunt grew more distant. Assured that I was not about to be trampled, I allowed myself to sink once more onto the leaves where I dozed uneasily for a time.

Then suddenly—so close it seemed as though it all happened inside my own skull- a horse's scream, a human cry, the snapping of branches and bracken, and a thud that resounded throughout my being. Wrenched awake, trembling with fright, I stared at the form of a youth, lying only a hare's leap away from me.

At first I took him to be dead, and dread of death held me still as a small wild creature that fears to move lest flight draw his enemy upon him. Then I perceived his breathing and crept closer. His features were rounded, gentle as a babe's. The hair on his cheeks and chin, meant for a man's beard, was yet golden and downy for all the hair on his head was so dark. I felt a great curiosity to know the color of his eyes, yet I feared that he should wake and look on me with horror. Somehow I resisted the impulse to steal away, for a stronger urge bade me stay to tend and protect this boy-man.

I tore a strip of fabric from my skirt and went to the stream to wet it. Returning to his side, I bathed the scratches that abounded on his face and arms. Gingerly, I felt his bones to know if any were broken. Then what I so dreaded and desired occurred: he opened large, drowsy eyes of hazy, golden green, like sunlight filtered through thick leaves. The eyes showed bewilderment but no fear as they looked into mine.

"Who are you?" he wondered.

"No one."

I felt the answer to be truthful but then considered it might not be helpful to one already in a daze.

"You fell from your horse," I explained. "Likely you were stunned. I chanced to be nearby. I cannot tell how badly you are hurt. Are you in pain?"

"Not much."

He moved tentatively, wincing as he sat up.

"My left arm and shoulder seem to be sprained," he concluded, smiling ruefully. "Just my luck to be left-handed."

"Ah, but that has been my luck, too!" I exclaimed, and for the first time it did seem lucky. For was it not a sign, evidence of some bond between this boy and me? Then, embarrassed by my eagerness, I added hurriedly, "Let me make a sling for your arm."

Before he could protest, I tore my skirt again, revealing my legs nearly to the knees, so that my shriveled limb was in evidence. I could feel the heat of shame, such as another might feel at nakedness, beginning in my face, spilling through my body.

My efforts to bind his arm could only be described as clumsy. Not only did I lack skill, but never before had I been so close to another's body. Though I did not touch his skin, I could feel the warmth of his flesh through his garments. All this was such a wonder to me, I had to exert more will than I knew I possessed to keep my fingers from trembling. Yet when I sat back and dared steal a look at his face, I found him smiling on me.

Even then, with no vast experience, I knew: some smiles mask; his revealed.

He could not, like Aurelie, bestow a smile. His smile bestowed him, gave him away utterly. The one who beheld such a smile could but reject or receive that gift. And I received. How gratefully, how joyfully, how fearfully I received. For I had nothing to give in return. I dared not even smile; for my face was unused to such contortions and might appear merely grotesque.

"I do not mean to rejoice in your misfortune," he said, "but I confess it eases me to meet another who favors what my father calls the sinister. Yet you seem in no way hindered by your left-handedness, while I am forever bumbling. My father has tried and tried from my earliest youth to force me to use my right, but I fear I am incorrigible," he sighed. "Father will be vexed that I have fallen from my horse again. He is such a fine horseman, himself. What is more, I greatly fear that I am lost as well. My horse has bolted, and I haven't a clue as to where I am or which direction I should take."

My curiosity and sympathy mounted with his every word. Here, it seemed, was one who had suffered, even as I had, despite his pleasing appearance and clothes which, dirty and torn as they were, suggested he was well-born.

"Where do you live?" I asked. "Perhaps I can tell you how to get back." He hesitated for a moment.

"I come from the Castle."

That explained his clothes; he was doubtless the son of one of the King's retainers. I stifled an impulse to laugh. The castle was so near! But then likely his fall had befuddled him. I must not mock him.

"It's not far. I will take you there myself."

As I spoke, a plan began to form in my mind, and the thought of solitary wandering lost all allure. Surely at the Castle, a big and bustling place, there might be work for someone with deft fingers. I would toil in the kitchens or scrub the garderobes if I could only be near this sweet youth. Just near him, so that I could glimpse him from time to time, for I had no illusion that there could be anything between us beyond this moment.

"Can you walk, do you think? Come," I beckoned.

I gave him my hands and helped him to his feet. Then I slipped my arm about him and bade him rest some of his weight on me. Slowly we made our way up the slope.

"But you are hurt yourself," he protested, detecting my limp.

"No," I answered. "It is only that one leg is shorter than the other and has been from my birth. I'm accustomed to it."

"Who are you?" he asked again when we paused to rest at the top of the hill.

"I want to know you by name, so that I may thank you properly. I swear I'll tell no one, if for some reason your name must be kept secret."

I felt a hot pricking sensation behind my eyes that I know now was the beginning of tears. Before then, with all my unhappiness, I had never wept.

"I would tell you my name if I could." I spoke with difficulty. "But I have no name."

I never thought to invent one for convenience sake. A name, a true name, must be given.

"No name!" He sounded grieved for me. "But that is not right!"

My heart beat hard. Now he will grant me a name. I know. It is for this that our paths have crossed.

I waited. When he spoke again he only queried, "Why do you have no name? Are you an orphan?"

I considered saying that I was. It would have been a neater explanation. But there was something about this boy, his simplicity, his trustfulness, that encouraged confidence.

"It's only that my parents had too many daughters. They were angry at yet another. Then, too," I added shyly, "they found me peculiar, because of my eye and all."

I felt that heat in my cheeks again, and I cast my eyes to the ground. Never before had I invited scrutiny.

"Oh but I like your eye. Do let me see it better."

I could refuse him nothing. I met his gaze. I felt the warmth of it penetrate my very bowels.

"It keeps changing color," he marveled, delighted as a child. "It's like a rainbow in a pool. Does it let you see things others cannot?"

"I don't know," I mumbled, ecstatic and embarrassed to an excruciating degree. "I have never thought so."

"Where are you bound?" he asked, and we began to walk once more.

I longed to put my arm about him again, but he no longer seemed to need my help.

"To seek my fortune in the wide world," I replied. "And since you are bound for the Castle I will accompany you there. You have had a bad fall and may feel faint before you reach the gate. As it happens," I added, "I am a skilled needle woman. Do you think I might find work at the Castle to keep me for a time?"

To my astonishment, my companion stopped abruptly. Taking my shoulders in his hands, he turned me towards him.

"You must not go to the Castle." He spoke with an earnestness I could not comprehend. "Particularly not in my company."

"If you do not wish ...." I stammered in dismay.

"It's not my wishes that matter. I like you very well. Seldom have I felt so happy and at ease with another. It's my father."

"I don't understand," I said.

Nor wished to. My greedy heart had seized upon those words 'I like you,' and I wished to hear nothing else.

"If you were with me when I returned," he spoke slowly, "everyone would see. They would tell my father. He would blame you for my fall. He is always seeking some explanation for why I am not as he would have me."

What he said aroused in me mixed passions. I was accustomed to being blamed for catastrophe, yet it hurt to know that this boy, who had seemed to regard me as but another fellow creature, had guessed that others would not see me so. Yet if he knew that most looked on me as a freak, was it not all the more wonderful that he did not? Then there was this father. I disliked the man intensely, sight unseen. Let him blame me for what he would. I longed to defy him.

"I care nothing for that!"

Could it be that I actually tossed my head? I only know that despite my marred face, my uncanny eye, my mud-colored hair, my uneven limbs, I felt, for an instant, as beautiful and strong and bright as Aurelie.

"Blame has been mine since birth, even as my limp. Neither can hinder me. If you are ready, come."

I turned towards the castle. Boldly I took his arm. He liked me. Had he not said so? But for all he was so slightly built and weak from his fall, I could not make him budge.

"You do not understand," he said. "My father—"

I made a ludicrous attempt to stamp the foot of my foreshortened leg in my rage at that phrase 'my father.' I was beginning to loathe the man.

"Your father! Your father! Just who is your father that I should fear him?" Even as I raised my voice, he lowered his.

"My father is the King."

I felt the high color in my cheeks drain away. Here I was, face to face with the Prince of the realm. Only a moment ago I had shouted at him as if I were his equal.

"Oh, why did you make me tell you," he moaned. "It was so delightful to be with someone, even for a little while, who thought me but a fellow being. That is why I did not tell you my name. When people know who I am, all they see is the King's son, the Prince, what I ought to be, that is, what they want me to be. Not who I am."

"Forgive me, Julian." I deliberately called him by his christened name and not by his title. My hand reached for his without my leave. "Believe me," I spoke slowly, groping for words, "I know what it is to be unseen. I swear I see you as yourself."

And you see me, I told him silently.

"I will come with you," I declared, refusing to remind him of his highness by asking permission. "Your father cannot frighten me."

"I forbid you," he said, assuming, all of a sudden, his royal role. "My father in a rage is unpredictable. He might even kill you."

"I tell you I don't care. I—"

"And if did he spare your life, he would never permit you to remain at the castle. The least of his servants must be ... " he hesitated, plainly pained at what he had to say, " ... perfect."

For love of him—yes, I knew by then that it was love—I looked at him and did not flinch.

"Only I, of all he possesses, lack perfection." He sighed again and turned away, beginning to walk. "He blames my mother for my weakness. Hard a man as he has become, I believe he loved her and has never forgiven her for dying. She died of me, you know. Folk wonder why he does not marry and get more heirs. I am not considered hardy, you see. Yet he will have none of marriage and turns to women only for sport.

"War is more to his liking." Julian shuddered. "I believe, even now, he is stirring up trouble in the borderlands so that he may take me into battle. He has some near mystic belief that when I'm blooded, as he puts it, I will magically become a man after his own image. Then will he see to my marriage. He says I am too unmanly now to foist upon a lusty wench. For he has in mind no princess, for all he would enlarge his holdings, but intends to search the land for the most perfect among the peasant stock—in order to strengthen the royal breed, he says."

I wanted to hear no more. What he told me of his father sickened me. Better the man had been kennel master than king.

Nor had he more to say. We walked in silence for a time, the heat of day beginning to penetrate the leafy cover of the Wood. Within my breast was yet greater heat, born of the struggle that ensued there. I yearned to say to him: Come with me. You need not go back. Come let's run away, far away, where we may both be free.

Yet strange as it may seem, I found I loved him too well to beseech him so. I knew, with the knowledge of love—for true love is not blind but sees all and forgives—that he was weak, though I loved him no less for that. And I had not the power to make him strong. He would long to go, and he would be afraid. Ever after he would wonder: what if I had? He was already so beset with doubts, I could not wish another upon him.

We reached the edge of the Wood and paused together, looking out on the fields. Some distance away peasants labored, scything the second growth of hay. I felt rather than saw him turn towards me, and like a plant to light, I turned to him.

"So we must part ways here, Girl with the Silver Eye. Blessings on your way."

"And on yours," I murmured, though his, I thought with sudden bitterness, was all too well charted.

But my bitterness turned all to sweetness as I looked once more into the green warmth of his eyes. So we stood for a time I cannot reckon, exchanging the gift of sight.

Then he did what no one else has done before or since, and, after all these years, all that has passed, the memory of that moment is still warm to the touch: he took me in his arms and kissed me full on the lips.

Before I could cry out or cling, he turned away and left me alone in the Wood.

I watched him make his halting way across the fields. Soon a sturdy peasant—too perfect in build to fear the King—offered him a ride in a cart. Even at a distance I could detect the clumsiness with which he clambered onto the cart, and my heart was sore for him.

With all my might, I willed him to look back. Just once. He did not, and soon he was lost to my sight.

CHAPTER THREE

STUNNED BY SUDDEN JOY AND GRIEF, I stood where I was as the sun climbed to its full height, scorching the earth and all who labored there. I stood as one of the trees, unmoved, unmoving, not stirred by so much as a breeze or a thought. I do not know what was in my mind. Likely I hoped to take root and remain where the love of my life had come and gone. I stood, and my shadow followed the shadow of the trees as they swung full circle to stretch out behind me, pointing the way to the deep Wood. Still, I gazed stupidly towards the Castle, and its huge shadow moved nearer, menacing, as if it would blot me out if I did not depart its domain.

At last, my body, impatient with my mind and compelled by the urgency of its needs, turned me abruptly from my useless vigil and brought me back to the stream, where it insisted I drink, then eat. Though I yielded to these corporal demands, I resented them profoundly, for I could find no reason for my continued existence. Yet I welcomed the stupor that followed this refreshment, and I sank into sleep as a millstone into a still pond, my last thought a wish that I might never wake again.

I did, of course, with the light of the just waning moon beaming merciless on my face. The wily moon seemed to know her way into the Wood better than the sun did and had sought me there on purpose to make a mockery of me with the cool loveliness of her light: light that gladdened the hearts of fortunate lovers. I returned the moon's stare angrily. I had woken in a rage, and, for lack of a better object, directed this passion towards the moon. I could not turn my fury on my beloved, though, in truth, it was he who had undone me. I believed I had perfectly resigned myself to a life bereft of human love and comfort. Now all my hard lessons were unlearned, my bitter strength laid waste.

Restless, unable to return to sleep, I rose and began to follow the stream once more, vowing that if I had not died of natural causes before I reached the sea, I would hurl myself into the water that foamed and churned—so I had heard tell—with a power a thousand times greater than the mill wheel. For a time, anger gave me great vigor, but as I walked, stumbling in my foolish haste, anger ebbed and desolation seeped in to take its place. Near dawn, wearied with pain both of body and soul, I sank in my tracks and allowed myself the comfort of leaning against a small boulder.

It was an extraordinarily comforting rock, strangely soft and yielding, warm. Warm! I snatched myself from the drowsy ease that was stealing over

me. Rocks are not warm save when they've been drenched for hours in sunlight, and the sun had not yet risen. My body went rigid; my eyes opened
as if they would never close again. I drew away from the rock and forced
myself to look.

At first what I saw maintained the appearance of a small, gray boulder, covered with moss and lichen in varying shades. I wondered if the
warmth that had seemed to emanate from it had only been in my fancy.
Perhaps I was going mad. Then, with the gathering light, the rock began
to change. Or my vision of it changed. To this day, I am not sure where lay
the transformation.

Out of the shape and shadings of the rock, meaning emerged: a face,
long of nose, round of cheek, eyes deep set; white hair, smooth, straight,
flowing over broad shoulders and down a humped back. From beneath the
hair, arms reached around legs drawn up against what appeared to be large
breasts, though the figure was obscured by a loose, course-spun grey shift.
Bare, knobby feet, gnarled as roots, peeked out from beneath the garment.

The woman, for so she must be, remained as still as the rock I had taken
her for. If she breathed, I could not discern it. I began to fear that I had
stumbled upon some dreadful enchantment and had better get away before
I became entangled in it. Yet curiosity held me, and when I studied the face,
I could find in it no terror, nor rage, nor anguish. Indeed, I knew no word to
describe what I saw in that face, but I sensed at once that it was something
I did not have.

And, at least at that moment, I wanted it, but it was a different sort of
wanting than I had ever felt before. It lacked the greedy desperation that
so marked my character. It was a humble wanting. Though you may think
I have scant cause for pride, humility has never come easily to me. Nor has
patience. Soon I could no longer endure waiting for something to happen.
Summoning all my courage, I reached out my hand and gently, gingerly,
touched the woman's shoulder.

As if it were some long awaited sign, her head turned full towards me,
and I found myself face to face with the woman. I could not have been more
shocked if a real stone had moved. For, in spite of the form, which I had
recognized as human, and the warmth of the body, which could only mean
life, I had felt that I was alone. Now, suddenly, for the third time in my life,
I was not.

Eyes looked into eyes. Hers were black, like the sky of a clear, moonless night, a blackness pierced with points of light. But where the dance of

the stars is stately, the light in her eyes danced merrily, more like light on moving water. Though she kept silent, I had the distinct and disconcerting feeling that she was about to laugh, and I could not fathom why.

"Hail, Daughter, and well met," she spoke at last.

Daughter is a customary form of greeting from an older woman to a younger one, yet no one before had so addressed me, not even my own mother. Her voice had a homely, comforting quality that made me think of loaves, fresh and warm from the oven.

Then she reached for my hand, and I helped her to her feet—or she helped me to mine—for we both rose and continued to regard one another standing. We were almost of a height, but she was stooped and I straight, so I stood taller. Because of the hump in her back, which swelled just below her neck, she could not tilt her head but peered at me from beneath heavy, over-hanging brows.

"Yes, I think you are ready at last to accompany me," she pronounced. Now it was my turn to play the boulder, for her words rendered me stone.

How had it taken me so long to recognize her? I forgot the warmth of her voice, the mirth in her face, the mysterious quality in her bearing that so attracted me. I knew with the cold certainty of fear that I had been tricked.

"I know you!" I accused. "you're the—" I bit back the word witch. "The Wise Woman of the Western Wood."

"Indeed, that is my title." She smiled, not at me, but to herself. "One of them. Yes, Daughter, that is what I am, but it is not who I am. You do not know who I am, for I have not told you my name." She paused for a moment, then added, "No one living knows my name."

She fell silent again, and I sensed she was waiting for me, neither impatiently nor with patience. She did not seem to dwell in the same sort of time that most mortal folk inhabit.

As for me, what she had said sent me reeling. Here was one who knew the power of names, or else why would she keep her own a secret? Nor had I any intention of wresting that secret from her. Truth to tell, after buzzing about her curiously, my thoughts had flown back to myself. It was my own name I craved to know, and I vowed, could she tell me, I would accompany her to hell, if such were her pleasure.

"Mother." I addressed her thus without a thought, and at once it seemed right to do so. "I beseech you to tell me my name!"

In answer she studied me, as if seeking to find my name in my face.
"Daughter, I tell you plainly, I do not yet know your name, but this I promise you: When it is given to me to know, you shall know, too, and bear your
name from that day forward."

I could scarcely bear this answer: the joy that one day my name might be
bestowed upon me, as a true name must be, and the anguish of this undeter-
mined span of time until some mystic knowledge—in which I confess I had
little faith—came upon this strange woman, whose own name I did not
know. Nothing in life had taught me to trust other people.

My longing to know my name had, for an instant, banished caution.
Now my native wariness returned.

"What is it you want of me?" I demanded rudely.

She appeared to take no offense but answered straight away, "I need an
heir to my arts. Ever since I received you from your mother's womb, I have
suspected that you might be the one who was meant to come after me."

That she was midwife at my birth came as news to me. True, my mother
had scattered dark hints about that event, intended to exonerate herself
of blame for my sinister being, but, like other women who had turned in
times of trouble to the Witch, my mother had never admitted it in so many
words.

"And it seems I suspected rightly," she went on, "for here you are at the
appointed time and place."

I could not altogether doubt her pronouncement, but I liked it not at
all. I had accepted my fate as cruel at worst, indifferent at best. To discover
that there might be some purpose to my life, of which I had no knowledge,
discomfited me.

"Now yours must be the choosing, Daughter."

Here was a coil! First, she informed me that I had arrived at some foreor-
dained destination. Now she asked, no, commanded me to choose. It was
in no way just. Was my life my own or was it not? Of one thing only was I
certain: I wanted to know my name. This woman held forth a promise of
that knowledge, though likely only as bait to lure me into her trap.

"Tell me when you will know my name, and I will go with you," I
bargained.

"Daughter." She looked at me with a mixture of merriment and sadness
I could not comprehend. "I cannot tell you the time, only the task."

Then, in a low voice, she began to sing:

Take the dung and make it flower,
Take the pain and make it power,
Let your own fear make you bold,
Take the straw and spin, spin, spin the gold.

It's as I thought, I told myself, she's mad, chanting her nonsense rhymes. I gazed at the ground and paid her no heed, but she sang her rhyme again and then once more, until, against my will, the words lodged themselves in my mind and sang themselves.

Though I knew there was no meaning in the rhyme, the very lack of meaning maddened me. Oh, to be sure, animals were let to graze in fallow fields so that their droppings might enrich the soil, but did anything follow from that simple fact? I knew well enough my pain had nothing to do with power. It was precisely that I had no power that I knew such pain. As for fear, a cornered beast is bold enough, but what of that? And straw spun to gold was nothing but a child's tale, unless—

Truly, folk did fear her and call her Witch. Could it be that she might teach me something of use? Why not find out? What had I to lose? Taking my time to empty my face of any thoughts that might have lingered there, I lifted my eyes to hers at last.

Then that quality about her, for which I yet had no name, took me by surprise and held me captive. But, no, that is not so. She in no way imprisoned me. It was I who sought to chain her with words like witch and madwoman. For my own ease I must make her as small as my puny understanding. But when I looked up, there she stood, utterly undiminished.

"I am ready, Mother," I spoke at last, more humbly and willingly than I had intended.

"Good. Let us go then, Daughter."

The Mother turned and led the way to some shallows where it was possible to ford the river. Knee deep in water, I followed her to the other side and scrambled up the bank. In years since, I have crossed that river many times. But I know now, as I did not then, that for me there is no return from the Wood.

CHAPTER FOUR

W E REACHED THE MOTHER'S DWELLING after an hour's walk, sometimes climbing, sometimes on the flat. To me the place seemed nothing but a forest glade sheltered by some small cliffs. Yet there could be no doubt that we had arrived, for out of various shady places in full, glad cry came goats and chickens, rabbits and cats, and even a snake, to greet their mistress. Casting my eyes about the clearing, I spied a great blackened cauldron. Coals smoldered beneath it, and steam wafted from it. She must have left something to simmer all night. Close by was a bread oven. In the midst of the clearing, where the sun would shine all day, lay flax drying on a brake, and on a worktable stood a scutching board. Under a crude shelter, a roof of woven rushes hoisted on saplings, stood a spinning wheel and a niddy-noddy. At the far end of the glade, near where we had entered, was a large garden. Some vegetables and herbs I recognized at a glance, but many were unknown to me. Still, the clearing looked much like that of any good wife, save that there was no cottage in sight, not even the meanest hut.

"Come, Daughter," the Mother called. "The goats are in sore need of milking. Do you know how to milk?"

In truth, I did not, though I would not have said so if she had not asked me straight out. Our family was poor, and we were lucky if we had anything to trade for milk. Sometimes, in charity, someone gave us a sickly beast, goat or cow or sheep, but I was not allowed to touch it for fear the creature would take fright at me and go dry.

"It is time you learned, then."

Thus began my apprenticeship, though it was a long time before I acknowledged that homely lesson as my first.

"Now, Daughter, let us get within and break our fast. Nor must we leave the milk to stand in the heat of the day."

To my bafflement, she began to walk straight towards the cliff. Before I could understand what she meant to do, she reached out her hand, parted the flowering vine that covered the rock face, and disappeared. Ah, I thought, with mounting excitement, my lessons in magic now begin. I will learn to rend rock. Then I, too, found the opening the vines obscured and stood within the Mother's cave, a natural cave, though to me the cave was novel enough to stem, for the moment, my craving for the supernatural.

As the Mother moved about fetching food and drink, my eyes made adjustment to the dimness and took measure of the place that was to be my home. If any cave can be said to be airy, this one was, to my relief, for I had no desire to live like a rat in a hole. The roof, if you could call the carved expanse of rock overhead a roof, was high enough so that at the zenith another as tall as I could have stood upon my shoulders. Gingerly, as someone else might have touched a toad, I extended my hand to feel the walls. Though they were pleasantly cool, they were not damp. My nose told me that the floor was strewn with fragrant herbs—rosemary and thyme, perhaps. The Mother's pallet appeared to be skins spread upon bedstraw. There were two stools and a low table before a vast hearth hung about with herbs and onions and cookery pots. Daylight trickled in through a natural chimney. To the left of the hearth, taking up nearly a third of the room, stood what I took to be a loom, idle now. Doubtless she did her weaving in the winter.

"Sit down, Daughter," she beckoned me.

I took the empty stool beside her, and after a curious silence, which I came to understand took the place of the garbled Latin hurriedly mumbled in village homes, we broke together a loaf of tasty black bread.

IN ALL HER GESTURES AND DEEDS, the Mother made me welcome most graciously, though she was always sparing of words. Yet for a time so long I cannot with any certainty name its span, I felt like a guest who had but come for a rest though to be sure I worked hard enough. What I thought of as my real life, if such a thing there was apart from my daily being, hovered at the edge of my thoughts, a vague mist. And, like a mist, whenever I sought to step into its midst, it seemed just a few steps further yet, its substance a mockery.

Meanwhile, I waked and worked, ate and slept in the Mother's world of Wood and Cave. All that surrounded me was so much one with her that I could readily believe that either she sprang from it, birthed by the cave that sheltered her, or that all of it emanated magically from herself. If there was more to her tale, if it had some commonplace beginning, I never knew it; for she told me nothing of where she came from or of what people.

Do not suppose that I complain or that I was ungrateful for the shelter and companionship or for the livelihood she set about to teach me. It was only that I felt I lived within another's life, as if I had been drawn inside some vast and all encompassing womb—as perhaps I had.

For all the Mother appeared to me, in some ways, as an enchanted being, she taught me nothing of what I considered magic. I still thought of a
witch as someone wantonly powerful, able to grant wishes or wreak havoc
on whim. I wanted useful knowledge, such as how to turn people into toads
or at least to inflict them with boils. Of course, I was willing to learn helpful magic, too. I would disenchant the deserving who had run afoul of other
sorcerers or help them to gain their heart's desire. In short, I wanted crude
power without any price attached to it. Indeed, I felt I had already paid
quite enough. If I was fated to live as an outcast like the Mother—and I
confess I still thought of her that way despite my deeper, truer sense of how
at home she was—then life must make it up to me in some way.

I dared not question the Mother in these matters, however, nor would
she have answered me if I had. She was never one for answering questions,
save those that had to do with the matter at hand, such as how long to
boil Our Lady's Bedstraw for the making of purple dye or where to gather
Lovage or what phase of the moon is best for planting beans. Such was the
nature of her teachings; for she taught me to know every plant that grows
in the forest or in the garden and all its properties and uses, how to prepare
all manner of medicines and potions, tinctures and dyes. Learning to brew
what common folk call a love potion was the closest I came to the sort of
magic I had in mind, but the Mother left me no illusions about its working.
It cast no spell over the beloved nor gave magic allure to the lover. It but
increased health in both sexes, potency in a man and fertility in a woman.

The Mother used all things for healing, and yet she showed me also
the ways to harm. That baffled me for some time: that she possessed and
proffered knowledge of which she herself intended to make no use. What,
then, was I to make of it? Over time, I began to understand that this was
the question she wordlessly posed me, and I myself must answer it with no
help from her.

Yet I felt no inclination to answer to anyone how I would use the knowledge that with each day became more and more mine. I saw no need for
such absolute decisions. To be sure, I did not intend to go out of my way to
harm anyone, but neither did I feel obliged to help if it did not please me.
Why should I not be like the plants, which were neither good nor evil in
themselves but only in the intent of those who used them? And if someone
used me ill, was it not right that he should reap evil as his reward?

One day, on return from foraging in the Wood as we sat in the clearing
sorting mushrooms, I ventured this argument with the Mother.

"You are not a plant," she answered.

Nor would she say one word more. When it came to philosophic disputation, the Mother had the knack of turning into that stone I had first taken her for, and this habit I found maddening. In so far as I was able to fathom a mind that did not reveal its workings to me, I reckon she believed I had too much to learn to waste my time with wastrel thoughts.

To my great delight, my evening lessons included reading and writing. I had never known anyone who could do either, and she never told me how she came to learn. She would sit spinning and carding while I labored over my letters. Thus, wordless as she was, she gave me the gift of words, words that opened other minds to me. The Bible, I discovered, was a greater and more varied book than any priest had led me to suppose and full of tales of the most wonderful wickedness, even—or especially—among God's favorites, and this I found most encouraging. The Mother had two other volumes, one of the practices and philosophy of alchemy, one full of the poetry of courtly love. The last I read only when the Mother was absent at child bed or sick bed, for the words woke my longing for the Prince, and I feared, were she witness, the Mother would be able to decipher the meaning of the hot ink that stained my cheeks.

On fine nights we often left our work, ignored our beds, and studied the sky. She revealed to me the dance of the stars and as much of its meaning as mortals know. From her I learned the laws that govern earth, wind, water, and fire. I believe she knew as much, no, more than any priest or scholar, any alchemist or philosopher. Yet she neither regarded knowledge as a possession nor was she possessed by it. She was guardian, steward, midwife of knowledge, bringing it forth from the secret places of the earth to a life in the world, and the purpose of that life—of her life—was not sovereignty but service.

Do not mistake me: time has told me these truths about the Mother. Then I guessed only one thing: no matter how much she might teach me of natural fact or universal law or even what ignorant folk might call magic, there was more she did not teach me, and, as I believe now, could not. Words could not remedy this unknowing of mine, and thus it became a source of chronic, if vague, unease.

The Mother was often silent, not because she hated speech, but because she never wasted words nor any form of power. Each word, each movement, each act was deliberate; she knew exactly what she spent. I came to understand that silence renewed her as rain renews earth. When she was silent, I had little choice but to be silent, too. Mostly I did not mind. Even when I had lived surrounded by people, I led the life of a solitary, however much against my will. For me silence was merely a convenient habit. In the Mother's silence I sensed something rich and powerful.

Sometimes as we sat wordless with our carding or spinning, I mused over the myriad lessons I was learning from the Mother and pondered the mystery of what I was missing. I was an apt enough pupil, quick and retentive. It was not dull wits that stymied me. Yet when I considered the knowledge I had amassed, it appeared to me random, disordered. It was like having quantities of fine wool and not knowing how to spin.

My puzzlement, however, was only a temporary diversion from my preferred pastime: daydreaming—or that is what I call it now. Endlessly I relived my moments with the Prince, and when the memories showed signs of wear, I would let them rest and restore themselves while I turned to pure invention. There was the continuing tale of our life together had we run away that day instead of submitting so meekly to our dreary destinies. But the most poignant fancy of all, so sweet I could scarce endure it, was that he should, by some marvelous chance or design, find his way into the Mother's clearing and, seeing me once more, know he could never again be parted from me.

These reveries were as much a source of pain as pleasure. I knew full well that fancy could never be fact, and yet the knowledge never failed to wound me afresh. Nor did I seem able to banish these sorry daydreams. Love had risen in me, and it raged. I raged in turn at Life or Fate or God, all more or less one to me, that my love should be denied its object. At times I felt sick with love, sick of love, and these daydreams were my only medicine, though they offered no cure, only temporary ease. And, indeed, like many medicines, they became themselves a poison.

How much of my inward state the Mother guessed I do not know. She was no more inclined to ask questions than to answer them. From time to time, I found her watching me, but I had no means to know the meaning of those looks. I was apt to ascribe my own harshest judgments to her, and I imagined that she always found me wanting.

I know now that I all but made the Mother my god—or rather goddess. Despite her drab robes and utter indifference to her appearance, she was deeply female in an elemental way, like a furrowed field of rich, dark earth. Thus I resented her as heartily as I loved her, all the more so because the severity I insisted on seeing in her glance was so often undone by the sweetness of her smile. There were times when I could not avoid knowing that she loved me, though I believe she wondered more than once whether she had been mistaken in thinking me her successor.

Yet, mistaken or not, the Mother loved me. For one with all the arrogance of self-hatred, such love, so freely given and having nothing to do with my deserving, was hard, indeed, to bear.

CHAPTER FIVE

FOR MORE THAN A FULL TURN OF THE SEASONS, I saw no one but the Mother; or rather, spoke to no one. Folk came to our clearing from time to time seeking her succor. Mostly they came early or late, before or after the work of the day, in the shadow times when they might steal away unseen. For as I well knew, no one openly admitted association with a witch. Most were ill or injured; some were carried on pallets by their desperate relatives.

Whenever possible, I was present as the Mother tended broken bones, cleansed and dressed festering wounds or sores, diagnosed lung fever or traced trouble to the liver. Always, either as she worked or immediately afterwards, she explained as best she could how she had made a diagnosis and why she had prescribed a particular remedy. Helping her tend the sick was part of my apprenticeship, and of herbcraft as well as the healing properties of mold and dung, I learned all the Mother could teach.

But in healing arts, as in others, I had the same uneasy sense that what was most important, indeed the heart of the matter, she could not convey. I would either one day know or I would not. How this knowing happened seemed the most impenetrable magic. More than once the Mother was at a loss to explain how she came to her conclusions. Watching her feel of a sick person, I guessed that her whole being became concentrated in her fingers. She listened with them. She quested and questioned, and to her hands the body revealed its secrets.

It was not only the visibly ill who sought the Wise Woman. There were others, men, women, youths, in whom I could discern no sickness of the body. These she saw alone, and she would never tell me afterwards what had transpired, though I pestered her like a child. I was alarmed to think I might have to succeed her in this mysterious office.

"Nothing will be asked of you until you are ready to give it" was all the Mother would say.

That first year she showed great wisdom and forbearance in her demands of me. She knew that I was not yet ready for intimate traffic with the human race. Thus midwifery she taught me first with the goats. When folk came, as they often did in what is called the darkest hour, to beseech her aid for some woman who labored at the border between life and death, she left me sleeping.

Nor, to my relief, did she ask me to accompany her on her journeys to market day in my village. Much as I loved her and swore to myself I was not ashamed of her, I had no desire to return to my native place in her company. I knew too well how she appeared to the village folk and how they treated her. Most showed her the wary respect they might accord a dangerous wild beast, but no one hailed her as a fellow creature. I feared that once people saw me as her chosen successor, my fate would be sealed. Human congress, though never offered, would be lost to me forever. I could not bear it yet. I needed hope, however false.

When I had been with her almost a year, the Mother returned from the Midsummer Festival with cuts and bruises on her arms and legs, and a nasty gash on her left cheek. Seeing that she was weary and disinclined to talk, I summoned a restraint alien to my nature and forbore to question her while I applied to her wounds the healing arts she had taught me. When, after plying her with food and drink, I saw some color returning to her un-molested cheek, I could contain myself no longer and demanded to know what had happened to her.

"It was no great thing, Daughter. Just a handful of children playing dares, each afraid to go against the others."

The rage that had always simmered in me came instantly to the boil, scalding the cool walls of the cave.

"Had I powers I would have turned the lot of them to the swine that they are! But you, Mother! I suppose you did nothing!"

"Swine are useful creatures to be sure, Daughter. But no doubt their parents would prefer them to remain as they were made, in God's image."

I could not tell if she were laughing at me or reminding me gently that even vile children have some sanctity or if she was simply evading my point.

"If God bears any resemblance to their like, then a pox on him!"

I stopped for a moment, shocked at the blasphemy that sprang so easily to my lips. The Mother, however, seemed untroubled: by the children's cru-elty, by my all but cursing God. Her calm made me yet more furious.

"I don't understand you!" The cave resounded with my shouting. "Have you never known anger or hatred!"

The Mother laid aside her carding, which she had taken up despite her fatigue, and looked me full in the face.

"Daughter, I have known all passions in their season. But there is a knowing beyond that. I am who I am. I know my own name."

"But I don't know mine!"

The Mother made no answer save to let her gaze linger on me a moment more. Before I could fathom the meaning in her eyes, she picked up her combs again and continued to card. I had lived with the Mother long enough to be certain that I might rage all night long if I chose, but not a word more from her would I get for my pains.

Summer passed, then autumn. One night, without warning, the Mother decided it was time. At the coldest hour, I found myself being shaken, none too gently, awake.

"Come," she commanded.

Still in a stupor, I rose and wrapped myself in a heavy cloak as the Mother swiftly—yet without the clumsiness of undue haste—gathered various herbs and potions and put them into her sack. Shrinking against the wall near the entrance, so that I did not notice him at first, was an ashen-faced young man. His build and scanty beard, the look of pained bewilderment on his face reminded me too sharply of the Prince. I looked away. But I'd needed only that one glance to know that the youth had come to fetch the Mother to a child-bed, likely his wife's.

The world hovered at the brink of Winter. We followed the young man into a night of killing frost. Fallen leaves softened our way through the Woods, but crossing the fields, crops plowed under, we bruised our feet on the frozen hummocks. I marveled that grain could grow again or that anyone would dare be born into this dead world.

At length we came to a peasant's hovel, one of the rudest I had seen. Even the Mother had to stoop to enter. At once our senses were assailed with the stench of sweat and blood and fecal matter. The room was smoky, too, for, like many huts, this one had no chimney, and the smoke had to find its way out of numerous cracks. And smoking was about all the fire was doing. The warmth of the room came mostly from the bodies, both animal and human, crowded inside it. I could not even see the laboring woman, surrounded as she was by what seemed to me a shapeless mass of women, a grotesque body bobbing with too many heads. They drew aside as the Mother approached the pile of straw where the woman lay. She beckoned me to follow her, oblivious to looks of hostility and suspicion. I felt them, for some of those glances found their mark in me. I tried my best to ignore them; I knew I was here to learn. What I needed most to study was the Mother's utter concentration. Nothing distracted her. She was a force directed unswervingly towards the sorry creature of the straw.

From the slenderness of her limbs, I guessed the wench was young, younger than I maybe. But her face, drained of color, taut with suffering, made her look older than the Mother. A pain seized her, and her face contorted in a grimace so hideous that she resembled nothing so much as the painting on the wall of our village church of the damned soul in torment. Between pains she whimpered softly, but she scarcely seemed conscious.

I expected the Mother to do something drastic, immediate. Instead she knelt by the woman and stroked her face, as if smoothing the untimely lines that sought to engrave themselves there. The woman quieted, then opened her eyes and looked directly into the Mother's. I watched but saw no trace in her face of the fear that customarily greeted the Witch. With death to one side, this woman knew life when she saw it. Still the Mother did what I considered to be nothing, though behind me the other women muttered about spells and snake's eyes. In truth, the Mother's eyes bore no resemblance to a snake's, and, in my opinion, if the Mother could cast this pitiful woman-child into a trance, it would be a mercy.

Another pain gripped the woman. I saw her face tighten. This time instead of crying out and gasping, she remained silent, and it struck me that she and the Mother were breathing slowly, deeply, as one creature. When the pain released her, the woman appeared to sleep.

Turning to the other women, the Mother questioned them about the labor.

As if they were the single body they had seemed, the women spoke, one after another, not interrupting but combining their words in a continuous flow that told the story.

It's three days now. Yes, her first, poor lass, and the pains coming hard since dawn. We've tried raspberry leaves and ragwort, but that's not what she needs for her trouble. She's been wide open and ready since dusk, but the babe won't come. We broke the waters to hurry it along. But she's past her strength. She can't last long. It's open her up and save the babe or out with the hooks perhaps to save the mother. She's just too small I told him, so make up your mind. But, poor lad, he's fair lost what mind he had. He would run to fetch you, Mother.

I could also hear what they did not speak, this chorus of doom: Someone must die—mother, babe or both, and the blood be upon you, Witch, the blood be upon you.

Without a word, the Mother parted the woman's rags and laid her ear on the swollen belly.

"The babe still lives," she pronounced. "Daughter," she directed me as she stroked the great roundness which had tightened with another pain, "in the sack, find a bowl and a flask of spring water. Heat the water, then mix it with fermented wood spirit."

I obeyed, realizing with shame how heavy was the sack the Mother had carried all that way over her humped back while I went empty-handed. I did not bother to ask for more fuel to heat the water—I suspected they burned animal dung—but raised the fire instead with some of the wood spirit. No doubt the onlookers thought it sorcery.

Then I brought the Mother the bowl and the clean cloths she also requested from the sack. With one cloth she washed her hands and with another she daubed the woman's privy parts, none so private now. I felt the suspicion of those around us mount. The Mother believed that disease grew and spread in dirt even as plants do. But the watchers saw her every move as part of some aweful and inexplicable rite. Why didn't she teach them, tell them? Did she want folk to think her a witch? I wondered.

Soon I became absorbed in watching her feel of the woman, one hand inside and one hand over the woman's belly. Then she bade me examine her. I was not so awkward as I might have been, for I was familiar with female animals and had delivered a breach kid. Still, I was discomfited at being so close to another human being—a woman, made as I was made—close enough to feel her pain as I laid my hand on her struggling body. So close that I could not escape the knowledge that here was another single suffering being, like all the rest, like no one else, like me.

"Find the child's head," the Mother prompted, "and tell me why the child won't come."

I understood that the Mother already knew; she wanted me to learn. I reached inside the woman, trying to be gentle, and marveled as my fingers touched a soft skull. I closed my eyes as I felt, trying to see the shape of it.

"The face is looking up."

"Yes," said the Mother, "and the chin is caught. I must turn the babe. I will need help." She motioned to the other women. "You must lift her a little higher than your waists."

More slowly than I thought respectful, the women moved to do the Mother's bidding. Uncertain of my role, I made to join them.

"No," the Mother stopped me. "You are to watch."

To the women, she said, "Hold her as still as you can. Brace yourselves against each other and against the wall."

At last she spoke to the laboring woman, "I am going to reach inside you and turn your babe. You will feel more pain." Oddly the woman seemed reassured rather than alarmed. She must have been glad that something was to be done, however dreadful.

I watched closely as the Mother, facing the woman, reached in her hand, palm upward. For a moment she groped; then, it seemed, she found a purchase. The muscles of her arm and shoulder tightened visibly beneath her robe. She waited for a moment, in absolute stillness, waited for the perfect union of body and spirit that is power. Then, suddenly, the woman shrieked, and the Mother turned full about, facing away from the woman, her arm stretching out behind her. When she withdrew her hand, it was palm down.

"Lay her on the straw again," she instructed the women; then she knelt next to the lass. "Your babe is ready now. Rest, and I will give you a drink to strengthen you. Then you will bring forth your living child into the world."

To me the Mother said, "In the sack find mandrake, wormwood, burdock, thyme, and elder. Use more spring water and brew tea. When the drink is warm, break an egg into it. You'll find one wrapped in lamb's wool."

When the drink was brewed, the Mother supported the woman as she sipped.

Now, between pains, the woman's face smoothed and rounded so that it looked like a child's. Surely she was years younger than I. Then, all at once, her eyes widened, and she struggled to raise herself.

"Ah!" the women murmured with grudging admiration for the Mother's feat, "the babe is coming now and certain."

The Mother directed two women to support the lass that she might squat.

She herself knelt at the woman's thighs and showed her how to grip them with her hands.

"When the next pain comes, bear down with all your might," the Mother said.

The woman obeyed, and then I beheld a wondrous transformation. Until now, for all the Mother's comfort, the woman had seemed a pitiful thing, helpless, trapped within the pain. Now even as she groaned and pushed, she appeared, all of a sudden, powerful, perhaps as powerful as the Mother herself. Unbidden, the Mother's rhyme came to my mind: Take the pain and make it power. For the first time I saw the meaning, saw it with my own eyes.

"Rest now," the Mother told her when the pain had passed.

Obedient, she sank back into the arms of the other women, limp as wet wash.

"Get oil," the Mother instructed me. "And ready the blade."

Soon the woman was pushing again, making fierce animal sounds, grunts and growls. No wonder men were barred from witnessing birth: they would be afraid, afraid of this pain become power, afraid of this magic women make. For though I knew birth to be part of the natural course of life, it seemed more magical than anything called by that name.

Then, as I squatted myself the better to see, I glimpsed a tuft of the hair that I had felt with my fingers. It was dark as the woman's hair. With the oil I poured on her hands, the Mother began kneading the woman where the babe would come, firm rhythmic strokes, oiling the doorway to the world. I peered around the Mother. The sight of the babe's head stretching and straining that opening was marvelous, monstrous. I had always thought of a newborn babe as tiny, but as I watched the head emerge, it seemed enormous. How was it this little woman did not break in pieces, shatter like the egg that holds the chick?

Then the woman unleashed a scream that seared the marrow of my every bone. Surely, I thought, she's dying. No doubt the poor wench thought so, too.

"It's the head," the Mother told her. "Bear down again. Your babe is all but born."

A terrible noise issued from deep within the woman as she fought to cast forth the child. All at once the head was fully born. I had a glimpse of a face, all closed, like a fist, like a bud. Then with lightning swiftness, the babe fairly sprang into the Mother's hands and gave its first cry.

"Lack-a-day," muttered one of the women. "All that trouble and only a girl." That these should be the first words to greet the child! I wanted to strike the old bitch. But more than that I wanted to take the tiny girl—so white, for a moment, I feared she could not be living but already turning rosy—into my own arms. I wanted to croon to her and sing her a name. Here was the miracle:

Out of the dung—smoke, blood, filth, pain, fear—out of it all had come this flower.

I watched the Mother cut the cord then wash and oil the babe. Of their own foolish will, my arms reached out. No one noticed my futile longing. They were all too busy clucking their disapproval of the Mother for handing the babe, naked as she was, to her mother, instead of swaddling her first.

I stepped back into the shadows but could not keep my hungry gaze from the meeting of mother and child. My own breasts ached as the Mother helped the woman guide the babe's mouth to her breast. The new mother did not seem at all dismayed by the sex of her babe. She smiled at her and made the cooing sounds that were caught in my own throat. For a moment, I wanted to rejoice with the new mother, to tell her that I understood the glory of this girl-child.

The impulse passed and seemed as foolish as had my outstretched arms.

For who was I? This young mother had no need of me. Her arms encircled a world. Why should I make glad when my own arms were destined to remain empty? Bitterness, comforting in its familiarity, beckoned me to sink into its withering embrace. I began to yield, but the Mother, impatient, motioned me to come and watch her deliver the afterbirth.

CHAPTER SIX

SO BEGAN MY APPRENTICESHIP AS A MIDWIFE. From that night forward, I accompanied the Mother to all childbirths, bearing myself the marvelous sack, whose contents I came to assemble with a deftness that matched the Mother's. I learned all the complications of birth and how to remedy them if remedy there were, for we were never called save in extremity. Little by little, the Mother turned over more tasks to me. So gradual was this shift that I was hardly aware of it.

Then one day, I found myself receiving a babe from the womb into my own hands. And with the child: joy. A joy so great that I could not hold it as I held the babe. Rather it was as if joy held me, cradled me close to its heart. For an instant. Then the moment vanished, and joy, as if a womb, cast me forth from blissful warmth into the dull chill that seemed my natural atmosphere.

That experience was to repeat itself again and again. Each time I presided at a birth, I had the same terrible longings. I was certain that if only I could keep a child, joy would be mine forever. I would dwell in it safe, as in a fortress, defended against all assaults of pain.

So overpowering was my exaltation at each birth, and so bereft did I find myself afterwards, that I was often silent and downcast on our journey home. I took little notice of weather or season and felt impatient with the Mother if she discoursed on birds or plants that we passed. I had heard all her lore, knew most of it by heart. It annoyed me that she should repeat herself or assume that I needed further instruction in these elementary lessons. It did not occur to me that there might be another cause for her redundancy; nor did I notice how her step had slowed, and her breath grown labored. I was too absorbed in my own grief—or rather grievance.

Once, in early summer, we left a happy childbed at break of day. Briar rose ran riot in the hedges; cottage gardens blazed with poppies. The wild strawberries grew so thick in the meadows that we could not help but trample them. The Mother insisted we pause every few steps to feast. When she had eaten her fill, she joined the birds in a paean of praise; not quite a song; for it had no tune. It was free flowing verse, a chant that took its rhythm from the very pulse of life; words that did not break silence but rose from it, like flowers crowning a deep-rooted plant.

Against my will, I listened, determined, however, not to join the chorus. Joy was a cheat. Misery, at least, could be depended upon. And so I held fast to it.

I was relieved when the Mother's hymn ceased, but only for a moment. The silence grew loud. Though she did not turn to look at me, I had lived with her long enough to know when she had fixed her mind on me.

"Daughter," she said, "why do you sorrow?"

Her questions were as rare as her answers. I never knew what to make of them. I suspected that she already knew: not my answer but the Answer and only wanted me to speak it to discover the truth for myself. Part of me rebelled against such questions as an invasion of what I exalted as my private thoughts. But another part, smaller yet stronger, craved whatever healing she could offer.

"Mother, nothing is all mine!" I burst out, instantly regretting my words and wishing I had taken time to phrase my feelings more eloquently. "What I mean to say is, when I hold a new babe in my hands, it's as if I hold the very secret of life. And then my hands are empty again. Time and again they are empty."

"Hands are made to do two things: to hold fast and to let go." Sullenness overcame me once more. I wanted comfort, not proverbs.

To my surprise, for it was out of character, the Mother continued, "Do you think the woman whose full arms you so envy will not also have to let go?"

"Yes, yes," I said impatiently, though I had not thought about it, nor did I believe it. "But she will have had a child for awhile. For a long time!" My awareness that I sounded like a child myself only made me angrier. "I will never have the chance to be a mother."

"And what is a mother?"

"Someone who has given birth to a child, who has a child," I insisted stubbornly, refusing to give the Answer.

"All that anyone has is a gift," said the Mother, "and every gift is to be given again."

The Mother's wise sayings so irritated me that I lashed out at her. "I tell you I have nothing!"

Not even a name, I added silently, bitterly.

"If you believe that, Daughter, then you are both stupid and ungrateful." Never before had the Mother been so angry with me. I was both chastened and curiously eased by her anger. Though to all outward appearances I continued to sulk, I began to take some pleasure in the fine morning. When I found a fallen bird's nest, I took it home and helped the eggs to hatch.

IN TIME I BECAME AS SKILLED A MIDWIFE as the Mother. She herself commended me with unusually lavish praise. Then came the day when someone called us to childbirth, and the Mother sent me alone. I told myself that her trusting me to go without her was merely a last test, a means to mark the end of my apprenticeship, as perhaps it was.

Not long after that, the Mother asked me to go to the village market day in her stead. It was late afternoon. The Mother sat on a bench carding wool, keeping me company while I brewed dye in the cauldron. The day was warm, the season poised between summer and fall, the hazy air suffused with light, so that light seemed an element of substance, something you could breathe or touch or drink. I looked at the Mother and saw that the light did not merely touch her surface; she partook of it. Meeting no barrier, light flooded her.

In that moment, I saw that she was old. I knew that she would die. For many dying is another battle, and some are stronger fighters than others. In truth, I often find it hard to know which is the enemy: life or death. I have seen so many women wearied with childbearing, even if no one birth went hard, women almost welcoming death as a way to get some rest. But in the mother I sensed no struggle. She saw no enemy in life or death or any fellow creature. Perhaps living her life among plants and loving them as she did, she would die like one as well: like a leaf becoming dryer, lighter until one day the wind would take her, scattering her substance, returning it to the elements.

For an instant, her death held no threat for me. I could see it as part of the great circle in which one thing becomes another and yet goes on and on. Then, in the next moment—was it just that the light changed with the sinking sun, the warmth of day yielding to the evening chill?—the idea of her death became intolerable to me. My childhood had been so lonely and strange; I was, for all my knowledge and skill, so much a child still. My mother had no right to leave me.

"No!" I spoke aloud.

"I'm sorry to ask it of you, Daughter, but—"

"No, no," I cried, dismayed that she had misunderstood me, amazed that she had not heard my thoughts when they'd sounded so clear in my own mind. How could she believe that I would refuse her request? "Oh, Mother," I said, "I would go to market a hundred times over. It's not that."

"What then?"

But she must know without my saying. Why did she, of all people, force me to utter words? Silent fears were bad enough. I did not want to name them, for then they could never be unnamed.

"Daughter, I have been old longer than you have been young," she spoke to my silence. "I have made friends with death."

Truly, the Mother would make friends with a viper—and had, for that matter.

"It's not you I'm worried about!"

Oh, but I had not meant to say that! How heartless I sounded. "I didn't mean—" I began.

"You did," she countered.

"Then, Mother, you must know that I would hate for you to suffer, and I trust you to tell me how I may serve you. What I meant is, I know you're ready ... ready for anything that might befall you." I still would not say the word she used with such ease. "But I'm not ready—or at least I don't know that I am."

I waited for the Mother to make some reassuring, if cryptic, pronouncement, but she said nothing. I brooded over the cauldron bubbling with black elder, heather, and pomegranate to make purple, the color both of royalty and repentance.

"You have learned much," the Mother spoke at last. "Everything that I can teach you."

I knew her well enough to know that she had not uttered all she thought. I felt, not angered as I so often had, but desperate, as if she were about to leave me in some wild and desolate place with no one, no word to guide me.

"But there's more!" I cried. "Those people, the ones who come not for tonics or potions, who have no bodily ills, no wart or baldness or headache." I named half a dozen ailments more that I myself could easily treat. "What do they want? What do you give them? You say you can teach me no more. But there must be more, some greater magic. Indeed, you have taught me no magic at all!"

"All that I have taught you is magic."

"Then what do you mean by magic?"

"Daughter, do you still not know?" Then she began to sing.

Take the dung and make it flower,
Take the pain and make it power,
Let your own fear make you bold,
Take the straw and spin, spin, spin the gold.

That rhyme again. When I witnessed childbirth, I thought I knew what it meant, what it could mean. For other people. But my own pain seemed so vague, so uninteresting, more like toothache than birth pain, though toothache could be excruciating. Yet what came of it, save, like as not, a gaping gum? Where was the magic in that? I was no longer so crude as to desire seriously to change those who irritated me into toads, yet was that so very different from turning straw to gold? Of course, I had learned to take plants and make them into medicines and dyes. Perhaps that was all the rhyme meant.

I glanced at the Mother, intending to gauge from her face the likelihood of getting more answers, but the weariness I saw there made me forget all my questions for the time.

"Come, Mother. My dye is set, and the night draws in. The pottage is simmering on the hearth, and I've much to prepare for my journey tomorrow."

I helped her gather up her carding and urged her inside, my touch gentle, my determination to care for her, fierce.

CHAPTER SEVEN

I ROSE, NEXT MORNING, BEFORE THE SUN and milked Marguerite and Delilah, our goats, who would pull the cart. The trip to town was a treat for them. Market day was always something of a festival, and the Mother gave the goats the freedom of the streets in exchange for their services. They would roam about to their heart's delight, foraging for delicacies: spoiled fruits and vegetables, sweets and spicemeats. Some cart was forever being overturned by excited children or their brawling elders. All save the Mother's cart. I hoped I would appear as formidable as she.

I had loaded the cart the night before with cheeses and herbal concoctions of all sorts, including the ever-popular love potion. Since flasks and bottles were hard to come by, these were mostly stored in leather pouches, carefully labeled, though few folk could read. We also sold cloths of all weights and colors and weaves, mostly spun, dyed, and woven by me. For in the making of fabric, my genius, the Mother readily admitted, far surpassed hers.

Alone in the Wood, I often wore my own more fanciful creations, changing my garments to match season or weather. I was no worldly beauty to dress for the eyes of others. Indeed, few saw me, save the Mother, nor did I have a glass. The sight of myself in my outlandish rigs would have made me feel foolish and spoiled my fun. I had no desire to see myself from the outside, and I forbade myself fancies of what the Prince might see. I adorned myself as the earth adorned herself, as if I were a cluster of bright toadstools or an outcropping of moss-covered rock.

For this journey to town, however, I wore a simple brown shift and borrowed from the Mother her grey cloak, which I intended to keep about me even if the day should grow warm. I did not hope to disguise myself. We were not much alike, the Mother and I, save that we were of a height. I merely thought to shield myself from the curious, hostile, or even startled glances that were sure to rain down upon me.

The Mother gave me a hearty breakfast and blessed me on my way, pressing a fresh-baked loaf—made with the last of our meal—into my hands. I set my face to the northeast, just as light began to brim over the rim of the earth. I was now accustomed to the uneven terrain of the Wood, and, despite my limp, I was nearly as nimble as the goats, who knew the way to the village better than I.

With no need to mark the path, I was free to follow my thoughts as I followed the goats. With some surprise, I noted that this visit to the world aroused not fear alone but also eagerness. The Mother never brought back with her much news from the market. I reckon folk were too wary of the Witch to do more than transact their essential business. Nor did the Mother possess that sort of curiosity that delights in gossip. To gossip with the Mother would be like chattering to a tree or a stone. You'd feel a very fool in a matter of moments.

But, in truth, I had never plied the Mother with questions on her return from the village. My longing for news of the Prince was so intense that it became a kind of dread. It was not simply that I feared to hear of some injury or infirmity or, worse still, to learn of his marriage to some worthy wench selected by his father. It was that I did not want the fact of his continuing life—which surely went on quite easily without me—to belittle a memory I had so enlarged. As I left the wood where my fancy, unfettered, had the power to make the past, at least, in its own image, I felt the challenge of the world, of the present. Something in me rose to meet it.

The sun was just over the horizon when I left the trees for the fields surrounding the village. Already the grey cloak felt too warm, yet I resisted the temptation to remove it, for I soon found myself part of a growing procession of peasants and peddlers all making for the village gate.

Many people, I noted, pulled their own carts. Some, like mine, were drawn by goats. I saw only a few donkeys, no oxen, and, of course, only the nobility could afford horses. The carts seemed not so heavy-laden as I remembered from my childhood. Vegetables looked puny, and the livestock, mostly chickens and geese, a few sheep, undernourished. Such leanness at the end of summer was surprising. As far as I was aware, the weather had been favorable for crops. Why these signs of hard times?

I wanted to ask, but I observed that folk kept a marked distance between myself and them, though they were in no way disrespectful. A few even offered swift nods, careful, however, to keep their eyes averted. They must have recognized the Mother's cart and goats and taken it for granted that I was she. Of course, I had known mostly village folk, so there was no reason for these peasants to remember me.

Their scrupulous avoidance of my eyes left me free to look about, though I was careful not to look at any one person too long, lest someone notice and accuse me of casting the evil eye. It dawned on me, after a time, that the crowd consisted mostly of women and children, a few old men. I wondered at the absence of men in their prime. But it was a clear, warm day. Perhaps they were at work scything the second growth of hay in the King's fields.

As we drew nearer the village, the throng swelled as one rutted dusty lane after another joined what could almost be called a road. Nearing one such intersection, I almost forgot myself and cried aloud, for surely that was one of my sisters approaching the mainstream from a byway. Like many other women, she pulled a cart, but despite the strenuous labor, she was fat. Perhaps she was unaccustomed to such work, for she looked cross and weary and paused often to mop her face with the corner of her apron. As often, she shouted to a swarm of children who dashed ahead, too excited to slow themselves to her pace. Surely she should have a son or daughter old enough to pull the cart for her. Come to think of it, I believed she had married a prosperous man who kept more than one beast of burden. Could she have been widowed and forced to sell her stock?

I had never had much depth of feeling for my sisters, nor they for me. Still, they had never been cruel to me. It saddened me to see my once-pretty sister—Griselda I took her to be, though I could not be certain; there were so many of them, and they all looked alike—grown coarse and harried. Should I address her? Some family feeling, dormant so long I had never guessed its existence, made me want to ask how she did and what had become of my other sisters and my parents. I also longed to know the names and number of her children. I would have liked to make her a gift of some fine cloth and some medicines that, as the mother of so many, she doubtless needed.

On the other hand, I dreaded the questions she might ask and the interference with my life that might follow. Then, too, I reasoned, to be seen with me might do her no good in her neighbor's eyes. Unable to decide upon a definite course, I resolved to adjust my pace so that she would draw her cart alongside mine. I would let her see my face. Then, when she recognized me, she could choose for herself whether or not to know me.

Her frequent stops made it take longer for her to reach the main road than I had anticipated. Thus, when I got to the lane, I came to a halt myself, to the annoyance of those behind me, on the pretext of adjusting the goats' harness. As my sister neared me, I straightened and turned my face fully towards her. We were close enough that I could see the beads of sweat that stood on her brow and the grimy tracks the sweat left where it streamed. She paused again to puff and mop. Then, briefly, her eyes brushed my face in a manner that made me think of a cow flicking its tail to rid its back of flies. When she spoke, she, like the others, kept her eyes averted.

"Is there something amiss, Mother, that your cart stands so in the lane?"

Her tone was deferential but impatient.

I was too stunned to speak. Did she truly take me for the Mother or was she feigning? Surely I had not changed as much as she. Slowly I shook my head, more in amazement than in answer to her question.

"Then I pray you, Mother, move along, or else all the best places will be taken."

"Do-you-not-know-me?"

I spoke without volition. My throat, parched and dusty, made my voice sound ancient and unfamiliar.

A look of fear crossed her face. "Mother, I meant no disrespect."

Her fear convinced me. Without another word, I turned away, signaled the goats to go, and moved on as swiftly as the crowds and my limp would allow. I did not need to wonder if she would notice my ungainly gait. I could hear her bellowing to her children, directing them to run ahead and hold the spot by the tavern or, failing that, the one by the bakery.

I knew which place would be mine, and so did the goats. Since before my memory, the Mother had set forth her wares in a narrow alley that was always in shadow, though it did open on the market square. No one else wanted the spot, because there was not much coming and going along that lane. Also the money-lender lived there, and he was held in almost as much fear as the Mother. She did not mind these drawbacks. The spot was cool and restful in the summer and sheltered from the wind in the winter. Any-one who wanted what the Mother sold knew where to seek her, and folk were more likely to do so in the seclusion the alley provided. With a shawl or cloak over your head and your back to the square, no one could easily mark you as a patron of the Witch.

All day, while the goats sought their pleasure, I sat in the Mother's al-ley listening to the din of the market place: vendors crying their wares; occasional loud disputes; musicians—pipers, drummers, strummers, sing-ers their music mixing with the bleating and squawking of livestock. From time to time, children peered into my alley for the fun of frightening them-selves. To one of these children who was bolder or greedier than the rest, I tossed a coin and bade him fetch me a tankard of ale to drink with my bread. I ran the risk that he would simply steal the coin, but he must have feared my wrath, for he returned speedily, gawping as I thanked him and tried to make pleasant conversation.

So close to all the human bustle, I felt lonelier than I ever did in the Wood.

The stillness of the dim alley, which the Mother found restful, oppressed me. I found myself wanting to befriend the boy. I rummaged in the cart for a gift I might offer and discovered the perfect new-shed skin of a snake I had found that morning and kept; for snakeskin is an ingredient in a number of potions. I held the skin out with what I hoped was a smile—I have never been able to gauge the effect of my face. His eyes widened with desire and fear. No doubt he thought I was trying to entice him, and, in a way, I was, though not for the evil purposes he must have imagined. He stood frozen for a moment; then he snatched the skin and dashed away, squealing with fright and pleasure.

Grown folk came to my alley in ones and the more fearful in twos on their swift, furtive errands, often walking the long way round to avoid entering from the square. Many of my customers were women, drawn by the medicine and cloth. The tavern keeper sent a young man to purchase most of the cheese. He was the only one to pay me in coin; the rest paid in kind. I did not drive a hard bargain, and no one dared barter; they would as soon have tried to cheat the Devil. So I amassed millet and lentils, which we did not grow ourselves, tallow for candles and soap, and tanned leather and fleeces. The latter, I noticed, were of markedly poorer quality than last year's.

After the first few transactions, my heart ceased to hammer. No one recognized me. Everyone treated me with the deference and fear folk usually accorded the Mother—to her face. A few covered their fear with a fine disdain. There were advantages to the awe I inspired. No one jeered in my face, yet the effect of this awe was the same as that of the outright cruelty I had suffered as a child. Both kept me at a remove from humankind, as if I were some strange being beyond mortal ken. As a child I did not fully understand why I provoked such cruelty. Now my understanding was complete, and yet the pain was as deep, deeper. Protected by a misbegotten innocence, I used to believe in my strangeness. Now, to my sorrow, I knew I was not so different as I seemed. I longed to share in the common loaf, but no one would break bread with me.

I made no attempt to reveal myself to those I recognized that day, and there were many: older folk and children grown into men and women, some in unexpected, others in predictable, ways. I know now that I was afraid. Bad enough to be shunned as the Mother. To be spurned once more as myself, I could not bear. At the time I reasoned that it was useless to identify myself. Surely the Mother had cast a spell on the cloak. That was why people mistook me for her.

Yet I did not risk removing the cloak.

CHAPTER EIGHT

WHEN I HAD TRADED ALL MY GOODS but one cheese and a potion to make the bowels move, I called Marguerite and Delilah from their debaucheries. We had yet to stop at the brewery for a keg of ale, after the brewery a trip to the mill for flour, then home. Yes, home, for so the Mother and the cave had become. But when she no longer shared the hearth?

I shook the thought from me and made my way across the square where the crowds parted to let me pass. My business at the brewery was easily dispatched. The Mother always purchased a keg, and the brewer expected her. Like the others, that I was not the Mother escaped his notice utterly. Indeed, I was beginning to wonder myself. For who was she? Who was I?

I knew neither of our names.

As I proceeded to the far side of town, I passed the village green, usually, on a market day, the site of drunken revelry, but now oddly deserted. Memory stirred and made me see Aurelie in the midst of a gay throng. I saw her leading the May dances. And then, still more clearly, I pictured her grey eyes looking straight into mine, seeing me as I had never before been seen. I turned my head away and passed by swiftly, but I could not escape the vision.

My agitation mounted as I neared the mill, though, I reasoned, there was no cause. I would not find Aurelie there; she was long since of marriageable age. With her beauty and at least a modest dowry, she must have married well, a freeman or perhaps even a knight. Whoever he was, she had doubtless borne him half a dozen lusty sons by now.

The crowd at the mill was smaller than I would have expected for a market day. I could see a woman at the scales; for she worked on a platform in the yard that raised her just above the crowd. It was not the stout serving maid the miller used to employ, having no wife to fill the office. Even when this woman stooped to read the scale, it was evident that she was tall and slender. Her coifed head was bent; I could not see her face. Then she lifted a sack of meal from the scale. Light ignited tendrils of red-gold hair. I knew I looked on Aurelie.

For all she was but a miller's daughter weighing out meal and flour, to me she appeared as a goddess balancing the heavenly scales of justice. Such was the severity of her beauty. Here was no passing flower, blooming for a season. I had seen plenty of that kind, my sisters among them. Aurelie's beauty was of bone—hers were strong and well-proportioned—and bearing. She stood straight as a young tree and moved as if she danced. Beauty would still be hers when that fiery hair had burned to ash. Nor had she changed much from her earlier youth. She was one of those who knows from birth who she is and never questions the supreme importance of that being. I doubted the power of time or catastrophe to work a change in her of any depth.

I had no such certainty about myself, no way to measure my own changes.

That she would know me or that she would not: both possibilities seemed equally terrible. To distract myself while I waited, I listened to the talk about me and soon discovered that something was amiss.

"Are we to starve then?" demanded one woman, her voice edged with anger and fear. "I brought five bags of corn to grind, and you're telling me two sacks of meal is all I can claim? I've got children to feed and winter coming on!" Her voice rose and threatened to become a wail.

"Your quarrel is not with me, Dame," Aurelie answered. "It's the King's new tax."

"The old tax was bad enough," an old man grumbled. "Near half of what a man raised."

"Men!" snorted one woman. "What men? Unless you count yourself one and a man's work the lifting of a tankard. It was women raised these crops."

"Aye," agreed another. "First they take our men and now our bread." "I've got hard coin!" shouted someone just ahead of me. "I'll buy as much as I want!"

Aurelie shook her head. "There's a ration. You can offer a King's ransom, and the most I can give you is two sacks."

Then everyone spoke at once, each attempting to out shout the others with tales of need or deserving.

"Silence!"

Aurelie raised her palms, then pressed them down towards the people as if to hold them in place. For a young woman, she had a commanding air, and the crowd heeded her.

"I tell you again, I did not make these rulings. Look you," she pointed, and all turned to see a horseman, wearing the royal insignia, trotting towards the mill, followed by several ass-drawn carts and some peasants.

"There is one stands nearer the King than I. Take your complaints to him. If you dare."

No one did. Folk remained silent as they watched the knight directing the peasants to load the carts with sacks of meal and flour—for the nobles must have white bread! Only Aurelie did not stare. She went back to the business of weighing, and soon, I marked, the knight was eyeing her. She appeared to pay him no mind; she was no silly village lass to blush and simper at the notice of a man, however high his station. She did toss her head now and again, and those loose tendrils of hair danced on a breeze that seemed to stir for her alone. If possible, her movements became even more deft.

At last came my turn to be served. To my surprise—for I had made no plan, having been diverted by watching the knight study Aurelie—I heard myself speak.

"I'll take but one sack, though I'll pay for two and in coin. Give the other to someone who has greater need."

I still do not know whether I was prompted by charity—for with the grudge I held against my neighbors, why should I care to ease their hardship at my own expense?—or whether I spoke in hope of attracting attention from Aurelie. But whether I honestly intended the one, I succeeded in the other. She paused in her task and looked me full in the face.

"Oh!" she exclaimed. "I know you!"

Cloaked as I was, I suddenly felt that I was standing naked before the earth.

"Do you not know me?" she demanded. "You once gave me such a pretty shell. I believe I have it still."

My heart seemed too small for the joy that swelled it.

"Folk say the Devil lured you away." Her tone was merry and mocking. "Tell me, is the Devil as handsome as they say?"

I wanted nothing more than to banter with her, but I had no practice in quick repartee.

"Did you forfeit your tongue as well as your soul?"

"No," I managed. "It is only that I am unused to speech."

That was not precisely true, but my occasional discourse with the Mother could hardly be accounted lively conversation.

"Stay a moment then." She handed me my sack. "You must tell me your tale, for there is hardly any news here worthy of the name."

I drew aside, abashed yet pleased. By rights I should be starting home, or else darkness might overtake me and the Mother would worry at my lateness. But I had no power to deny Aurelie.

"Sit down," she said when she was able to join me, and she led me to a bench built into the wall. "I put aside the extra sack you gave, or else we might have had a riot on our hands. I'll see to it that the right person gets it at the right time."

"Why this new tax?" I asked; for in my alley I had heard nothing.

"The war, of course! The King must feed his army as well as keep alive the peasants who are building a stronghold in the mountains."

"Why are we at war?"

Aurelie shrugged, and if she had been younger and fuller of face, one might have said she pouted.

"Who knows? Some say one thing. Some another. The King does not keep counsel with common folk. There are those who say the King of Gule is greedy for more land and disputes the border. Some even say there have been raids and peasants taken for slaves. There are others who whisper that it is the other way around. It's common knowledge that the King and his knights were restless at home and spoiling for a fight. Then, too, it's rumored that the King is impatient for the Prince to win his spurs in battle and prove himself a man."

Then likely Julian was not yet married! My foolish pleasure in that temporary state of affairs was severely marred by the thought of my sweet Prince, who had trouble keeping his seat during a hunt, blundering his way through a bloody battle.

"I neither know the cause of the war nor care," Aurelie concluded. "So long as it comes to a speedy end."

"Yes," I nodded. "The people suffer for it."

"Not only that," Aurelie sighed. "It's deadly dull here. Have you noticed? The only men about have to gum their bread like babes."

"Are you not married then?" I ventured.

She shook her head and half-smiled.

"Before this wretched war, I had suitors in plenty. I could not take a step without tripping over one or another of them. But father found fault with every one. He is loath to part with me. And, indeed, I knew no reason to make my marriage bed too soon. I saw how it was with my friends. Brides one season, crones the next, worn out by bawling babes and brawling brats, nor talking nor thinking of anything but breeding and birthing and breach-ing. I was content to bide my time.

"And now I think maybe I've waited too long." For a moment she looked wistful, then her face hardened with defiance. "But I'll not marry an old man. I need no husband to keep me. My father, having no son, has taught me all his skill. I know I can run the mill alone. And shall, if need be!"

Aurelie appeared to have forgotten me for the moment, her eyes turned on some future time. I took the chance to admire her, so beautiful, so strong, set apart, as she always had been, from all the others.

"But you were going to tell me your tale," she remembered. "And a strange one it must be if you know nothing of the war."

"It's not so strange," I began, wishing that it was. "So far as I know the Devil never deigned to tempt me. My parents could no longer keep me and bade me go offer myself in service to some sister. The plan did not suit me, so I simply left one night."

"Alone? Out into the world? With no destination?"

Aurelie's eyes widened, and I puffed up like a toad.

"And so what happened?" urged Aurelie. "Were you fallen upon by thieves or ravished by roving knaves?"

Her eager incredulity made me see Aurelie in an unexpected light. For all her beauty and the authority she had displayed at the mill, she was still a child craving a story, a virgin in awe of the world beyond the village walls. I considered for a moment inventing a lurid tale but feared I had not the swiftness of mind and would be caught in a lie. Then what a fool I would feel.

Of course I could have told her of meeting the Prince, but beyond that fact, what could I say? That I loved him on sight and loved him still? That he gave me a kiss and turned me away? No, not even to impress Aurelie would I unstop my most precious memory and disperse its essence on the indifferent air.

"Well, go on," she prompted.

"Do you know the Wise Woman of the Western Wood?" Aurelie nodded, "The Witch, you mean?"

"If you will have it so." The word witch, I decided, did add some glam-our. "I met her in the Wood and became apprentice to her. I came to the Village today in her stead."

"Oh, yes." She sounded a trifle disappointed. "I should have recognized the goats."

"Most folk recognized the goats but did not know me. I have wondered at it. I thought the cloak must be magicked—but then," I added, "you knew me."

For me that fact held a thrilling significance.

Aurelie shrugged. "Most folk do not use the sense or senses God gave them and thus are easily deceived by the simplest spells." She brushed aside a straying tendril of hair as if brushing aside all such inconsequential persons. "But tell me, how did the Witch bind you to service? Are you under some enchantment?"

"If I am, I don't know it," I said, feeling that I could not defame the Mother merely for the sake of spicing my story. "I was alone in the world. She offered me a home and many skills."

"She has taught you magic then?"

"She calls it magic," I answered cautiously.

"Ah, I will remember that." Aurelie smiled. "It's good to know a fledgling witch."

But I am not a witch, the words almost spoke themselves before I checked them. I did not want to be a witch to Aurelie. I wanted to be my unnamed self. Yet how could I deny all I had just told her and keep my credence.

"I would gladly serve you if ever I could," I mumbled instead.

Yet I could not imagine Aurelie lacking in anything that I or anyone could give. She was perfect, complete in herself.

"Strange," Aurelie mused. "I remember you so clearly. I can still picture you as you held out the shell to me. But I do not remember your name."

"Not so strange, as I have no name to forget."

"Oh yes," she laughed, and though her laughter seared me, I earnestly endeavored not to begrudge Aurelie her merriment. "Now I remember. Your parents had too many daughters and ran out of names. It was a village joke for many years."

In so far as one I worshipped could give offense, I took it.

"If it was a joke, I recollect most folk did not find its butt so funny."

"True," agreed Aurelie. "You were quite the little hobgoblin. But I never feared you. I knew all the while you were but playing your part, even as I played mine."

She did understand! She did know me, even as I knew her. In her mind, as in mine, we were linked in our distinction from the common herd. Here was my sister, my other self. My opposite. My twin.

"Night draws in, and you've a journey ahead." Aurelie rose and smoothed her skirts. "But we must speak again, Girl with the Silver Eye."

I did what I could to answer her parting smile. Then she turned away. The audience was over.

CHAPTER NINE

I WAS GLAD TO RETURN TO THE CAVE and to the Mother, who awaited me with a simmering stew seasoned with restorative herbs. She knew better than I did how tired I was and wasted no time in talk as she busied herself with my bodily comfort. Her ministrations seemed magical to me. Without knowing quite how it all happened, I found myself spooning stew by the fire, my feet soothed in a tub of warm water steeped with mother-of-thyme. The Mother, who had removed the cloak without my noticing, was rubbing liniment into my neck and shoulders, untying knots I had not known were there.

The only impurity in my pleasure was my awareness that I had never welcomed the Mother this way on her return from market. Oh, I had always prepared a hot meal, but I had never guessed how bone-weary she must have been, Indeed, my own fatigue took me by surprise. I had traveled greater distances to childbirths, remained longer, labored harder, and had never felt so spent as I did now. I must have dozed as the Mother kneaded my neck, for I startled awake as my bowl and spoon slipped from my hands and landed with a soft thud on the earthen floor.

"No, Mother, let me." I stopped the Mother as she bent to pick them up. "I am much restored now."

She did not protest but returned to her stool and took up her everlasting carding while I wiped clean the bowl and spoon and put them away.

"Well, Daughter, how did you fare at the market?" she asked when I had sat down again.

"Well enough, Mother. I trust I brought back everything we need for the winter, though not so much meal as we usually have." I paused, but, unlike Aurelie, the Mother seldom prompted. "It seems there is war and the King has levied a new tax. I did not buy even as much as I might. There is hardship among the people, and so I bade the miller's daughter give the extra meal to the needy."

I felt anxious, for in what was, perhaps, but a ploy for attention, I had taken bread from the Mother's mouth as well as my own.

"It was well done, Daughter."

I waited for her to say more; I wanted her to, though I knew well enough she would not. I must speak myself if I had anything to say. For that very reason I held my peace, though I was not in the least peaceable. Sometimes I liked the silence, too; it flowed between us, a span of space and time that both separated and connected us, like a body of water between two islands. But tonight that water foamed and churned where my impatience met with her imperviousness.

I sat, too tired and fretful to soothe myself with spinning, and listened to the fire crackle and hiss, telling the secrets of the wood it consumed. The Mother's lack of curiosity made me more and more curious. Did she know what had happened to me in the village that day or did she simply care nothing for what transpired beyond the Wood? I wanted to know. The day had taxed me greatly, and my thoughts were as tangled as a skein of yarn that's suffered the attack of a litter of kittens. It was all very well for the Mother to tend my body, but what of my mind? At last I could contain myself no longer.

"Why didn't you tell me that you cast a spell on the cloak!" I demanded, not at all sure that she had, but hoping to startle her into some unplanned revelation. Foolish hope for one who had lived so long with the Mother. If she had been a pond, I would scarce have seen a ripple.

"Tell me what happened, Daughter."

"Everyone thought I was you. No one recognized me, though I saw many I remember. Even my own sister did not know me, and she looked me full in the face. Only one person knew me. The miller's daughter. Do you know her? Aurelio." I said her name slowly, savoring the syllables with my tongue, as if they had some fine and delicate flavor. "So I thought there must be some magic in the cloak that blinded all but her."

"There was magic, Daughter, but not in the cloak."

"Where then?"

"In the eyes of the people who beheld you, in the inner eye behind their eyes."

"I don't understand. How did you cast a spell over so many people? Surely it would have been simpler to magick the cloak."

"Daughter, Daughter," she said, half-laughing, half-lamenting. "Why must you insist that I cast a spell at all?"

"Why? Because everyone saw you though they looked on me."

"Why are you so certain they saw me?"

"They all called me Mother."

"Mother is not my name, nor Witch, nor Wise Woman. I have told you before: that is what I am, not who."

"But no one knows your name!" I cried.

"I know my name."

She knew her name! She knew her name. Bile rose in my mouth; I could not speak. For once, without my pestering her, the Mother continued.

"Within the inner eye of all, there dwells the eternal image of the Mother or Witch or Wise Woman. Most folk know nothing of such visions. They only know what they think they see. And so they seek the image in the world without. That, Daughter, was the magic at work today. And magic it is, though it is simple, too simple for most people to understand. And it is powerful, terribly powerful."

The Mother had never revealed so much at once. I wanted to shout: Stop! Wait! as if my very thoughts were out of breath.

"In my time I bore the image. Now it is your turn."

"But I never asked to bear this image!"

"Image bearers do not choose; they are chosen. No." She shook her head before I could form the question. "It was not I who chose you. I do not know the name of the power that chooses, but chosen you are. Your choice, Daughter, is how you will bear the image: as a curse or as a gift, as pain or as power, for evil or for good."

The Mother fell silent at last, and this time I welcomed her silence. Her words gave me much to ponder. They illumined my childhood. If they were true—and loath as I was to admit it, they had the ring of truth—then I had always been an image-bearer, or an incipient one. So far, I had borne the image as pain and a curse; nor could I deny that evil tempted me.

But it had never occurred to me that I had chosen pain. I had suffered it rather, and most unwillingly. Nor had I ever felt very powerful, save, perhaps, when I deliberately frightened someone. I suffered still. The Mother made such a fuss over the difference between who and what she was. I was sick to death of what I was. Whether I called that 'what' image-bearer or outcast, I'd had my nose rubbed in it all my life. I wanted only to find out who I was, and I yearned for someone to know me by that name.

I knew very well from my lessons with the Mother that to know a name was to see. Had I not seen the Wood, once to my eyes a simple mass of green, transformed into a complexity of plants and trees I called by name? The indiscriminate dazzle of the night sky, that, too, had taken on meaning and precision with the naming of the stars. To be known by name was to be seen. Without a name, no one could see who I was. I was invisible within the image, a cloak that hid no face. Then I remembered Aurelie.

"Mother, the miller's daughter, she saw not the image but my very self."

"Well said, Daughter. It pleases me that you make the distinction between the image and yourself. Not to know the difference or to forget is dangerous."

"Yes, yes," I brushed the words aside, impatient. "But what of Aurelie? How is it that she saw me?"

"I believe it must be that she, too, is an image-bearer."

"Mother!" I was offended. "Aurelie could never be taken for anything like a Witch."

"No, Daughter, I didn't mean that. There are other images. The miller's daughter might bear the Maiden or perhaps the Queen."

"The Queen!" I agreed delighted. "It must be so. But then she and the image she bears are one, for truly she is a Queen."

"The who and the what are rarely one," cautioned the Mother, "even with folk who do not bear the great images."

I was no longer paying the Mother much heed, intrigued as I was with these new ideas.

"Mother, are there men who bear images?"

"Yes," she nodded. "Many. The Priest, the King, the Prophet. The Prophet is closest to the Wise Woman, save that time is kinder to prophets. Their words may be written down. They may come to be revered, even worshipped, like the Nazarene. But in their day they, too, are outcast and reviled."

But I had neither care nor pity for prophets. I was thinking of my poor Prince, so gentle, so meek to bear the image he was born to. How clearly I had seen who he was. And he had seen me. He had! If only I could have told him my name, so that he could keep it for me, always.

"Mother, I pray you, name me soon or else must I name myself. I am weary of waiting for a name. You know yours, as you keep telling me."

"But have told it to few. An image-bearer must take care who knows her name. Nor can you name yourself, not your true name that is yours alone. Have patience, Daughter. The name will be given to me, then I will give it to you."

"But will it be soon, Mother?"

"Daughter, the hour is unknown to me, but I trust it will be soon."

With that unusual measure of reassurance, I had to be content. The Mother set aside her work and rose to bank the fire. I fell asleep that night, day dream drifting into dream of how one day I would tell my name to Aurelie.

CHAPTER TEN

I HAVE NEVER TOLD MY NAME TO AURELIE; nor after that night had I much time for dreaming. The Mother did not rise from her pallet again. That morning I found her stricken in her left side, so that she could scarcely move any limb. After I had done all I could to attend to her comfort, I sat beside her in an anguish, fretting that somehow my left eye or left-handedness had afflicted her.

The Mother, always adept at reading me, taxed what strength she had—for speech was a great effort—to make me understand that she believed she suffered from a thickening of the blood. So I gave her infusions of sweet clover for thinning the blood, but I sensed that she neither desired nor expected to get well. She only regretted how much care she required of me and worried that I was overworked, what with the animals, harvesting the plants, cutting wood, tending the sick, and going to childbeds.

In truth, I welcomed the never-ending work, for it left me no time to wonder what was to come. And I never tired of tending the Mother, though she doubtless tired of my attendance. I was always mixing brews to stimulate her appetite, to help her sleep, to relieve the constipation that so afflicts the bedridden. Daily, I washed and massaged her. All the healing arts she had ever taught me I practiced on her poor, dying body, and she suffered my ministrations more for my sake than for her own. I was far more anxious to keep her in life than she was to stay. Though I had proved myself able to accomplish all our tasks unaided, I still felt a great inward lack that, like myself, had no name.

Never did I feel that lack more acutely than when there arrived at the break of day a certain woman seeking audience with the Mother. It was one of those clear mornings that dawn in deep winter when the air itself is hard as crystal. The bare branches of trees stood so sharp and still against the sky they looked like the characters of some ancient writing that—could one but decipher their meaning—would reveal the secret of the world's beginning. I was outdoors a short distance from the cave gathering kindling when the woman hailed me.

"Mother, a word with you."

I did not startle now when one called me Mother.

"Is it childbirth or sickness?" I asked as she drew near.

"Neither. Only...only that I must speak with you or I don't know what I'll do."

Her eyes met mine for an instant too brief for me to read anything I might have seen there. Then she cast them down as folk always did. I took a moment to study her face. I could not tell whether it was young or old, only that it appeared to be frozen. Who knew how far she had journeyed in the coldest hours of the night?

"Come then," I inclined my head towards the cave.

I led the way, a step or two ahead of the woman, grateful that she could see only my back. I did not trust my face to conceal the panic mounting within. Surely here was one of those who sought the Mother for reasons I had never known. What was I to do? She had taken me for the Mother, and I had not contradicted her. Should I disabuse her when we reached the cave and turn her over to the real Mother while I fled to tend the goats?

As we entered the cave, I cast a glance towards the Mother's pallet, and all hope of escape died. She slumbered still, and I had not the heart to wake her. Moreover, her speech was slurred and cost her much strength. I turned towards the waiting woman, and as I did, I heard within me the Mother's voice: "It is your turn to bear the image."

I felt neither willing nor able, but what could I do? I did first what the Mother would have done before all else: I sat the woman down before the fire while I stoked it. Then I brewed some hot spiced wine and gave her a hunk of bread and some cheese. While the woman ate and drank, I watched her. Though the color returned to her face, it still appeared stiff, save for moving as it must to take the food and drink. I guessed her to be just past her childbearing years and in good health, no teeth missing, a little thin but by no means starved. Her clothes were simple and somber but in excellent condition and of good quality. A widow perhaps of a wealthy merchant or a landed knight? A respectable woman, not in any obvious need. What could she want with the Mother? What had driven her to journey alone through cold and dark and deep woods? She had finished eating and had cast down her eyes again. Clearly she was waiting for me.

"Daughter, how may I help you?"

My words and the gentleness of my tone surprised me; for I was feeling more curious than compassionate and the woman I addressed as daughter was likely old enough to be my mother.

"Mother." At last she lifted her eyes to mine; they were ordinary eyes in all respects, save for the depth of their misery. "I am in such terror of death that I cannot bear to live. Help me or I shall be driven to end my fear with my life."

Here was a coil: someone who would kill herself for fear of death! And I was to save her? From death? From fear? How I wished the Mother would wake and speak wisdom from her bed. She, so fearless of death, would know how to banish fear.

"Do you suffer from any fatal sickness?"

My own healer's sense told me that she did not, but I did not know what else to say.

"No, but I live in constant fear that there will be an outbreak of plague or a perilous storm or fire or barbarian hordes." Her face remained immobile as she chanted this litany of disaster.

"Surely," I reasoned, "all these things may chance to happen, and we cannot know when they will or stop them if they do, so why trouble to fear them?"

Her only response was a soft whimper, and I felt I had spoken stupidly. It was precisely that she had no power to prevent catastrophe that she dreaded it so. Yet other folk went about their business as confident as she was fearful that such accidents would never befall them. There must be some deeper reason that she shrank from death before it had even approached her. Unshriven sin perhaps?

"Have you seen a priest?" I asked, thinking to rid myself of this woman and all obligation to her.

"Oh, yes, and more than one."

Her tone and her face became more animate with scorn, and I warmed to the woman. I have never cared for priests nor they for me.

"They keep asking me about my sins. I confess everything I can think of, and they press me for more. They tell me only mortal sin could make me so afraid of death. But, truly, I do not think so. I have had uncharitable thoughts, but never did I act on one. I was ever a chaste and obedient wife. I am no glutton; indeed I find no pleasure in food or drink but only take what I must. Nor envy, anger, greed, nor lust have ever moved me greatly. I am not clever enough at anything for pride to tempt me. As for sloth, I perform all my duties. I go to Mass, observe all fasts and feast days. There are many more sinful than I, and sometimes the worst sinners seem the merriest."

I understood better now why her face appeared so frozen: It was not just fear but an utter lack of enjoyment. As yet I had no idea what I could offer this woman beyond a tonic brew, such as I had given many women when they felt low during the change of life. I toyed with the idea of reciting some impromptu incantation and assuring her that I had thus dispelled her fear. But this woman was no fool to be impressed with sham magic.

"Tell me more of your life," I said, partly to gain time and partly in hope that I might discover some clue to the mystery of her fear.

"There is nothing to tell. Most would call me fortunate. I have never known want nor any suffering beyond the common lot. I am a yeoman's daughter. I married a neighboring lord who wanted to enlarge his holdings with our land. My husband, dead now these ten years, God rest his soul," she added perfunctorily, "was neither kind nor cruel; I neither loved nor hated him. I bore eight children, and I know I am considered lucky to have five living, though I have never ceased to grieve for the lost ones. I have always been afraid of death, but when I was younger and had the babes to tend—I did love my babes—and the household to manage, I had less time for fear.

"Now my children are all grown, three daughters married and gone. I scarcely see them or their children. My younger son is a knight in the King's service, and the elder is Lord of the Manor, now that his father is dead.

"He is married, and my daughter-in-law runs the household with more zeal and skill than ever I possessed. I would not dream of interfering with her. She is most considerate of what she calls my age." Here she gave a wry smile that made me aware of the wit and intelligence that lay unused in her. "So I am allowed to do nothing unless I beg her.

"I suppose that is my own fault. There is nothing much I want to do. The various household tasks I performed for so long were never pleasures. I work on the tapestries, like all the ladies, but I confess it bores me, and the others are all more nimble with their needles. I would like to spend more time with my grandchildren, but they are all boys, and since they were out of swaddling, they've been perpetually schooled in all the manly arts. I used to play upon the lute, but my daughter-in-law has her own musicians, and I cannot practice my poor skill when they are about.

"So you see, there is nothing for me but old age, infirmity, and death. I live in terror of all three, but death most of all. I don't know why death seems so dreadful to me, since I care so little for life. They say we shall be happy in Heaven—if we ever get there; I know my children would buy masses for my soul—but I have scarcely known earthly joy. How can I believe in the joy of Heaven?

"No matter what the priests say, I fear death may be nothing but deeper nothingness, and I cannot bear it or the fear of it another day. In truth, I cannot bear to live or die. I have heard that you are a Wise Woman. So I rose while everyone slept—my son and daughter-in-law would never countenance such a journey—and asked the way here of one of our serfs. Help me if you can, though doubtless you cannot."

She fell silent, her head bent again, her face set in those grim lines as she waited, it seemed, for me to concur that she was beyond hope. Her certainty that I could not help her vexed me, though I had no reason to believe I could. Still, I was determined now to try, to prove her wrong and because her plight touched me. Truly, as she had said, according to the facts of her life, she could be called fortunate. Yet how often the truth confounds fact. Here was a woman in whom I could discern tact, intelligence, maybe even talent. Yet she could not—or would not—value herself at her worth.

Finding little to guide me in the woman's account of her comfortable and exemplary, if joyless, life, I began to search my own life for the source of such fear. I did not believe myself to be as afraid of death as this woman. And yet, of course, I was afraid. I pondered what it was that troubled me most about my own death, and very soon I knew: my greatest fear was that I should die without knowing my name.

"Is there," I spoke slowly, groping for words, "is there some one thing you always wanted?"

The woman shook her head. "I hardly know what it is to desire. I have told you, I do what I must."

"But there must be something." I pressed her, feeling desperate. "Or if there isn't now, there must have been once. Some dream that you forced yourself to forget. Remember it now. I charge you." I made my voice stern, as I took on all the authority of the Mother. For a moment, the woman looked balky and stubborn as an old mule. Then something in her yielded, and, before my eyes, she seemed to grow younger. When she smiled to herself, I saw another woman, the one she might have been, the one she yet could be.

"Well, it's very foolish," she began, "but I do remember. When I was a girl in my father's house, there came, from time to time, wandering minstrels —not like the ones my daughter-in-law boards. They were not so fancy but rather raggle-taggle folk, men, women, and children. They journeyed from castle to castle, from village to village, from festival to festival, singing and playing for their bread, sometimes telling stories or acting plays. When they were there, all was merry, and no one minded what we children did. We stayed up until we fell asleep under the tables with the dogs.

"The next morning, or in a day or week or two, depending on the weather or the season, they would leave again, striking out across the fields, as if they feared no one, as if they walked in the company of angels. Indeed, the way they came and went, the wondrous beauty of their music made me believe they were angels.

"Now I know they were a scruffy lot with common ways and low morals. Then I wanted nothing more than to join their band. I practiced upon my lute and dreamed how I would run off with them next time they wafted through, but always, when it came to the moment, I lacked courage. At last I grew old enough to understand how foolish were my fancies. As the daughter of good yeoman stock, I was destined for the very life I have led."

She had told me what I needed to know. I was certain of what I must say. For the rest: that lay with her.

"By your own account, you have discharged your duties as wife, mother, and lady of the manor. If no wandering minstrels come to your castle, then go to the nearest town next feast day and find there a band to join. In the meantime, practice upon your lute and ready yourself for your calling."

The woman looked on me aghast.

"Mother, some call you wise, but maybe you are mad. I was but a silly maiden when I entertained that fancy. The life such folk lead in truth must be both rough and dangerous, not at all like a young girl's daydream. I have told you how fearful I am. How could I brave the perils of a wanderer's life? Death would beset me on every side!"

"And so it does now, and so it does everyone. You can hide from death and cower within your castle walls, but death will seek you in due season. Or you can go out and face death on the open road. Maybe you will meet life there as well."

The woman was silent for a time, but her face worked. I felt frightened by the feeling I had stirred in her.

"Mother." She looked at me with full eyes. "If I only had the courage, I would do as you say."

"No." I shrank from the authority with which she had endowed me. "Do not what I say, but learn to listen to yourself. That's all I meant, Daughter."

"For so long I have heard only my own fear. Can you not give me courage?"

The woman wanted me to work magic. And why wouldn't she? Was I not a Witch for all she used the polite title Wise Woman? Wouldn't folk be shocked if they knew this Witch did not know the meaning of magic? Skeptics sneered at magic as deception; the devout condemned it as the Devil's art. Most all, at one time or another, even the skeptical and the devout, looked on magic as a way to get what they wanted—at a price, perhaps, but without their own effort. If that were magic, then I was no magician. To be sure, I had a hazel wand for the divining of water, another service for which folk sought the Mother, but I could not wave it over this woman and make her brave.

I glanced at the Mother asleep on her pallet. What would she do? She insisted she had taught me magic but would never say what magic was, save to repeat that maddening rhyme. Silently I chanted it again, desperate for a hint.

> *Take the dung and make it flower,*
> *Take the pain and make it power,*
> *Let your own fear make you bold,*
> *Take the straw and spin, spin, spin the gold.*

The rhyme seemed as pointless and useless as ever. For all my pain, I felt powerless to transform this woman's fear into boldness. I would have to resort to trickery. The woman was waiting, and the goats were bleating for me to come and relieve their swollen udders. I would give the woman something, anything. I cast about in my mind for exotic ingredients to mix in a potion and elaborate instructions to accompany them. Then, amidst all my mental scavenging, there rose an image, so vivid, so potent, that it stopped my frantic thoughts in their tracks.

Against a background of autumnal colors: gold, russet, brown, glowing with the rich light that suffuses that time of year: a lute, and where the hole of the lute would be, the great sign of healing: the mandala.

"Wait," I said to the woman as I rose. "I have something for you."

I went to the wooden chest where I kept my finished cloths, and the pungent smell of the herbs I used to keep away the moth greeted me as I opened it. Though there was not much light in the cave, I knew my weavings by touch and swiftly found the one I had envisioned. I had sewn it to a drab grey backing, because I delighted in the contrast. As I lifted it from the chest, only the grey side was visible. Then I took it into the fire's light, held it up, and let it open before the woman's eyes.

She drew in her breath, and her face was again transformed; it took on the warmth and richness of the weaving's colors. I understood that these colors were hers, though perhaps she had never worn them.

"This cannot be meant for me," she protested, and in her voice I heard both joy and wonder.

"But indeed it is. I wove it for you against this very day."

As I spoke, I knew my words were true. Was this magic then? This purpose, this pattern, so rarely apparent to the mortal eye, and yet always present?

"You knew I would come," she marveled.

I did not answer yes or no. That much I had learned from the Mother: timely silence does wonders to preserve a reputation for wisdom.

"Take it, Daughter, and make it into a cloak. See? The other side is grey as rain and will draw no attention to you."

She received the cloth from my hands and held it close to her for a time, as if it were one of her lost babes.

"I must go now," she said, rising to her feet. "Or they'll be plumbing the wells for me." She actually grinned.

I wondered that she could make such a joke! There must be magic afoot.

"I don't know how to thank you or repay you. I have coin—"

"No, keep your silver." I stayed her hand.

True, I had given her one of my finest weavings, but I was in no way certain that I had helped her. If she followed my advice, then I had sent a respectable woman to lead the life of a vagabond. No wonder the priests thought the Mother an evil influence on the people!

"Only tell me your christened name that I may remember you by it."

"My name is Amelia, Mother."

"Go now, Amelia. If you find what you seek, return to me when you are able and play for me upon your lute."

Amelia still cradled the weaving in her arms as I walked her to the door and waved her away into the fine morning.

Then I heard a sound I had never before heard in all my days, and yet I knew it from before time and for all eternity.

It was the Mother's voice, clear for the first time since her illness began, the Mother's voice calling me by name. Again she called my name as I turned to her in the fullness of my joy.

"Come," she said. "I want to tell you who I am."

CHAPTER ELEVEN

FOR LESS THAN A FULL SEASON, we knew one another by name. Then, one morning in early Spring, my Mother, she who named me, called my name and asked me to move her to the open door. She longed for the light, she said, though it was so strong she had to close her eyes and let it stream through lids that were thin and dry as parchment. I sat beside her, and we shared a silence alive with the sound of things waking and stirring in the earth.

She did not have to tell me that this was our last time.

Just before the sun reached its height, I turned to her. She still breathed, but her breath had the stillness that comes at dusk and dawn, at noon and the dead of night. I spoke her name, and I blessed her journey. I let her go, and she was gone.

The Mother had instructed me to burn her body. I was grateful. The ground was still frozen, and I would have had a hard time digging a grave, but without her bidding, I would never have dared a fire. Burning the body is a pagan custom, and if any priests had found out, they might have made trouble for me.

The Mother refused to believe that God would require a rotting corpse for resurrection on Judgment Day. Strange how the priests professed to despise the flesh while it was living but set such store by its remains. No one had tended the living body more lovingly than the Mother, but the body belonged to the earth, she said. Death but reclaimed it and returned it to the elements from which it was made, whether it burned or decayed. And so with her teaching, she strengthened me for this last service I would render her.

When her body was burned, I took the ashes and scattered them in a favorite place of hers, where she used to gather the herb called life everlasting, and where I gather it to this day.

BOOK 2

MOTHER

CHAPTER ONE

THUS I BECAME THE MOTHER.
And yet I remained myself, different from she who bore the title and the image before me. I was always aware of the difference, all the more so because I now knew my name. Yet no one else appeared to notice. Folk came as they always had, seeking the Mother as midwife, healer, wise woman. Most of the time, the service required was simple enough, and what I was sufficed to meet the need.

Every now and again, one came, like Amelia, with trouble not of the body but the thing that makes the body a unique being. Priests call it a soul, and they say it is eternal. I know nothing of that, but I do know that nothing is tougher or tenderer than what I might as well call spirit. When it is wounded, the wounds are deeper and harder to heal than most suffered by the body. I do not know whether I helped to heal all or any of those who came to me. I only know that the work of healing put my whole being to the test. For the one who sought my wisdom, I had to be the Mother, bear the image. Yet for the healing word or gift, I had to delve into my own depths, down deep to the very dwelling place of the Name.

That Spring and Summer, living alone as the Wise Woman of the Western Wood, I felt that I aged many seasons. I worked hard, but it was not the labor alone that changed my face so that I startled to see my image in a pool of water. Nor was I displeased with the difference I perceived. I could not mourn the passing of beauty I'd never possessed; my bodily strength, far from abandoning me, seemed at its height. No, the change was subtler, not merely a matter of slack or wrinkled skin. It was that I was beginning to look the part of a wise woman; I was growing to resemble the image I bore.

To be sure, I did not radiate the calm that was not only the image but the essence of the Mother before me. Still, I thought, I looked inscrutable. I had disciplined the muscles of my face never to betray fear or hope, anger or delight. My birthmark had faded as my skin weathered, though it was still discernible. My silver eye, stark and startling in a child's face, now seemed a fitting repository for my mystery. I would not cower within my cloak next market day. I had become my own disguise.

Judging by the dwindling of supplies, I must soon make that journey again. I looked on the prospect both with less eagerness and less alarm than I would have dreamed possible a scant year ago. Curiously, now that I had a name, I was no longer certain that I wanted to tell it to Aurelie. The pain of namelessness had become the power of knowing my name: knowing that I had something in reserve, a secret that I could reveal or keep as I chose, a prize possession that no one could wrest from me against my will.

Nor did loneliness frighten me now that I was alone. It was like looking at last in some dread comer where you feared to find a bogie and discovering only darkness, darkness that was there all along, and only fear gave it the power to take shape. It was not that I suffered loneliness cheerfully. I missed my Mother sorely, and I grieved for her. It was only that loneliness had become not a fear but a fact, and I had neither died of it nor gone mad.

Much of the time I did not feel lonely, even though I was alone. I had shared a daily, yearly round of tasks with the Mother for so long that the work still seemed companionable. Sometimes, in the evening, as I spun or worked at the loom, the silence felt not empty but full, as though the Mother shared it still. Then, of course, I had the goats and the other creatures for warm-blooded company. All in all, I congratulated myself, I had made an admirable peace with my lot in life.

Then, at harvest time, I made my visit to the village. As soon as I reached the outskirts, I noticed the changes: the animals looked almost as lean as the year before, but there were more of them, and not so many women acted as beasts of burden. Donkeys, and even some oxen, pulled carts that were heavier laden with all manner of goods. But the greatest change was in the faces. Grim matrons who last year barked orders to their children had turned jolly and indulgent. Children scampered about, shouting their joy, getting in the way, exciting the animals, but no one chastised them. Young girls tried to be careful of their new dignity but their blood betrayed them, racing back and forth between flushed cheeks and restless feet that longed to dance. I had only to look at the women to know: the men were back. The air of festival was like strong drink. I wagered with the babes begotten this day, I'd get little rest come June.

I tried not to begrudge folk their merriment, as I sat apart in my alley all day. Men and women alike had lived through a bitter time. No one needed second sight to know that hard times would come again. Winter could be cold and full of sickness. Floods could rot the seeds in Spring. Drought could crack the earth and wither the crops in Summer. Early frost could blight the harvest; untimely storms ruin the grain. Then, too, the poor had always to contend with calamity imposed by the King: heavy taxes and harsh laws. Indeed, one could argue that as an outlaw, of sorts, living deep in the Wood with my goats and my honey bees and with my knowledge of herbs and wild foods, I fared better than most folk and seldom knew want in the worst of times.

And yet I held my grudge—or my grudge held me. I could all but smell my sourness, as if I were curdled milk or rank cheese. The memory of the Mother's kindliness and good will towards all only made me feel the meaner. As I yielded to my bitter mood, I strove to justify myself. True, everyone suffered, and, in material ways, more than I. But other folk had recompense for their suffering in days like this one: in mirth and camaraderie, in song and dance, in the bliss, however fleeting or foolish, of coupling.

As the day grew older and drink made lads and maidens bolder, I saw more and more lovers. Yet I felt so far removed from the rites of courtship that I observed them as I might the mating dance of birds. Nor was there much difference, I sneered to myself, save that the human females were more brightly plumed than their feathered counterparts. As for the males, they strutted and brawled like barnyard cocks. In time, it seemed, no one lacked a mate. Many a pair slipped through my alley, seeking seclusion for kisses or heading for the orchards and haystacks at the edge of the village.

And I lie when I say the sight of youthful love meant no more to me than the mating of birds. The memory of the Prince, which in the Wood often slept because I was too busy to attend to it, stirred and stretched as if it had been wakened with a kiss, as truly, in my fancy, it had. And I found my heart was as sore as ever from my long and hopeless loving. At least this day, I vowed, I should have news of him, however much it hurt me to hear it. For surely he must marry now.

"What of the Prince?" The question leaped to my lips each time someone came to buy from me, and each time it died there unspoken. I feared I could not hide my love-longing. No one offered news unasked. Therefore, I set my hopes on Aurelie, for with scarcely a question from me she had told me much last time we met.

Late in the afternoon, I made my way to the mill. The yard was crowded, more crowded than the marketplace. After the austerity of war, folk had much need of meal, but peace only partly explained the throng. I could scarcely see Aurelie, the men swarmed so thick about her, a wild hive following their queen. When I came in full sight of her, I, too, was ravished anew by her beauty.

The year before, though nothing could disguise the fineness of her bones and features, her beauty had been subdued, like a church in Lent. Now it blazed, a daystar that made the bright world dim beside her. It was partly the effect of her red-geld hair, uncovered—likely some mischievous knave had snatched her kerchief as a prize—streaming in the wind like a long-tailed comet. A common wench thus uncoifed might have appeared a strumpet. Even in her disarray, flushed with excitement, Aurelie looked regal.

When it came my turn to be served, Aurelie gave me a nod of recognition and a fleeting smile. With that I had to be content; clearly she had neither leisure nor desire for conversation with me. Slowly, I wended back through the streets towards the main gate, reluctant to leave unenlightened about the Prince. As I crossed the market square, it occurred to me that I might bide awhile and drink some ale in the tavern. No one was likely to bother me: times were good, folk were merry, and inclined to leave well alone. So I secured my cart, bade my goats stay, went inside, and bought a tankard. In the comer nearest the door, I drank with my cloak pulled close about me. I believed I might be acquiring the Mother's knack of blending with surroundings, and I hoped to be taken for a large keg.

For a time there were too many different conversations for me to follow any, and I thought to myself: What a yammering these humans make, worse than the chatter of squirrels and to less purpose. All at once I longed for the quiet of my cave. What could I possibly learn of the Prince that could make any difference to me? The pattern of my life was as set as the natural cycles. The seasons changed; the moon waxed and waned all in accordance with unvarying laws. Human irregularities were not for me.

I set down my ale unfinished and stirred myself to go when in through the door burst the miller and a band of boisterous companions. He was plainly the leader and meant to hold sway in the tavern as well.

"A tankard of ale for every man!" he shouted to the alemaster.

"Business must be good, Miller."

"That it is, lads, that it is. And it's only right, after all, as father-in-law to the crown prince, that I should bestow my generosity upon you peasants."

He roared with laughter to show he meant no offense and reached for a huge tankard the alemaster's boy had fetched, downed it with what seemed a single gulp, and handed it back for more.

"Slow your swilling, Miller!" someone shouted. "You must have been in the drink since dawn with your royal airs. We all know you got a fine wench, but unless your goodwife, God rest her, was telling you lies, she's common-born like all the rest of us."

For a moment the Miller turned red, and his huge fist tightened on his tankard so the knuckles showed white. Then he appeared to change his mind, and he let forth another blast of laughter.

"I forget you're but poor ignorant folk that cannot read, so likely you know nothing of his Majesty's proclamation."

I doubted the miller could read either. Most villains could not. A herald must have sounded it abroad. I had more than an inkling of its purport.

"Oh, that," said another, determined to steal the Miller's thunder. "Of course I read it. I don't recollect it said anything about you being father-in-law."

"Goes without saying," rejoined the miller, unruffled. "The King seeks a strong young woman of childbearing years, fair of person, sound of limb and mind, to be wife to his only son and heir, his Royal Highness, the Prince Julian.' Now I know you've all been pestering me many a year to marry my Aurelie to your own, but you must see it's my duty to consider the claims of royalty first, eh lads? The King's our sovereign lord, after all."

There was some laughter, but it was strained.

"So when's the wedding to be, Miller? I suppose we're all invited?"

"His Majesty will set the date when—"

"When he's chosen the wench," interrupted another man. "The proclamation was only made today. There's King's men all about the place on a tour of inspection. My daughter or yours is likely as his to be the one."

"You all know as well as I," the miller raised his voice over talk that grew louder and louder with excitement, "that once they've seen Aurelie, there's no contest. There's been King's men at the mill all day."

"There's been King's men at my shop, too," someone rejoined. "My lass may not be a walking torch, but she's a good girl, sturdy and pleasant, obedient, too. Knows her place—not like some," he added with emphasis, his meaning plain.

"My girl is handy, too," another chimed in. "She makes pies fit for Heaven's table."

""But, sir, you know she's promised to me," objected a young man, built like an ox, the sort who seems perpetually in a sweat.

"Yes, but you'd not stand in the way of her becoming the highest lady in the land."

"That I would, sir."

I could well imagine him doing just that, and wide enough he was that any girl might have difficulty getting round him.

"And you just ask her," the young bull continued, "whether she'd have him or me. I've seen the Prince. He's nothing but a weakling, all pale and girlish. Now take that battle. It's being sung on every street corner as how he won it. But I was there—"

A companion jabbed him violently in the ribs, whispered something and gestured, directing his gaze and mine to a corner where two men, dressed in the livery of the King, listened attentively to the talk. The rash young man, who was already ruddy, turned the color of a purple cabbage and mumbled something about his loyalty to the crown and meaning no offense. But most of what he said was lost as other men vied with one another, plainly for the benefit of the royal proxies, extolling and enumerating their daughters' virtues.

"Mine can sew the straightest seam."

"Mine can get milk from a cow gone dry."

"You should see the candles my daughter makes. Why the priest himself said, just the other day—"

"Fools!" the miller broke in. "Do you think the King seeks a common housewife for his son? The King has servants in plenty to sew and bake and milk. As for my daughter, she can do all that and more. She can do whatever she sets her hand to. Why, she can take straw and spin gold!"

My heart jumped to hear those familiar words in so strange a setting. But the pounding of the blood in my ears was overmatched by the guffaws that met the miller's boast.

The miller was a big man, well known among village folk for telling tales taller than himself. Often folk were willing to add a pinch of salt and enjoy the tales for what they were. That day, angered by his arrogance, they goaded and teased and drove him to defend a claim he might otherwise have forgotten the moment it was made. Thus, he went on to spin a lengthy yarn about a fairy woman who came to his daughter's christening and gave her the gift of spinning straw to gold that she might make her dowry. Unknown to the now thoroughly drunken miller, the two King's men hung on every word.

I crept away unnoticed before the Miller's foolish talk was done. I neither believed nor disbelieved his story. There were reputed to be a few fairy folk left in our countryside—or those with fairy blood. Indeed, perhaps the Mother had been such a one. Now and again, it was rumored, fairies did bestow gifts or call down curses at christenings. But whether he lied or spoke the truth or knew not which he did, the miller was a lackwit to open his mouth.

What need had Aurelie to spin gold with hair like hers? Her face and figure, the vital grace that animated both, these were riches to rival a King's wealth. Of course Aurelie would be chosen! There was no contest; in that the Miller had spoken truly. Indeed, now that I knew, I felt as though I had always known: that she was the one, the chosen one.

As I made my way across the dusky fields, I pondered this old-new knowledge. Was it not fitting, I asked myself, that these two should marry: the one I admired, the other I adored? And both had seen me, known me when I scarcely knew myself. Was there not cause here for satisfaction, even rejoicing? Yet as I reached the Wood, I could feel bitterness seeping into my soul, cold and corrosive as brackish water.

Until now I had contrived not to grudge Aurelie her good fortune. I had gloried instead in our bond, our distinction from ordinary folk. Were we not both image bearers? Yet the image she bore exalted her, while mine debased me. Hers fitted her more perfectly than the finest raiment, while I felt imprisoned within mine, distorted, grotesque.

To think that this Summer I had almost begun to relish the image, to fancy that I had some likeness to it. What a dupe I had been! Now, trapped as I was, I recoiled from the image, tried to shrink myself to mere nothing that it might not touch me: me, the one who knew her own name but could not, would not, tell it. My name was my last freedom, my only refuge from a fate I knew full well I could not escape. No more than Aurelie could escape hers, I reminded myself. I ought not to blame her. But I did. For hers was a fate to be envied, as pretty as a child's tale.

That night as I lay on my pallet, seeking sleep in vain, I could not cease picturing their wedding day. Underlying my jealousy was a feeling of unease that had nothing to do with my own thwarted desire. Something was wrong with the vision that rose again and again. There was Aurelie, her hair fiery and free, in a gown of deepest blue embroidered with gems as stars in a night sky. My difficulty was with Julian; next to Aurelie, he was all blurred and shadowy. Try as I might to clothe him in garments that befitted a bridegroom, when I managed to make him come clear at all, he would appear each time, as I had beheld him, in his torn and stained riding clothes, his cheeks soft and downy, and in his eyes that look of sweet bewilderment with which he had first greeted me.

Maybe it only was that to me he was still a lad and did not look right beside Aurelie, whom I had seen but that day a grown woman. Yes, that must be it, I thought, crossing at last the borderline into the land of sleep.

But the odd foreboding followed me, and, in the days to come, I grew so used to its presence that I forgot it was there at all.

CHAPTER TWO

O F NECESSITY, MY LIFE CONTINUED with all the familiar
tasks the Mother had taught me. Most days I had no more need
to consider what to do next than the trees have need to think to
shed their leaves or put forth new ones. Like all the other creatures of the
forest, I made ready for Winter. I gathered wood, smoked cheeses, dried
herbs, washed and aired the wool I would weave, made dyes from the late
Autumn flowers and berries, and did my best to pretend that I was no more
lonely and restless than I had ever been.

But I was. Despite my sure knowledge that Aurelie would wed the Prince,
I craved the news. Like any common village wife or maid, I longed for such
details, real or invented, that are the stuff of gossip. Yet for this petty curiosity I despised myself and thus refused the opportunities for talk that
came my way.

Then one evening, just as I had finished tending the animals, a child
came seeking me, a lass so pale and scrawny I took her to be some woodland
wraith. Indeed, she stood so long unable or unwilling to speak, despite my
entreaties, I did not know what else to think.

"Are you the w-witch?" she stammered at last.

"So I am called by some," I answered. "But you need not fear me. Come,
maiden." I tried to make my voice sound kindly, but it so rarely sounded
that note, I could not be sure if I struck the right pitch. "Have you need of
me? Or have you been sent to fetch me?"

"The Lady," she managed.

I waited in vain for her to elaborate. "What lady is that?"

"She says you are to come to her. She bade me give you this."

The childish fist, which must have clutched the object for the entire
journey, unfolded stickily, and the lass extended a cautious hand, as if she
held out food to some dangerous beast who would as soon devour her as any
morsel she might offer.

In the dim light I could not identify the object by sight, but touch told
me that it was small and curved—rough on the outer curve and smooth on
the inner. I also knew that I had held it before. I let my fingers trace and
retrace the shape; then I remembered: another child's hand had clutched
it long ago and offered it not in fear but in homage. I did not need to
see to know that in my hand lay the very shell I had given Aurelie, come

back to me now to plead or perhaps to command that I honor the bond it betokened.

"Where is the Lady?"

"Why, at the castle," the girl answered, as if all the world, and certainly a witch, should know.

"Is the Lady sick?"

Although I feared she wanted more of me than herbcraft, I reckoned I should prepare myself if, mercifully, medicine were all she required.

"Sh-she did not say so. She only said that you were to come."

"Well, I will make ready. And you, child, must rest and have something to eat and drink."

"No! No!" the child cried, if possible even more alarmed. "She said we must haste."

"As you will," I shrugged. "I must fetch my cloak."

I went within where the child plainly preferred not to follow me. While I did not dally, neither did I hurry myself. I opened my chest and tucked the shell away among my weavings. Then I cut hunks of cheese and bread for the wench and me to eat along the way, and I filled a leather flask with wine. I half expected the girl to have vanished before I stepped outside once more but she was waiting in a wordless dither over the delay.

To my surprise, the girl proved a swift and decisive guide. I followed without further question as she led eastward. It was not quite midnight, by my reckoning, when we came in sight of the Castle. Once again I was struck by its resemblance to a horned beast crouched and ready to spring. The torches of the watchmen on the ramparts glowed like the eyes of a night creature.

As we drew nearer, I could see that the gates were closed for the night, though the drawbridge was down, there being peace in the land for the moment. We did not approach the Castle directly but rather skirted it, taking care to remain obscured by the tall marsh grass that grew about the moat. When we had walked halfway round the Castle, we made our way to the water's edge and found there a little boat, scarcely larger than a tub, hidden among the reeds. In this vessel I crouched as the lass poled us across the moat. On the other side, she felt about the wall with her pole until she found an iron ring to which she made fast the boat. Near the ring I could just make out a door, which she proceeded to unlock with one key from among a bunch she wore about her neck beneath her shift.

Who was this little shadow of a child to be in possession of such keys? No doubt she had stolen them. She moved soundlessly enough; that I had observed on our long walk. There was a stealthiness about her that I sensed came not only from shyness but from fear.

The door proved to be barely above water level. It gave with a sound that bespoke slime and opened inward. Immediately, my nose was assailed with the stench that dwells in damp, unaired places. It seemed we were entering the castle by way of the sewer or dungeon or both. Rats! I recoiled at the thought. I fear no creature that dwells in forest or field, in den or burrow, however fierce it might be. But rats, who scorn the wide world in preference for the foulest comers of human habitation, fill me with uneasiness. They were at once too strange and too familiar.

To my relief, my guide preceded me. I do not think I could have nerved myself to step alone into that noisome unknown. But then, to my dismay, she disappeared completely, leaving me half-in, half-out of the boat. Nor did I commit myself to any course until she returned, bearing a small lantern in one hand and, with the other, gesturing frantically for me to enter.

Once within, I found myself at the top of stairs that led downward below water level. With profound misgiving, I watched the girl lock the door behind us. But if I had qualms, it was soon too late to heed them. The wench led me through such a maze of twists and turns, down in the castle's bowels, that I knew I could never find my way out unguided.

At last we began to climb again, at first merely an earthen incline. Then we came to another door, which the lass unlocked. It opened onto some stone stairs that wound upward in a spiral. We passed two doors on landings at different levels, but at these we did not pause. Up and up, we climbed into what could only be a tower. At last I saw light round one of the curves; the stairs ended in a round chamber.

There I beheld Aurelie, slumped against a stool, her head cradled in her arms, asleep before a spinning wheel, and surrounded by distaff upon distaff dressed with straw.

CHAPTER THREE

"SHE IS HERE, MY LADY."

Aurelie startled awake and stared at me. Her eyes were rimmed with red as I had never before seen them, whether from weeping or weariness, I did not know.

"Thank God," she said. Then she spoke to the girl, "Go now, Gretal, and wait at the bottom of the stair until I call for you."

The child disappeared at once, and I thought to myself that it was hard that she should have no thanks or praise from one who had sent her on such an errand. But then, I reasoned, Aurelie had only just wakened and must be full of fear for her own plight. I needed no telling to understand that the miller's boast had been empty.

"You know why I sent for you," Aurelie addressed me, wasting neither time nor words.

"Yes. I was there when your father told any who cared to hear that you can spin straw to gold."

She gave a bitter laugh. "I can scarce spin flax to save my life." She grew earnest. "And it's my life that's at stake. I don't know how much you've heard."

"Nothing since that market day."

"Sit down then." She offered the stool. "I will tell you all quickly. The King made a great show of looking over all the village maidens. He's like a great cat playing with a mouse before he kills it; for everyone knew he had his eye on me. Sure enough, before long, the summons came. Father and I were brought to the castle in a fine carriage to be feasted and to meet the Prince. The banquet went on for three days, and there was all manner of revelry. I was supposed to be making the acquaintance of his Highness, but he is terribly shy and scarcely spoke a word with me, though we supped together each night. And a clumsier partner for dancing I have never had."

I winced for Julian.

"Of course, it matters not a whit whether the Prince and I have any liking for one another if the King desires we shall marry. But he gave no hint of what was in his mind until the last night. Then, amidst the feasting, he rose to declare that the Prince and I would be wed at Christmastide.

"Everyone cheered, and I felt so giddy that had I been sitting on a common bench instead of a chair, I would have fallen over. I glanced across the hall at Father and saw him mop his brow with his sleeve. For an instant we both dared hope that the King had forgotten Father's foolishness. But when all the cheering had died away, the King added, 'provided the lady can fulfill the terms of her dowry.' Then he turned and spoke to me alone. 'My dear'—he dared to call me that!—'tomorrow you shall be escorted to a room where you will find straw and a spinning wheel. Spin straw into gold and you will be the highest lady in the land, wife to my only son and heir, one day queen. Fail, and you shall be put to death.' "

I gasped, "Utter wickedness!"

And gross injustice! It was her father who had made the false claim, not Aurelie. Then I understood. The man was a monster. What greater suffering could the miller know than to see his beloved daughter die for his folly?

Aurelie merely shrugged, looking so strangely unmoved that I feared for her sanity.

"It's nothing but greed. The war has been costly, and the coffers are nearly empty, they say."

I was about to protest, with vehemence, any excuse for such vile and contemptible cruelty, when all at once Aurelie lost her composure and clutched at me. In the intensity of her grip, I felt all her terror and desperation.

"So, you see, you must help me," she cried. "You can, can't you? Say you can!" she pleaded. She commanded. "Already one day has passed. On the third day they will come for me."

I gazed about me. On every side, we were surrounded with the distaffs. Panic mounted within me. Never had I felt less powerful. My image as a witch seemed nothing but a bad joke, a mere posturing.

"But can't we escape?" I asked, feeling as trapped as she. "That girl, she has keys—"

"Yes. She's the jailer's daughter. I made her steal her father's keys. But what would become of my father? He is still here at the Castle, and his life would be forfeit."

"The girl," I repeated, feeling increasingly feeble, "she knows her way everywhere. She could find him. We'd all go together—"

Aurelie moaned, "No, no, it's no use! Can't you see? Even if we could escape, where would we go? What would become of us? We'd lose the mill. We'd have to leave the village. The very kingdom."

I silenced myself before I could utter more foolishness. It was true. There was nowhere for them to go. I could hide them in my cave for a time, but for how long? And when I tried to picture Aurelie hidden away in the Wood, I found the image as impossible to hold as that of myself at the King's high table.

"Why can't you just do it for me?" Tears stood in Aurelie's eyes. She looked like a child who has been inexplicably denied. "You have powers," she insisted. "Don't you want to help me?"

She was puzzled, petulant, but, most of all, frightened.

"Of course I want to." That was no lie. "I will do what I can. You are weary. Lie down now and try to sleep."

I did not think I could work with Aurelie's anxious gaze fixed upon me. I wished I had brought my sack. I should never go abroad without my herbs and potions. I could have made her a sleeping draught. And, it occurred to me, a sufficient quantity of henbane might have provided a simpler solution to everyone's troubles. At that moment, I felt quite capable of regicide, and I cursed my lack of foresight. As a wicked witch, I was a wretched failure. But was I a witch at all? I had always wondered. Tonight, it seemed, I was destined to find out.

I glanced at Aurelie. To my surprise and relief, she had curled up on the floor, her breathing deep and even. So, for Aurelie, too, I had become the Mother. Like a child, she had cast all her cares on me and gone to rest. I took a deep breath, as I so often bid women take in childbirth. Then I turned to approach the spinning wheel.

Of course the wheel was set for a right-handed person. I went to work, adjusting the wheel to my left-handedness, forgetting, for a moment, the larger task that loomed before me. When I had arranged the wheel to my satisfaction, I could think of nothing to do but stare at it. My mind was empty as a pot that's been scoured and left to dry in the sun. Had I been asked, I doubt I could have recited a cure for warts. It was as if I had never learned anything from the Mother. I tried and tried to think. I wracked my brain so that I broke into a sweat, and my stomach churned with terror at my helplessness.

At last I stopped trying and simply allowed myself to be empty, to wait for whatever would or would not happen. I think I even dozed. Then into my stupor came a song; the song drew me slowly and gently back to full wakefulness. I realized that the song was drifting up from the staircase, and I knew it was the child, singing to comfort herself as she passed the long night alone on the cold, dark stairs. There were no words to her song, but something in the rhythm, the repetition called up for me the words of another song.

Take the dung and make it flower,
Take the pain and make it power,
Let your own fear make you bold,
Take the straw and spin, spin, spin the gold.

Within me the Mother's voice mingled with the child's. Empty no longer, I turned to meet the task, once more the Mother.

The straw was awkward to work. Soon the fingers of my left hand were covered with small cuts, and I felt no certainty that the fibers twisting between the fingers of my right bore any resemblance to gold.

Take the pain and make it power.

As I toiled, I summoned the pain of my childhood and lived it again. Again I lived my love for the Prince and the everlasting loss. I lived the pain of my empty hands and my empty heart. All the pain of my life I lived, pain that had taken me against my will.

Now I willed to take the pain. With the whole of myself I offered that pain: for the Prince, for the Mother, for Aurelie, for the child on the stair, for myself, for the very life that was within me and around me. As if it were a burnt sacrifice, pain was consumed, and power leaped like flame. I needed no wand. I needed no word. The magic was within me; I was within the magic. I, the transformer and the thing transformed.

I took straw. I spun gold.

I must have worked in a trance. I had no awareness of day following night or night, day. Time did not pass but rather gathered itself, as the gold wound onto spindle after spindle, into one unbroken moment. Spinner, wheel, straw, gold merged in unceasing motion. Nor do I remember collapsing when the task was done. Memory begins again with Aurelie bending over me, her bright hair brushing my face as she pleaded with me.

"Wake! Oh, please wake! They will come soon, and they must not find you here."

I sat up in some confusion and looked about me. My vision blurred, and it seemed at first that Aurelie's hair, grown impossibly long, filled the room. Then my mind and sight cleared, and I knew I gazed upon the reams and reams of gold I had spun.

"Yes, you have done it," said Aurelie. "You are a great and powerful sorceress. I owe you my life."

There was a new tone in her voice: awe. I was not displeased to hear it. "Name your reward, and when I am wed to the Prince, you shall have it. But

now, I beg you, hasten. The third night is almost past. The girl is waiting.
She will guide you."

Aurelie helped me to my feet then lowered her voice as we crossed the
room.

"One more favor I must ask: Get rid of the girl."

"Get rid of the girl?" I repeated, still feeling dazed.

"Ssh!" she hissed. "Yes, before she talks. No one must suspect it was not
I who spun the gold."

"But how do you mean? Get rid of her?"

Aurelie gestured, half-fearful, half-impatient, then grimaced, and I
understood she meant me to kill the child. But she did not want to say it.
Let my hands, already bloodied and blistered, bear the stain.

"I'll do what I must," I muttered, and that seemed to satisfy her, for she
began to descend the stairs.

In those few moments, as I followed her, my mind whirled swifter than
the spinning wheel. No, the motion was not so ordered as the wheel's, for
the havoc it wreaked within me. My golden idol, so long enthroned, toppled
all at once and lay broken and tarnished in the dirt.

That part of the story, of her ruthlessness, born of a sordid marriage
between greed and fear, is never told. No one knows it, save Aurelie and me,
and I don't doubt she has forgotten that evil command in the wake of her
other misdeeds. I tell it now, for in the common tale, sung in the streets, it
is of my wickedness folk clamor to hear. Yet even in sin I remain unseen,
unknown, unnamed. Worse: misnamed. Was it she who put it forth that I
am a small, misshapen man, fearing that to name a woman would turn all
eyes to the Witch? And did she lie to protect herself or me?

To this day, I do not know, but as the story goes, I am supposed to have
bargained with her before I touched the straw. I make it known, now and
forever: there was no bargain. I did not spin gold for gain. Had I tried, the
magic never would have come to me. That deed was purer than its doer.
That one time, I was greater than I am or was or ever will be. As you will
see. As I must tell.

I watched Aurelie wake the child, whom she would send without a qualm
to death at someone else's hands, and I resolved to make Aurelie pay and
pay dearly for my services. I had power over her. I could talk, and it had not
occurred to her that such a mighty sorceress, as I appeared to be, could be
threatened with death as any mortal woman.

"Swiftly, sweeting."—That she dared call the girl a name of endearment!

"Guide the Wise Woman to the water door, and see her home again. Don't be afraid. She'll not harm you."

Unknowing, Aurelie spoke the truth.

"A thousand thanks," she turned to me and took my hands.

Where once I would have warmed to her, thrilled at a rare human touch, I now had all I could do to keep myself from recoiling.

"Safe journey to you."

She withdrew her hands and turned to ascend the stairs. I remained still. "You asked me to name my reward. I am going to. Now."

"Yes, yes," she said, turning back, her hands pulling at each other, betraying her anxiety. " Any thing you like. But hurry!"

"When the time comes for you to bear your first child, you will send for me. I shall be the midwife. You will have no other attendant."

"Gladly."

"I further claim as my reward the right to name the child, whether the child be male or female."

"Granted." She already spoke like a queen, though I heard a trace of doubt in her voice. "Whatever name you choose. I shall put it forth as my woman's whim, not to be questioned by sovereign or heir."

She smiled, doubtless in contemplation of her womanly powers.

"And last—" I drew a breath and silenced any inner voice that would soften my decision. "If that child be a living girl, I claim her as my own to raise as I will."

I expected her to gasp, to refuse, to protest at least. She merely laughed.

"As you like. But, of course," she cautioned, smiling still, "I shall bear only sons. You will see. I shall send for you at my lying in."

"Until that time." I bowed my head in farewell, though she was already mounting the stairs.

Then, I do not know what made me think of it, nor yet to act upon the thought, perhaps some fleeting sense of honor. Whatever the cause, I found myself calling after her:

"Look to the wheel, Lady. Or else folk will say it was no maid but a very devil spun that gold."

I did not know how truly I spoke.

CHAPTER FOUR

IN THOSE DAYS AND NIGHTS that had passed unmarked for me in the tower, the world without had changed. We had come to the castle under a fine and starry sky. Now we emerged into a dawn, dun colored and damp. The heavy air settled on my skin like the scum that topped the water in the moat. With empty fascination, I watched Gretal's pole rend that foul mantle. Gretal, uneasy as ever, kept glancing over her shoulder, fearful lest we be spotted by the watch. Save for her sake, I could not care whether we were caught or not.

The seeming purpose for my existence had come and gone. I had known pure power—and power that is pure is rare indeed—and now here I was, myself again, none the greater for the greatness of my deed, nor the richer for the riches that had passed through my fingers. In truth, I was poorer, robbed of a cherished illusion, my only illusion, and without illusion, life is bare and comfortless.

Moreover, I had no Mother now to soothe or disgruntle me with her wisdom.

Oh, I had a life to live, of sorts, and skills to offer. I must not withhold the Mother's legacy from those it was meant to benefit. But my greatest gift had been given, no, squandered. Unless...unless I could have a daughter. The child of my dearest love. And he was my love, the only love I had left. My love, not hers. For she would never love him. Of that I was certain.

Intent on my sorrow, I followed Gretal through marsh and field to the very part of the Wood where I had met the Prince. I motioned Gretal to stop, and I crouched to drink from the river so that she would not wonder at the pause. I was thirstier than I had thought, and I drank for a long time. When I had slaked my thirst, I sat back on a rock and gazed about me, losing all awareness of Gretal. It was as if no time had passed since I had met Julian, and yet as if there had passed a thousand years. I was that girl who had bent over that dazed boy. I was old beyond age, the Mother. And for all the power that had passed through my fingers, turning straw to gold, for all my apparent wisdom, I could not say whether anything had any meaning at all.

A nervous cough recalled my attention to Gretal. She was crouching at her usual safe distance, tired and hungry, but not daring to let herself rest. I no longer needed a guide. How I wished I could send her home to her breakfast. What was I to do with her?

"Come, Gretal," I said, getting to my feet. "Lead me home."

There was no sense in alarming the child before I must. If I told her she must stay with me while we were still so near the Castle, she might run away, seeking safety where only danger awaited her.

We reached the cave late in the afternoon, and the animals massed on us, my poor nanny goats with their swollen udders bleating in pained and frantic reproach. I had not known I would leave them for so long. I hoped they would not go dry.

"Gretal can you milk?" I asked. "I need your help sorely. These goats have not been milked in three days!"

Gretal was not a peasant and needed teaching. Her help proved a hindrance, but she tried, and the chores forestalled the time when I must tell her that she was homeless but for me. By the time we were done tending all the animals, the sun was setting. Neither Gretal nor I had eaten that day, nor for days before that so far as I knew.

"Rest now, child," I said, half-pushing, half-leading her inside the cave, indicating a stool beside the hearth where I knelt to build a fire. "I will make us some lentil stew."

Gretal persisted in standing, one foot poised for flight. Her eyes kept darting, like a small bird's, from me to the doorway.

"Sit!" I commanded.

Whether from fear or hunger, she obeyed, though instead of trusting her slight weight to the stool, she merely permitted her scrawny hindquarters to hover over it. I felt both saddened and dismayed that she should continue to find me so fearsome. When the food was ready, she ate hers both eagerly and warily, snatching at it, as if she feared it might attack her. I considered making her a sleeping potion and putting her to bed, delaying my task until morning, but decided such a trick would only make her mistrust me more.

"Gretal." I spoke as gently as I ever have. "You are welcome here, and I will see that you do not go hungry or sleep without a roof over your head."

Her look was uncomprehending as any dumb beast's. No, more. I swear the goats understand human speech better than this child seemed to.

"I am telling you, Gretal, that you cannot return to the Castle. You know far too much about what has happened. It is dangerous for you there. Someone might try to hurt you."

"Oh, but the Lady wouldn't let them." Her eyes came alight with the word 'Lady.'

Inwardly I cursed fate and the false betraying images it wantonly made us bear. Passion warred with prudence, vengeance with pity. I longed to strip from Aurelie her adorable beauty and expose her to this child. Yet what had I to offer her in place of the Lady? Who would strip from me the ugliness of the Witch? I had tried to doff the mask and failed. Maybe only time would wear it away. Meanwhile, I must somehow persuade this child of her peril without calling it by name.

"The Lady could not help you, child. Even after she is crowned Princess, she is subject to the King."

A bolder child might have questioned me further. My explanation had been scanty and, if examined, would have been found full of holes. But Gretal, I was coming to see, had been taught to fear long before she stood quaking in my clearing. Looking at her more intently, I could read her history on her body. There were scars on her arms and legs that could only have come from beatings, and I wagered there were more on her back. She must have learned long since that grown folk were terrifying and unpredictable, not to be crossed.

"I tell you," I warned, deciding to play on her fear, "if you go back to the Castle something terrible will happen to you. The Lady wouldn't like that, now would she?"

Those honeyed words left a bitter taste on my tongue.

So Gretal stayed with me. Autumn's brief flame blazed in the Wood, but I was too desolate to marvel at it or to plot ways to capture its colors in dyes, its cast of light in warp and weft. Gretal appeared to be overawed to the point of fear by the brilliance of the season and seemed most at ease in the cave. I reckoned that until now, she had lived the life of a mushroom in the dank and sunless places of the Castle.

I soon ceased to worry that she would run away. I found her exceedingly docile and could not imagine that she had been beaten for disobedience. But she was absentminded and pitifully inept with her hands for one who had to live by their work. I thought at first that she must be simple-minded. In time I came to understand that she dwelt so much within herself that she all but unmade the outer world. When that world startled her with its demands, she was flustered and slow to respond. The punishments of the impatient folk about her must have come more swiftly than she could comprehend. So she had grown fearful, and fear made her clumsier still.

I guessed at her inner world, because she often sang to herself, though never when she thought I could hear. Her voice was clear as spring water, fine and distinct, such a voice as a star might have if it is true that the stars sing. She sang softly, unless she thought I was far away. More than once, on returning from a childbirth in the early morning, I heard her singing full-throat. If I had never seen her, I would have believed that some glorious, sparkling creature had strayed into the Wood from another world instead of wan little Gretal with her dull hair and her small watery-blue eyes that always looked swollen and red. Rabbit eyes, I called them to myself.

Some of her songs had words, and I surely overheard her sing more words than she ever spoke to me. Sometimes she simply sang about what she was doing or rather to what she was doing: a little song to the wool she was carding or to the seeds and the leaves she rather sorrowfully crushed for the potions I made. Plainly the song engrossed her more than the task, and I would find her stroking the still-tangled wool or playing games with the seeds, but I seldom had the heart to chastise her.

Other times she sang herself stories, some of which must have been about her earlier life, songs of cruelty incongruent with her sweet voice. In these sung tales I came to identify a number of characters: her father, at best indifferent to her; the cook, a veritable ogre, whose slave she was; a stable hand, who, I feared, had forced his body on her.

Then there were songs about the Lady, many, many of them. These must have been made mostly from fancy, for she could not have served the Lady very long. Aurelie seemed to have been the one brightness in the child's dingy life. I was glad I had not dimmed that radiance, though it hurt me to hear these hymns to the Lady—for hymns they were—particularly as Gretal showed no sign of warming to me. Perhaps she was a trifle less timid, but no matter how constant my kindness, she seemed to regard me, at best, as an indifferent and unpredictable natural force, like the weather.

Moons waxed and waned. Winter came and kept us mostly within the cave.

I grew more and more disheartened. With Gretal, I had neither solitude nor company. The silence, unbroken except by commands or requests from me and the briefest of answers from her, was never shared as the Mother and I had shared silence. We were each alone and yet uncomfortably aware of the other. She, poor child, could not let herself sing and fidgeted at the tasks I set her. I had my weaving, but her presence distracted me, and I could not lose myself in color and pattern or in the rhythm of the shuttle

as I used to. So there we were, two human creatures, confined to a cave for
the Winter. I don't doubt we both wished we could sleep away the season, as
the bears and the badgers do.

My mind frequently turned on what was to become of her or rather
what I was to do with her. Hope that she might become my apprentice died
a swift and early death. Biddable as she was, she showed little interest in
mastering any of the arts or crafts I practiced and less aptitude. Her hands
were not sensitive enough for fine work with plants or even for spinning
and weaving. She liked collecting eggs but was never much good at milking
or at making cheeses or breads. She was far too frightened of people even
to begin to learn to treat sickness. In truth, she could never be anything but
an indifferent servant, and I did not want such a servant. Indeed, I did not
want a servant at all.

What I wanted was a daughter. Desperately. It was a cruel joke: here I
was called Mother, at least to my face, by all who met me, and yet I had no
child of my own. The Mother before me at least had me in her last years,
and I hoped I had been a good daughter to her. But I wanted more than
what the Mother had had of me. She had never needed me, except as an heir
to her arts and the thrice-cursed image. Oh, I know she was fond of me, yes,
even loved me, but she was complete in herself. At the heart of her was a
well of peace that never ran dry, its source within her, yet beyond her.

At the heart of me was not peace but passion, a hunger so fierce that it
frightened me. Before I spun the gold, I had been able to forget the hunger
at times, content with the bread and water of my solitude. Now my hunger
raged; it cried out for flesh. I even contemplated going abroad in the fields
for the heathen rites of May—which were still observed despite the priests
—and, cloaked by darkness, getting with child by the first man who would
have me. But for all that folk called me Mother, I was still a fearful virgin
and likely to remain so. I longed to be wooed; I could not forget the tenderness of Julian's kiss.

And now, now—though I hardly dared admit the hope—perhaps I
could be mother to his daughter. And how much better a mother I would
make than Aurelie. Nor did I consider that I would be depriving her. She
was strong and would bear many children. All I wanted was the one.

I could not help myself; I could not stop the images from forming: of a
cradle, made by my own hands, near my pallet so that I could rock my babe
whenever she waked in the night. In the daytime, too, I would keep her near
me, bound across my breasts or back. I believed, virgin though I was, that

with the right herbal potions and with the babe's sucking, I could make the milk come and nurse her myself.

Nor did the images cease with her infancy. I saw her crawling about the clearing, playing with the chickens and rabbits and goats, taking her first tipsy steps, then growing into a strong child, sturdy and graceful, becoming at last a wise and beautiful woman, free to choose her way in the world. For I would not force my own or any image upon her. I wanted only the chance to love her. I loved her already, fool that I was. For all I knew, she had not even been conceived, yet I had named her and called her by name in all my fancies: Marina, for the great sea that I had never seen, for the great sea of tenderness within me. I had forgotten, for the moment, the shell I had tucked away among my weavings, the shell from the faraway sea, the shell that linked Aurelie and me.

So the Winter wore on, I, dreaming of Marina, and Gretal, no doubt, of the Lady. And we were no use to one another.

CHAPTER FIVE

HEN THERE CAME, AS THERE SOMETIMES DOES in the midst of Winter, a tantalizing thaw. Tree buds swelled red. Frozen earth turned to mud as snow melted. The stream knew a day's freedom from its Winter bonds, and we fetched water without breaking ice. Sheltered in the Southern lap of a great tree, some snowdrops dared an early bloom. Even the sporous soul of Gretal seemed to put forth green shoots. We stayed outside all morning, bathing like cats in pools of light, feeling more camaraderie in this respite from cold than we ever had before. At midday we brought out bread and cheese and steaming mugs of broth and sat on the bench to eat. We had just begun our meal when Gretal stiffened. She was as good as any watch dog, alerting me to the approach of a visitor long before I would have sensed it myself.

"What is it, Gretal?" I asked, unable to suppress a sigh. At least she did not bark.

She pointed. I peered into the Wood and at length discerned a cloaked figure wending its way through the trees. Once it entered the clearing, I decided it was a woman of indeterminate age but exceedingly hale and hearty. Winter though it was, the woman's cheeks were brown and rosy, eyes crinkled with squinting or laughing. Her complexion bespoke a life lived in the open, but she did not appear destitute. Her grey cloak looked to be of good quality, and she had a bundle tied to her back. She paused upon sighting us, but her bearing suggested no trace of fear. On the contrary, even in stillness, she gave an impression of vigor and purpose. In short, she was unlike most who sought me, and my curiosity was aroused.

"Hail, Mother!" She raised her arm in greeting. The grey of her cloak lifted like a cloud; there flashed a sudden wing of deep red and brown and gold as her motion revealed the inside of her raiment.

"Amelia!" I cried, knowing the weaving and so the woman, transformed as she was. "Welcome!"

She approached, smiling, I noted, with lips and eyes. My own smile, rare and rusty and timid, threw off its uncertainty and spread itself over my face.

"You bade me come and play for you, Mother. It is small recompense for your wisdom, but here I am."

"But first you will rest and eat," I said, rising to my feet and daring to take her arm as I led her to the bench. "And tell me of your life since we spoke. If you are cold, we can sit within."

She shook her head. "I am used to life in the open, and the sun is warm."

"Gretal," I said. "Fetch more bread and cheese and broth, and some wine for our guest."

"Who is the lass?" asked Amelia when Gretal had disappeared.

"A homeless child," I answered with brevity and truth. "She is staying with me for a time."

"Are you teaching her your arts?"

I made a helpless gesture, but before I could find the words to explain Gretal, she returned, and I pressed Amelia for her tale.

"After I saw you, Mother," she began," I returned to my manor, my son's manor, I should say, and practiced upon my lute night and day. What is more, though my daughter-in-law scolded, I refused to sit at tapestry with the ladies. Since I was no longer dallying with my lute, I found a change: the more I gave myself to the music, the more the music gave to me. Oh, to be sure, at times I would fret and fall into my old ways. I would feel like a fool, trying to master the lute at my age and station. I could see no purpose to it. But then, instead of casting my lute aside, I would force myself to play on. Often I'd spread out the cloak where I could see it, and the magic you wove into it gave me courage. Somehow it always reminded me that it did not matter how good I was, as long as I strove to serve the music.

"But truly, I believe my skill increased. One day I dared to ask one of the hired musicians if he would hear me and teach me. I know he only agreed to humor the dowager lady, mother to his patron. His look of surprise when I played gave me hope. And so he agreed to instruct me. He took me to task for all my amateurish faults and vastly improved my counting. Best of all, he and the other musicians would play with me now and again. Thus I learned to play in concert.

"When Summer came, I rose one day before the dawn, dressed in my simplest clothes, strapped my lute across my back, and donned the magic cloak. I took some coin, a loaf of bread, a flask of wine, and set forth on my journey, heading for the nearest market town. And was I afraid. Indeed, I was. I believe there is no magic that can unmake fear. But in the past fear sat upon me, heavy as a tombstone. That day I shouldered fear, even as Christ his cross, if it is not blasphemy to say so, and though I staggered at first, I went forward. Nor did I look back. I dared not, lest the temptation to retreat to safety overtake me. I knew if I turned back then, I would venture forth no more.

"When I reached the town, it was already bustling. I walked about feeling more foolish than fearful. About midday I came upon a sorry band of minstrels, counting the few coins passers-by had tossed to see if they had enough to buy them drink. They were a rough looking lot, particularly the one I took to be the leader, a man a bit older than my son, whose three-day growth of beard did nothing to hide a nasty scar on his cheek that stood out white against his leathery skin. The others, two lads and two maidens, appeared younger. To my surprise, I saw no lute player among them. Summoning more courage than I ever knew I possessed, I addressed them.

" 'I'm sorry I did not hear you play, for I dearly love music.'

"The leader eyed me as if trying to guess where my purse was hidden and how many coins it contained.

" 'It's hardly your misfortunes Madam,' said one of the young men. 'We are all out of tune today. Our feckless lute player fell in love with the innkeeper's daughter at the last village and stayed to live a life of ease.'

"The leader growled something and then he spat. I was now not only fearful but affronted, yet I forced myself to speak.

" 'I can play the lute.'

"The leader sneered, and the others glanced at me curiously. Despite my plain attire, my face and hands and speech must have identified me as a gentlewoman.

" 'I have my way to make in the world,' I said. 'Will you hear me play?' "My boldness astonished me. I could feel my chin tilting in defiance, and I stared the leader straight in his bloodshot eyes. He looked away first, shrugged, and made a vague gesture that I took to mean I was to suit myself.

"My hands trembled so I could scarcely unfasten the lute from my back. They shook as I tuned it. Then I made ready to play, and somehow the feel of the lute in my arms, of my fingers on the strings, calmed me. I was no longer simply Amelia; I was Amelia playing the lute. I played well. I could feel it. This was practice no longer; I was playing for my life. The young folk smiled and began to dance. A small crowd gathered. More coins were tossed into the hat. When I had done, the leader nodded at me. Then I joined them in a round of ale, heavy and bitter, peasants' brew, such as I had never before tasted. Thus I became a member of the band, without hearing them play, without knowing their names or telling them mine, without taking time to wonder at my folly.

"I have wandered with them since. The leader, Rolf, is a fine musician, though not always a scrupulous man. He has nothing resembling manners, which is why he remains a wanderer without a patron, for he is not lacking in skill. The lads and lasses, of whom I have grown fond, all have talent and tales of woe to tell. All, like me, have run away, one of the girls from a convent, another from, well … " She glanced at Gretal. "I won't say it here. One of the lads is the orphaned son of a wealthy noble; he fled before his uncle could arrange his death. The other was apprenticed to an undertaker against his will.

"I have told none of them my own tale. I do not trust Rolf enough for that. Like as not, he would hold me for ransom if he thought he could make more money that way. But I will tell you," she giggled, "in one town I saw men from my son's castle. I am sure they were searching for me. I could not refuse to play without arousing Rolf's suspicion, but I did skulk in the background. They passed by where we were playing a number of times. One of them even looked at me but without recognition. I suppose," she mused, "they might not have known what I looked like to begin with. I was so very unobtrusive as the dowager lady."

"You have changed indeed, Amelia," I said. "I did not know you myself until I recognized the cloak. But tell me, if you can, what of death? Have you lost your fear of it?"

"Well you may ask, Mother, and I will answer if I can. I told you, I no longer believe there is magic to unmake fear any more than magic can undo death. They say our Lord vanquished it, yet even he submitted to it, as must we. I still fear death, but before it was a fear like a child's, who cowers beneath the bedclothes from a nightmare, afraid to sleep, afraid to rise. Now it is more like the fear a child might know in a game of tag or hide and seek. Death is 'it,' and one day I will feel his hand on my shoulder. Meanwhile, I am alive, and I will lead death a merry chase, sometimes so merry that it seems a dance, and one day death will be my partner. Yes, I am afraid, but where once I was timid in fear, now I am bold. That sounds like nonsense, that fear has made me bold, but I can think of no other way to say it."

"You have said it, Daughter." I managed to speak through the tears caught in my throat. "As well as the wisest of the wise.

"And now, Amelia, if you please, unfasten your lute and play for us. The afternoon wears on, and the light is losing warmth. Let us go within and sit by the fire. Or else your fingers will be too stiff to stroke the strings."

When we had rearranged ourselves before the hearth, Gretal and I watched while Amelia warmed the lute and tuned the strings. Then she began to play. The contours of the cave held the notes and extended their life, as does the stone in a church. The music expanded the cave: no longer small and dark, but dark and vast as the night sky; each sounding of a string, a star newborn. As she played the lute, Amelia seemed at once near and distant. To give oneself, as Amelia did, to the music must be like yielding to a lover. I felt close to her as I seldom do to other folk, save for women in childbirth. Yet I sensed she was far away, no, not far but deep, deep within the music, deeper than I could follow.

A movement close by distracted my attention from Amelia, and I turned to see Gretal creeping closer to the music. I almost cried out at the change I saw in the child's face. The difference between the Gretal I knew and the Gretal now revealed—or released—by the music was the difference between barren earth and a lush garden. Yes, it was indeed as if the water of life had drenched her soul and made it bloom. Never in her tremulous adoration of the Lady had she looked like this. Aurelie had been the child's idol even as she had been mine. Now Gretal was in the presence of her very god.

"Sing, Gretal!" The words spoke themselves, for they were not mine. I but gave voice to the command of the god.

Gretal sang. An hour ago I would not have believed it possible, but now I had seen the face that belonged to her voice. I glanced at Amelia and saw that she was startled, but trained musician that she was, she never missed a note. Content, I closed my eyes, so that I could see the music as it soared, flying from the mortal bodies of Gretal and Amelia on immortal wings. Silence, when it came again, was not an end to the music but a gathering of it back to its source.

CHAPTER SIX

TIME PASSED BEFORE ANY OF US STIRRED OURSELVES. At last I rose, poked at the dying fire, then went to peer outside the cave. The sky was dusky; the goats bleated plaintively. I turned to Amelia.

"You have kept your promise. Your music has repaid me many times. And Gretal." I paused, uncertain of what to say. "Thank you. Listen, dark is falling fast. Can you stay the night, Amelia?"

"I will gladly sleep by your hearth, if I may, but I must be up early, for we are moving on tomorrow. Lent is a doleful season. The King has no need of itinerant musicians now that Shrove Tuesday is past. We will wander South. I am to be at the crossroads by sunrise."

"You have b-been at the Castle, Madam?"

Despite her boldness in speaking, Gretal looked once more as timid and brown as a rabbit hiding in a thicket. I felt my old irritation stir.

"Gretal, go see to the goats," I said a trifle sharply. To soften my command, I added. "Maybe Dame Amelia will tell us more as we sup. Go now, Gretal."

She looked bewildered, but she moved to obey. Milking the goats was usually my task, and, indeed, I felt sorry for Marguerite and Delilah, Gretal being so clumsy, but I needed a chance to speak alone with Amelia about an idea that had taken root in my mind and swiftly flowered.

"The child has a remarkable voice," said Amelia as soon as Gretal was gone.

I stoked the fire and moved a pot of stew closer to the flame, pleased that Amelia was eager to talk of the very subject I wanted to raise with her.

"Can you not tell me where you found her?"

"It's a long story and not a pretty one," I answered. "The child herself does not fully understand. Her father is dungeon keeper at the Castle. Let us simply say that she ran afoul of one who is to be the highest Lady in the land."

"The wedding has taken place. Did you not know?"

"You must tell me about it. But now I want to talk of Gretal before she returns."

"How did she offend the Princess?"

For all its inevitability, it gave me a jolt to hear Aurelie's title.

"She but did that Lady a service and so knows something the Lady would have no one living know."

I was sorely tempted to tell Amelia all that had happened. She was the nearest to a friend I'd ever had, and it would have relieved me to speak freely with her. Yet it would be no friendly act to burden Amelia with un-needed, perhaps dangerous, knowledge. And no matter how much I liked Amelia, I was still the Mother. When no one knows your name, you must keep your own counsel.

"I see you are not at liberty to say more," said Amelia with the gracious tact of the lady she was and always would be. "Pardon my curiosity."

"No need for pardon," I assured her. "And though I cannot tell you much, I am going to ask much of you. Listen, Amelia, this child, I have taken her into my care and given her my protection, as I would any helpless creature. Apart from that I am no use to her, nor she to me. She has but one gift, and you have heard it. Will you not take her with you to join your band?"

Amelia was silent for a time.

"Do you fear that Rolf would not want her?" I probed.

"No, it's not that. He would want her right enough. Not one of our band has a voice to rival hers, and what is more, a child performer draws the crowds. It's only that, well, the way she sang just now; her voice is virgin as her flesh. And Rolf...I have told you, I do not altogether trust him."

"Her life has not been easy," I pointed out. "I doubt he could do more to her than she has already suffered. Yet you are right to fear for her. The child does not know how to protect herself. Is Rolf lecherous then?"

"No more so than another man, less than many. I did not mean that. But he would sell her singing as another man might sell her flesh."

"But what else can she hope for?" I demanded. "You yourself sell your music. Or Rolf sells it, if you will have it so. We are all bought and sold."

I was growing impatient with Amelia's scruples. For all she worked for her bread, she still had the delicate conscience of a lady, such as the likes of Gretal could not afford.

"Listen." I spoke urgently, for surely Gretal must return soon. "I can keep her here and protect her from the wickedness of the world. When I die, she will be destitute. While I live, she will languish. She has no love for me or my ways. She might well be a burden to you, and I will not blame you if you say no, but say no to spare yourself, not the child."

I argued more forcefully than I meant to. My own conscience, inclined to be lazy, stretched itself and woke from its usual slumber. Amelia had come only to play the lute for me. I had repaid her by foisting upon her an unwelcome choice.

"Forgive me. I have no right to ask—"

"No." She stopped me. "There is reason in your request. Let me think a moment."

I turned away and busied myself with stirring the stew.

"Well, Mother," she sighed. "I reckon it is not for you or me to protect Gretal more than she wants to be protected. Let her choose whether she would stay with you or go with me. Only, I pray you, let me be the one to ask her."

Later, when we were replete with stew, Amelia regaled us with tales of the wedding and festivities; for the wedding had taken place at the beginning of Yuletide, with the bride dressed in crimson like a Christmas rose.

"I should hardly think that color would suit with her hair," I commented.

"Oh, have you seen the Princess?" Amelia asked.

"We grew up in the same village."

Amelia looked bemused for a moment, as if she had never considered that the Mother might have had something so commonplace as a childhood. Then she went on.

"Indeed, it was not the best color for her. That hair that some call blonde, some red, always has more of what I call orange in it and sometimes looks well with rose or purple but never true red. They say, however, that the King himself chose the color and the cut, which revealed most of the poor lady's back and bosom, and no one dared gainsay him."

"And how looked the Prince?" I asked, bending my face over a hem I was stitching to hide the blush I could feel rising.

Amelia pondered. "Truly, I find it hard to say, for whenever the King is present, one hardly sees the Prince. It's as if the King were the sun and the Prince but a pale, daytime sliver of moon."

"I have never seen the King," I ventured.

"Oh, he is truly a magnificent sight," said Amelia, but I could hear the wryness in her tone. "Though he does not appeal to me, and his taste in music runs to vulgar extremes, either bawdy songs or mawkish ballads to make you weep. And, of course, battle songs, endless battle songs. But he is a wonder to behold. He scarcely looks old enough to have a grown son; for he is trim and battle-hardened. Any silver in his hair is lost in the gold, and his eyes are bright as steel in the sun. Even when he wears his court robes, he has the air of being armored and ready to fight.

"Now that the feasting is over, he will grow restless again, they say. He has paid his war debts with the gold the Princess spun, and there is more besides to pay for new weapons and lay in supplies. I've heard he is pressing his new daughter-in-law for her secrets, but she sticks to her story that the power to spin gold was given her by the fairy woman only to make her dowry. Now that she is wed, she can spin no more. It is not certain the King believes her, but he is content to bide his time, the coffers being full."

"But the Prince," I pressed. I had already heard enough of the King to despise him heartily, and I wished to hear no more. "You must have seen him on his wedding day. Did he look happy?"

"Anyone can tell he worships his bride. He is like a child or a puppy. He follows her everywhere. For once, it seems, the father's will and the son's delight are one. I fear the ribaldry that accompanies even a royal wedding was hard on the Prince. The whole court put the couple to bed. As a minstrel, I was there, too, and I pitied the poor lad. He blushed enough for himself and his bride, as the King, who was very drunk, bellowed his coarse jokes and tucked the pair in himself, giving the bride a smacking kiss before he went off to his own revels with two buxom wenches, one under each arm."

"And what of the Lady?"

"She laughed at the King's antics. Perhaps she was frightened and did not know what else to do."

That I doubted.

"At last, with the King gone, we left the couple to themselves, and I trust all went well. By the time our band left, there were some signs that she is breeding."

I thrust aside the unwelcome image of Aurelie and the Prince entwined and swiftly made count. If Aurelie got with child at Yuletide, then the child should be born in early Autumn.

"I must go to bed," Amelia was saying as she rose and stretched. "And you also, Gretal, if you would like to rise before the dawn and come with me to join the minstrels."

Gretal startled, then stared, first at Amelia, then at me, her small rabbit eyes opening nearly as wide as her speechless mouth.

"The Mother has said that, if you wish, you are free to come with me. I must warn you, Gretal, the wandering life is rough and sometimes dangerous. I will do my best to look out for you, but you will doubtless be safer in this cave. Hear me, Gretal, your voice is your treasure. You may keep it hidden or you may bestow it on the world that may receive it ill or use it harshly. Whatever you choose, child, remember that your voice is yours and no one can take it from you."

Gretal stood up slowly and, like a child taking its first steps, walked both with uncertainty and determination towards Amelia.

"I want to come with you, and please, will you take me to the Castle. I would dearly love to see the Lady now that she is a Princess."

"That she must not, Gretal." I spoke more sharply than I meant to. "Amelia, you must promise not to take the child there. If your band is to sojourn again at Court, bring the child to me while you're there."

Gretal looked bewildered and disappointed.

"The Mother knows what is best, Gretal. And now we must sleep."

Amelia spoke gently and firmly. She was just what Gretal needed. After all, Amelia had raised five children. She was a real mother, while I—what did I know?

But I would learn. Yes, I would learn, like any other woman with a new babe.

That night I slept on my side, my arms and body curved round the place where Marina would nestle.

CHAPTER SEVEN

I ROSE BEFORE LIGHT with Gretal and Amelia and gave them a hearty breakfast and food to take with them. Gretal I bundled as warmly as I could, and then I embraced her unresponsive bulk. As so often after a mild day in Winter, clouds had gathered in the night. I watched as Gretal and Amelia disappeared swiftly into a snowy dawn.

With a sense of relief, I turned back to my own life, the clutter of Gretal's continuous presence cleared away. Yet, to my surprise, as the days passed, I missed her. She had been a constant source of irritation. Now when I felt irritable, there was no one to blame. I suppose my condition was similar to that of someone who has suddenly lost a troublesome spouse. We grow comfortable with our petty crosses and feel cheated when we must lay them down.

Life was simpler without Gretal, my tasks completed with greater dispatch. Some days I found myself with time on my hands that I was disinclined to fill with the spinning and weaving that always awaited me. A bodily laziness I had never before known overcame me. I even took to napping, and instead of eating meals, I nibbled all day long. I found I felt queasy if I went any length of time without food. My lethargy and uneasy stomach caused me to wonder if I might be ill with some lingering sickness. I tried various remedies on myself. None of them had much effect.

Then one day a young woman came to me complaining of the exact same symptoms, and I knew at once what was wrong—or right—with her and hardly had any need to feel of her womb or question her about her courses. I gave her a mixture of goldenseal, anise, ginger, cloves, and raspberry leaves for making a tea and assured her that the symptoms would pass when the quickening came. The poor lass had never guessed that she might be with child, but she seemed pleased enough with the news. "For now he must wed me," she said. When she had gone, I laughed louder and harder than I ever had in my life. I laughed until I wept.

That night I wondered if Aurelie felt ill, too, or if I, by some magic, bore the symptoms for her. If that were so, I did not mind at all, for it made the babe all the more mine.

I spent what remained of the Winter making swaddling and other clothes for Marina whenever the weather kept me indoors. On fine days I worked in the clearing, chopping, sawing, and finishing wood for her cradle.

The sun journeyed northward, calling forth the Spring. Streams swelled with melted snow and buds with the sticky new leaves that curled inside them. I half-believed that new life, dream-nurtured, must swell in me. I was at once disappointed and relieved when my belly remained flat. My power, if you could call it that when it seemed so beyond my control, disturbed me. I had wondered: could longing alone cause the babe to grow within me? Had I stolen her straight from Aurelie's womb? Now I was reassured that the laws of nature were in working order, and my body was not to be the site of a miracle.

Yet at other times I fretted. Did the end of my symptoms mean that something had gone wrong with Aurelie and the babe? I longed to reassure myself, but I dared not visit the Castle. It would be a foolish mistake to let anyone guess my part in this birth in time to prevent me from playing it. I would have to bide my time and trust Aurelie to keep her word.

Come Midsummer, I decided to make a journey to the village. There was not much I needed, some ale maybe and some meal. I had made more bread than usual last Winter in an attempt to fatten Gretal. Nor had I much to sell. I had been so busy making baby clothes that I had neglected my weaving. But I had a passable quantity of herbs and medicines and had recently brewed more of the love potion that was so popular in the warm months. With Gretal gone, I could spare some cheeses.

The Midsummer festival is a jolly one. It was too early in the season to worry about the harvest, and the worst of the heat and the diseases it bred were yet to come. A day among merry crowds might make a welcome change for me.

By midmorning, alone in my alley, I felt disappointed with my excursion. If anyone is fool enough to envy what he fancies to be my power, let me make it known. It is exceedingly dull to be an image-bearer. Whether folk scorn you or worship you, they depend on you to remain unchanged. So I sat, as I always did, and served my furtive customers.

By noon I had sold most of my wares. I decided to break with my custom of eating the bread and cheese I had brought with me. Sallying forth—in so far as one with a limp may sally—I entertained myself by sampling food and drink at various stalls, doubtless disconcerting the multitudes with this departure from habit.

When I had partaken of more than my fill, I wandered towards the green where I knew I would find various sports and spectacles. At my approach, folk made way as if I were something mildly dangerous like a wasp. I was too accustomed to such a response to take much notice or offense. I found it eased my way to the fore of any crowd.

But a good view did little to enhance the entertainments. Most were glamorous only from a distance and appeared sordid under closer scrutiny. I was particularly distressed by the dancing bear, a mangy, flea-bitten creature, none too well-fed, who would doubtless turn rabid one day and serve his master right. I found myself watching the faces opposite me. A few seemed admiring, even awed by the bear. Many more laughed and jeered, and some pelted the poor animal with refuse. I looked at the bear again and imagined him as he might be in the Wood, his coat sleek, his belly full of fish and berries.

All at once I understood why people crowded round such a pitiful sight.

The bear bore an image, too. He was the Wild, the Dangerous, shackled with chains, subdued by a whip. I turned away sickened. If I were the witch folk feared me to be, I would dissolve the bear's chains and turn him loose on the crowd. But even if he were at large, the wretched beast's spirit and health were so broken, he could hardly have wreaked revenge.

There were other sights, less disheartening, among them a series of races, some earnest, some comic. Though I admired this one's swiftness, that one's grace, I remained alone in a crowd that cheered or hissed, laughed or roared. I had no stake in the outcome of any game. No one belonging to me—or to whom I belonged—ran or wrestled or danced.

By mid-afternoon, worn out with these feelings, I left the green and wended my way back to my alley to fetch my cart. Though I was curious to know if the father-in-law of the crown Prince was still the miller, I decided I could live with my ignorance. I did not need meal so desperately as that, and I was too weary to fend off the memories I would have encountered at the mill.

As I headed towards the gate, I was surprised to find myself in the midst of an excited crowd. It was too early for traveling folk to take their leave; the festivities had just begun, and there would be revelry well into the night. Some pending event must have occasioned this gathering. For once I found my fearsome presence ignored.

"What's amiss?" I demanded. "Let me pass." But no one heeded me.

Then I heard the blast of trumpets followed by a voice shouting over the din:

"Make way! Stand back! Make way for the Prince and Princess!"

My heart leaped. No, it flew. It soared high above the crowd, above the earth, melting in the light. I would see him! Then it fell, abruptly, as if struck by an arrow, and my heart was once again within my breast where it beat painfully. I would see her.

Soldiers parted the crowd with the flats of their swords, and I was squeezed against the wall of a house. Now I determined to exercise my grim privilege. I would see them. I would come close enough to touch them, even if my heart must break and never again be whole.

"Out of my way! Beware!" I snarled as I pushed my way to the front of the crowd just in time to see the royal coach enter the gate.

Drawn by four fine horses, two black, two white, the coach appeared to be made of gold, though likely it was only gilded. That pair could have ridden in my cart, pulled by my goats, and still they would have shone, shedding their glory as light on the dazzled crowd.

They were still some hundred paces away. I looked first to Julian. He had changed very little. If his face had toughened or creased during the war, I was still too far away to see it. He had achieved a beard, but it looked softer than most men's, and it was still much lighter than the hair on his head. I could not see the beautiful green-gold of his eyes from this distance, but in his bearing, in his every gesture was the gentleness I adored. As the coach drew nearer, I searched his face for happiness and could find no contentment there. He had instead a look of feverish joy, like that of a man in precarious possession of a rare treasure, who may never rest for guarding it. Though he was seated, he seemed to hover about Aurelie, moth to her flame, ready to render all sorts of unnecessary services.

The intensity of Julian's regard compelled me to shift my attention to Aurelie. With my practiced midwife's eye, I took in the swell of her midriff under the green fine linen gown, and I judged her to be about six months gone. Tall and big-boned as she was, she would not bulge much until the end. One look at her face, full of high color, with no trace of puffiness, told me she was one of those who carry with ease and grace, whose health and beauty, far from being marred, are enhanced. What might I not have forgiven her for a glimpse of a swollen ankle, the hint of a double chin.

But no, her condition crowned her as surely as the diadem set in her hair.

Unlike the village maidens when they married, she wore her hair loose to the waist, and tossed it as she turned this way and that, granting to all the privilege of beholding her newly royal face. Now and then she waved and even called out to some she knew. The crowd roared its delight and approval. She was declared "A fine lass! Still one of us!"

But I knew better. She had never been one of them, no more than I had. She had always borne the image of the Queen, crowned or not. Here was no great change—save, perhaps, that now she made the mistake the Mother had warned against and made no distinction between the image and herself. As I watched the crowd adore her, I had to ask myself: if I bore the image of Queen instead of Witch, would I bother with such fine distinctions?

Now the coach was thirty paces away. I looked again at Julian. At this range, I could see that his body had changed and hardened, filled out to a man's. But his face was still as tender and unguarded as an untried boy's. For an instant I understood and even shared his father's anger: "Cover yourself!" I wanted to shout. "You are not alone in a wood with your true love. You are the Prince of the realm appearing before your people. You have no right to scorn your image." Then the anger passed, and I desired only to gather him into my arms, take him far away from the world and Aurelie.

The coach was almost abreast of me now. Aurelie, seated on the side where I stood, loomed larger; Julian slipped into the shadow of her brightness. I fixed my gaze on her belly, for a moment forgetting everything but Marina. I fancied that I saw, beneath the smooth green linen of Aurelie's gown, the movement of a tiny limb. Then in a protective gesture I had not seen her make until now, Aurelie's arms encircled her roundness. I looked up and found that she was staring straight at me.

Despite the bright sunlight, her pupils had widened with fear, the grey of her eyes in total eclipse. As she passed me, I looked into that luminous darkness and beheld the image of the Witch.

Then I did the cruelest thing I could have done. No, I did not point a bony finger or utter any dreadful curse or dire warning. I merely smiled.

Aurelie shuddered and turned for the first time to the Prince. I could only see their backs now, as the coach proceeded down the street. But I did not need to see his face to guess the eagerness with which the Prince welcomed any attention from Aurelie. Before the coach turned into the square, I saw her lean against him. He put his arm about her and drew her close.

On my journey home, I probed my heart. It was not broken. Better that it had been. Instead it had shrunk, small and evil as a poisonberry.

CHAPTER EIGHT

SUMMER DRAGGED LIKE THE HEM OF A SKIRT in a dirty street, and the days seemed endless as the drone of insect song. Oh, I was busy enough with the tending and harvesting of plants and all the other seasonal chores, but I worked from force of habit, and my hands needed no instruction from a mind that was all too idle—or rather not idle enough.

I am sure I fretted more over the coming babe than any woman who ever carried a child. Nor could I reassure myself by running my fingers over and over that ripe roundness, alive with little stirrings. Now that the time for miscarriage had passed, I worried over stillbirth and deformity. A fine witch I was, afflicted with second sightlessness. To be sure, I sought visions. I visited every clear pool I knew at every propitious hour of the night and day, at every phase of the moon and got nothing for my efforts but eyes so strained I had to bathe them with a decoction of sticklewort.

My only comfort derived from a dream that came to me all too rarely. In this dream I rested my hands on a great, life-swollen belly: no face, not Aurelie's or mine, just a vast expanse, rippling and heaving beneath my hands, like the sea in the tales of the wandering bards, and in the deeps, raising the storm, my sweet leviathan.

I would wake from this dream weeping, my heart softened with the tears, but soon it would harden again, wrung in the grip of fear. I was in a dither lest Aurelie break her word. The terror I had beheld in her eyes that Midsummer day alarmed me. What had become of her arrogant confidence that she would bear only sons? Did she, too, sense that the babe must be a girl? And had some maternal feeling sprung to life along with the babe in her womb that made her dread to lose a daughter? Or did she simply fear what I knew, fear that if she kept her bargain with me the truth must out? Yet surely she was not fool enough to think that I would hesitate to use the truth as a weapon?

Her fear not only worried me, it also fueled my hatred. She, who had once known the image I bore for what it was, who had seen me, me—or so I had believed—had now turned me into the witch I appeared to be. She had wedded me to my mask so that I could not find the human face beneath it. Bitterly, I blamed her for what I had become. Hatred so flooded me that the tiny kernel where love still lived was in danger of being swept away forever.

Towards the end of the Summer, I felt lethargic. My ankles swelled, and so did my fingers, making them too clumsy for fine work. Though I did not have a great belly to carry before me, my back ached as though I had. Again I wondered about Aurelie's condition, and I wagered her ankles were as trim as ever. In the dog days, I gave myself over to sloth and spent most of my time lolling naked in a pool of the stream. Those who managed to find me there were generally too frightened to make their requests and promptly turned tail, crashing away through the undergrowth like outsized rabbits.

Then one morning I woke and looked about me, dismayed at the disarray in the cave. I spent the day in a bustle: sorting, sweeping, scrubbing, arranging the clothing for the babe. I sanded the cradle until the wood was smooth as satin, then I rubbed it with oils until it shone. In the late afternoon, a wind rose and the heat broke, shattered by the lightning that split the sky and loosed the waters above the heavens upon the earth. The world without was washed as clean as the cave. I retired exhausted but well pleased with my work.

For half the night, I slept the soundest sleep I had known all Summer. I was down deep in a well of sleep that knew no bottom. Then pain reached in with giant fingers and drew me out, squeezing all the while, as if to turn me to pulp. I woke with a scream. The pain vanished all of a sudden, as if it had never been, and I thought I must have had a nightmare. Then those hands gripped again: the heel in the small of my back and the long, wicked fingers reaching round the front. Again the pain released me, and I felt nothing at all. Moments later a third pain seized me with such force that I fought for breath. When it let go, I lay back panting and sweating, wondering if the hand of Death had been probing me for ripeness.

I braced myself to meet the next pain, but it never came. After a time I relaxed my watch and began to grow drowsy again. Images drifted. Again and again I saw the great belly rising and falling, rising and falling. Then all at once I knew. I sat up, wide awake.

"Why, the hussy!" I cried aloud, for I was convinced that Aurelie's hour had come, and she had failed to send for me. Truly, if she had meant to honor the bargain, she should have installed me as resident midwife this fortnight. Well, if she thought to escape me, she would soon know better.

In an instant I was dressed, the contents of the sack assembled. Hurrying out the door, I called to the goats. These worthy creatures I had arranged to leave with a woman who often sought my services and paid in kind. I did not know how long I would be gone, and I dared not run the risk of their going dry. Fortunately, the dame's cottage was not far out of my way to the Castle. Yet even the minor delay of tethering them in her yard was excruciating. Oh, for a wind-borne broomstick, such as witches are supposed to ride!

At the dawn of a perfect day, I came in sight of the Castle, rising with the sun from the meadows and marshes, casting its shadow for what seemed like miles. I was soon within its chilly reach, wishing I headed an invading army. How was I to storm this fortress? Accustomed as I was to inspiring fear in single persons, I had never had to contend with a garrison. As I approached, fear that I would miss the birth of my cherished babe emboldened me.

"Ho! Guard!" I shouted to the watch tower, astonished at the volume and authority of my voice. "Rouse yourself and open the gate at once!"

"Who goes there?" answered a voice, befuddled with sleep and hoarse with drink. A moment later the guard appeared, a handsome brute, no doubt to the King's taste. "State your business."

"I am the Wise Woman of the Western Wood, addressed as Mother, feared as Witch. I am come to attend the Princess Aurelie, who has dire need of me. Even now she labors to bring forth her babe, and no one may deliver the child alive save me!"

The man's answer was an insolent stare. Resting his chin in his hands and his elbows on the parapet, he leaned over to have a better look at me. I returned his gaze, but I was at a disadvantage, as I had to look up and squint. Eyeball to eyeball, I warranted, he would not be so brash.

"You may be a witch, old woman, but with a face like that, you'll not bewitch me," he guffawed at his own wit. "Only beauty passes through these gates. King's orders."

What a pity the Mother had never taught me useful magic. This young fool would make a fine toad. I bit my tongue to keep from muttering idle threats and took stock of the situation. The man was a bully and, therefore, likely a coward, too. In time I could intimidate him, but time was too precious to waste on this lout. I decided to gamble.

"Send a message to the Princess. Tell her that I am here, and that you have dared to keep me waiting."

"And just who are you to give me orders?"

I smiled to myself, for I knew I had succeeded in unnerving him. He was posturing now.

"I have told you what I am. No one living knows who I am."

My voice sounded ominous, even to me. After a few more feeble jeers, the guard disappeared. More quickly than I would have thought possible, the gates swung open, and the guard, all but groveling in his eagerness to appease me, escorted me into the courtyard where a chambermaid awaited me with her eyes downcast.

"This way, lady Mother," whispered the wench, her awe of me evident in every movement.

And so, I thought, if these two have taken their cue from their mistress, then I am dreaded by the highest lady in the land. Having no desire to dispel that fear, I stifled the impulse to question the maid about Aurelie's progress. No one must guess at my guesswork. I had a reputation for omniscience to maintain.

I diverted myself by looking about as we crossed a courtyard littered with molting peacocks. The gardens were gaudy with late summer blooms, but not, when one looked closely, well kept or well laid out. The gardeners here labored for someone with an indifferent eye who required display and cared nothing for fine detail.

Across the courtyard, we entered a corridor that was drafty despite the tapestries. The design of these affected me much as had the gardens: they were lacking both in subtlety and invention, conventional hunting scenes, varied with nymphs in the nude.

At last we came to the end of the corridor, mounted a flight of steps, and entered a suite of rooms. In the innermost chambers, where the fresh air brought by the storm—or, indeed, any fresh air—had not penetrated, in a bed hung with distinctly musty and lamentably moth-eaten velvet curtains, lay Aurelie.

CHAPTER NINE

S HE RESTED BETWEEN PAINS, eyes closed, body slack. As I neared her, I could smell the sourness of her sweat. Another pain took her; she clenched her jaw, and I could hear her grinding her teeth. All the lines and shadows, the puffiness here, the loose skin there, that would come with age were prefigured in her face. It was well the King could not see her now. When the pain passed, she opened her eyes and saw me standing over her. Tenderness and contempt warred in me, equally terrible. No one had ever been so utterly at my mercy.

Then Aurelie turned her head aside and vomited. The need for immediate action thrust all feelings aside.

"Is there no window in this room?" I spoke softly enough, but the ladies shied from me like so many skittish heifers.

"But, but we dare not let her near a window, Reverend Mother." She addressed me as if I were the head of a convent.

I remembered with exasperation the superstition that an evil spirit might fly in and enter the child with its first breath.

"She must have air. Fling open those doors and make yourselves useful with your fans. Fetch more water," I directed, glancing at a jug that was nearly empty and whose contents looked none too fresh. "Cold and hot, and see to it that it's clean."

While I issued orders, I noted that Aurelie's pains were coming swift and hard. I almost wished that she would scream and carry on, though it would make my work more difficult, for I longed to despise her absolutely. Grudgingly, I had to admit she seemed determined to labor like a queen. The fear in her eyes was of me, not of the pain. I sat down beside her and began to question her. Her waters had broken with the storm, and the pains had begun in the night, just as I had suspected. I made no accusations; she made no excuses. We both knew she had broken her word.

When I bent to examine her, I had to force my hands to be still; they trembled as much as they had the first time I ever examined a laboring woman. No, more: this was my own daughter I would bring forth. I laid my ear against the Belly—I did not, even now, think of it as Aurelie's—and my own heart leaped as I found the strong, steady heart beat of my child. My palm, resting near the top of the mound, met with the lusty kick of a little heel. As if in response, the womb tightened and squeezed again. When it let go, I felt inside and found all in readiness: the mouth of the womb open and Marina's head already there, thrusting from darkness towards light. Never had I attended so simple a labor—I will not say easy; labor is labor. Giving the lie to my dire pronouncement at the gate, Aurelie could have delivered herself as surely as a cat drops kittens. The King had picked a fine breeder. So had I.

"Someone fetch the birthing stool!" I roared. In peasant hovels, women squatted. Surely here there were more amenities. The women scurried to obey me. "Now you must help your body do its work," I addressed Aurelie.

Wordlessly, Aurelie allowed me to help her from the bed to the stool. I instructed her ladies to support her while I made ready my oils. Aurelie had only pushed three times, when I felt the soft, sticky hair of Marina's head as she crowned. I willed myself to remain calm. So intently did I concentrate that I fell into a trance.

Mine were the hands, blessedly skilled, knowledge in every bone and fiber, that eased the way. Mine was the body that pushed and burned and opened until I thought it must break. Mine, too, was the tiny being that suffered, without word or image or understanding, this first birth, this seeming death. So close were we in this timeless time, maybe it was no illusion that we were one.

And then we were three as into my hands sprang Marina: whole, separate, herself. Before I admired her, I made myself do all that was necessary, clearing her tiny, perfect nose with my own breath. With a cry more of surprise than of fear, Marina drew her own first breath. The cord gently ceased its pulsing; I cut it, and I held her to me, my daughter.

"My son," Aurelie struggled to stand. "Give me my son."

"This is not your son," I answered, holding Marina, carefully out of reach, allowing Aurelie to see the exquisite girl child, still covered with the bloody remnants of her birth but perfectly shaped and crowned with brown curls.

Aurelie cried out as she had not during her ordeal. Her ladies murmured comfort and reassurance.

"It will a boy next time, your Highness."

Aurelie moaned again.

"Quick you," I ordered a waiting woman. "It's the afterbirth. Deliver it." I held Marina close again; neither devil nor angel could wrest her from me. "When you're done, help her Highness to her bed and clean her up.:"

Aurelie kept her eyes on me, beseeching. I wanted to look away. What did I care for her sorrow? It came too late. Yet I was riveted. Vaguely, I heard whispering among the ladies, but the sound held no more meaning for me than the buzzing of flies. We were alone, Aurelie and I, as if no one but us had ever existed or ever would. Even Marina, stirring in my arms, seemed unreal.

I do not know how much time passed before I became aware that the ladies, having done what they could for their mistress' comfort, had joined her in staring at me.

"Send your servants away," I commanded. At a nod from her, they disappeared.

"The child's name is Marina," I told Aurelie. "Weep for yourself, if you will, but not for the babe. I will raise her as my own. For so she is, as you well know."

"No!" Aurelie struggled out of bed, but, like many women just delivered, her legs were weak; they crumpled beneath her. To my discomfort, and doubtless hers, she knelt before me.

"I will tell your ladies to help you back to bed. I am going now. Farewell."

"They'll stop you," she threatened. "They'll never let you past the gates." Marina slept now, and I reckoned I could easily conceal her beneath my cloak, but Aurelie need not know of this simple measure.

"No one will dare." I spoke with a brash assurance I hoped would convince her and anyone else who might seek to interfere.

"The King will ride after you with all his knights."

"And so bring upon his land pestilence, famine, and flood."

My threats sounded absurd to me, but I could see by the growing despair in Aurelie's face that she believed them.

"He will hang you as a Witch!"

"And learn from me before I die who it was spun straw to gold."

One of my hideous grins tugged at my mouth. It was she who feared death, not I.

"But what will I tell him!" she wailed.

I thought she meant the Prince. I began to panic. I must not think of him now.

"He'll kill me!"

My heart hardened again most satisfactorily.

"Tell him you made a bargain with the Devil," I said bitterly. "For so you believe me to be."

"Yes," she breathed. "Truly, that is what you have become."

She lowered her eyes at last and buried her face in her hands, exhausted, defeated. I struggled against the impulse to lay Marina in the cradle close by and help Aurelie to bed. If I had become a devil, then let me act the part. Yet something troubled me. That word 'what'. If only she had said the Devil is who you are, she would have sealed my hatred. Surely that was what she meant. But pity continued to buzz around me, like a fly trying to settle on my nose.

"I don't understand." She looked up at me again. Tears stood in her eyes.

Artful tears, I told myself.

"Once you did not hate me. You gave me a shell when we were children, and I gave it to you again as a token. Don't you remember?"

A cheap trick, pleading our childhood bond, our imagined bond.

"And when we met again at the mill, you seemed glad to see me. When I called for your help, you came. If you hated me, why did you come? Why do you hate me? Why?"

Why did I hate her? All at once I felt confused. Aurelie's face blurred. Images whirled. Aurelie dancing on the green, receiving my shell. I know you. I know you. I know you. But she did not. She had not. And I hated her. Had I not always hated her? But no, no, there was a reason. A good reason. What was it? What was it? I could not remember.

"Why did you spin straw into gold to save my life only to kill me now?"

"Kill you?" I repeated stupidly.

"Yes, you are killing me. For if the King does not decree my death, I will surely die grieving for my babe."

Her voice broke, and the tears began to stream.

"She is not your child!" I shouted to drown her sobs, to deafen a voice within that I must not hear. "You forfeited your right to her when you so lightly sacrificed another child to save your own miserable life."

She stared at me, bewildered. It was plain she had forgotten Gretal. But I had not, and I remembered with relief. For that was the reason I hated Aurelie, was it not? A good reason, a noble reason.

"You are not fit to be a mother," I told her. "Though I assure you, if the King spares your life, you will bear many healthy brats. But this child is mine, and so farewell."

I made to turn away, holding Marina tightly and drawing my cloak about me. Somehow Aurelie mustered the strength to crawl. Before I had taken three steps, I felt a tugging at my skirt, and there was Aurelie at my feet.

"Let go!" I tried to loose her hands, but she held fast.

"Please! Please!" she sobbed. "Don't take my babe. You cannot know what it's like. You cannot know how I feel—"

"Do not dare to tell me what I know or what I feel!" I shouted. "It is you who know nothing of feeling. Do you know what it is to be ugly? Do you know what it is to be despised? Do you—"

Abruptly I silenced myself. I neither wanted nor needed pity from Aurelie. I was the powerful one, not she. But I had spoken too much already. She seized upon my words.

"But I never despised you. I never thought you were ugly. Only different. Like me. I never feared you or made fun of you, like the others. I knew you. You knew me."

"No!" I spoke not only to Aurelie but to myself, to the power of the memories she invoked. "No!"

With my free hand I wrenched my skirt from her with such force that she fell forward on her face.

"You do not know me! You do not even know my name!"

The violence of my voice and movement woke Marina, and she began to howl for the first time. I felt both grief and shame that she, who had greeted life so peacefully, should find herself so soon in the midst of strife. Tears pricked my eyes and threatened to overflow. Aurelie, struggling to raise herself wept anew, and her beautiful, blue-veined breasts wept, too, causing me the bitterest envy.

"But you never told me your name," she sobbed. "You said you did not have a name. You were always the Girl with the Silver Eye."

"Ah, but I have a name now," I said. "Once I wanted to tell you my name, but you will never hear it from my lips. The Mother warned me not to tell you. My name is all my wealth, and I'll not squander it. No one living knows my name but me. I will give you three days, while I bide here and tend you. If you can tell me my name before that time is done, you may keep the babe. If you fail, be sure you will never see either of us again."

Aurelie gaped at me with mingled hope and horror. It was plain she thought me mad. So I believe I was. For those foolish words had spoken themselves, against my will, and though with all my will I wished I might, I could not take them back.

CHAPTER TEN

Y VOW TO REMAIN THREE DAYS kept me prisoner more surely than locks or chains. You may wonder, who follow this tale,
that one so debased as I had become could care for honor. Call
it pride then, the deadliest of the deadly sins, yet it kept me from stealing
away with the babe as I longed to do.

So wretched was I on the day of her birth that I could scarcely rejoice
in Marina's perfection, and perfect she was. Many newborns are mottled
and red, their heads squeezed into strange shapes, their features flattened
or pinched. Marina's easy entry into the world had left her smooth, her
skin with a luminous tone, like light shining through the petals of a rose,
her tiny features pleasing and distinct. The soft, brown down on her head
held a hint of red, but it was much darker than Aurelie's, and it curled, as
Aurelie's did not. Her eyes were newborn blue but might not remain so.
In shape they were large and long and heavy-lidded, like her father's. She
had a remarkably steady gaze, both sweet and serious. Already she seemed
to consider all she saw. In the moments when her eyes held mine, I forgot
everything else. It was as if she and I were alone in the Wood, alone in the
world, as I had so often dreamed.

Though I had the principal care of Marina—no one dared gainsay my
right—I was always aware of Aurelie's longing and dread. It hung in the air,
making the air dense and difficult to breathe. Then there was the practical
matter of Marina's feeding. In her determination to claim Marina as her
own, Aurelie had refused the wetnurse sent by the King.

Of course, I had planned to nurse Marina myself, certain that with
application of my herbal arts and the babe's vigorous sucking, the milk
would come. I had not reckoned on this delay at the Castle where I had did
not have the right herbs at my disposal nor the goat's milk to feed Marina
in the meantime.

Alone with Marina that first morning and afternoon, while Aurelie
slept the sleep of exhaustion, I offered my empty breast time and again. For
a while I dared to hope my plan would succeed. Comforted by the warmth
and cradling, Marina sucked and dozed, dozed and sucked like any tiny
nursling, but at last hunger roused her fully, and she roared. I knew very
well that Aurelie's breasts dripped with the nourishing yellow fluid that
comes before the milk. How could I deny Marina her proper food? Though
it galled me, I delivered Marina to Aurelie to be nursed. I could not bear to

watch, and so I left her chamber. Likely it was well for Marina that I did, lest my hatred wither the breast that must sustain her new life. I was too jealous to allow Marina to linger at that fount, and I returned to snatch her away as soon as I deemed the feeding done.

I laid Marina, sated and sleepy, in her cradle, and I took my place on the cot beside her, my head propped on one hand, the other resting on the cradle ready to rock it, for I had no intention of taking my eyes from her. My body had other ideas, however, and soon I was sunk in sleep as deep as the babe's.

I woke abruptly, hours later, in a state of alarm. Someone was bending over the cradle. I could not distinguish the face, for the dim light—which could have been that of dusk or dawn—was behind the figure. So befuddled was I with my sudden waking that I scarcely knew where I was or how I came to be there. I knew only that someone menaced my young; the hair rose on my arms, and on the back of my neck. I could feel a growl beginning in my throat. All my limbs tensed. When the intruder reached into the cradle to lift the child, I made to spring upon him.

Then he spoke, no murmured, for his words were for the sleeping babe alone. Nor were they even words but the softest sounds I had ever heard, sounds to make the mourning dove seem shrill. Yet this gentlest of voices, yes, the voice of my beloved, smote me the harshest of blows.

How was it I had given so little thought to Julian. Little? Say none, rather. Stunned, I retreated into myself where I watched in secret, stealing the sight I had no right to behold.

Cradling Marina in his arms, Julian carried her to the fading light that found its way through the window. I had known many a father afraid to hold a babe or holding one as if the tiny thing were like to shatter in his hands. My Prince knew he held a living, lovesome creature, and his arms and body curved to her small shape. He held her as a woman might with her head close to his heart. All this I could see, for he stood sideways, sheltering Marina's face from the direct light. I knew, too, the moment Marina opened her eyes to greet him, for his eyes spoke in return. For a long, long time they looked on one another, father and daughter. I commanded myself to look away, but my eyes would not obey my will.

At last Marina whimpered a bit. Her sire shifted her position, holding her closer, and rocked her from side to side as he paced. She quieted for a time and then cried anew. For the first time, Julian looked the part of the fearful father. I felt I no longer needed to conceal my presence, though to reveal it made me tremble.

"Likely her swaddling is wet, your Highness," I spoke, rising from my cot.

"And I don't doubt she is hungry again. Give her to me, if you please, and I will swaddle her with fresh cloth."

The Prince seemed both relieved and reluctant to relinquish his daughter, but he did not question my authority. Nor did he appear to recognize me, but then, I reasoned, the room was all but dark. As I loosed the swaddling bands, a torch bearer slipped into the chamber, making swift obeisance and leaving the room warmly illumined with candlelight. I kept my face bent to my task, wondering that the Prince did not leave while I did this woman's work. He not only remained, but I sensed he was transfixed. I had no need to look at his face; his adoration of Marina's naked perfection was palpable.

"You must be the midwife." He spoke pleasantly, as I fancied he would to any servant, while I began to wash and oil Marina's tiny body. "I have you to thank for the life and health of my wife and daughter."

My wife and daughter. The tone of his voice told me how he delighted in those words.

"Don't thank me," I mumbled. "It was an easy birth."

My reply was lost, for Marina, enraged at such prolonged exposure, began to wail. Swiftly I swaddled her in fresh bands. Then, without thinking, I picked her up and soothed her myself, dropping kisses on her fragrant head.

"Do you love all your charges so, Midwife?" queried the Prince. I could not speak for the tears caught in my throat.

"May I take her to be nursed?" he asked, always deferent.

Holding out his arms to receive the child, Julian came close to me. I could have touched him. As I yielded Marina, I let myself, for one instant, fancy that she was ours. Though I forbade them, my eyes sought his. At the same time he looked up to smile and share his delight in the babe.

"Oh!" he exclaimed. "Your eyes! They're of different colors. Or is that just a trick of the light?"

"They are." I scarcely breathed the words.

"I've met only one other person with eyes of differing colors." I stared at him, but he no longer looked at me.

"I fell from my horse in a wood one day long ago, and I was stunned. When I woke, I found her bending over me, bathing my scratches. At first I took her for a wood sprite or a fairy. She was a gentle creature, possessed of a strange beauty, like that of a twisted tree or a speckled pebble. But she turned out to be human sure enough, with a misshapen limb and all alone in the world. Long after, I sorrowed that I could not help her as she had so willingly helped me. I wish I knew what has become of her. I don't suppose you'd know, just because you, too, have eyes of different hues? Though I've heard it said that you are the Wise Woman of the Western Wood."

I lowered my eyes from his inquiring glance and fixed them on Marina, whose limbs flailed as she made to scream again.

"The babe hungers, your Highness" was all I said.

When he had gone, I gathered the soiled swaddling and put it to soak in a basin of water. Only my body seemed able to move: my mind was mired. When I had done what little was needed to set the nursery to rights, I sat down, wishing I had a wheel or a drop spindle or even a carding comb and some raw wool. I needed work for my hands in order to think. And thought—not some vague mental wandering but thought as movement of the spirit—was the task that loomed before me now.

Somehow, despite my helpless hands, I made myself begin. The Prince remembered me; the Prince did not know me. Though he looked into the selfsame silver eye he had once beheld in the Wood. And was my Beloved dullwitted, lacking in all logic to imagine that there could be two women in the world, hailing from that Wood, each equipped with a silver eye? How could he fail to know me? Unless he was right, and there were two different beings, not even related as mother and daughter. Indeed, if relation there were, it was a hideous reversal of that one; for the maiden had given birth to the crone.

But who was that nameless girl? A gentle creature, Julian had called her, possessed of a strange beauty. How could I say what had become of her? I did not know her; nor had she ever existed. Or else was my world unmade.

Before I had time to ponder further, the Prince returned with Marina asleep once more in his arms. I wondered that Aurelie had sent away husband and babe so soon, and I felt yet more justified in my claims on the child. A real mother, I reasoned, would have kept her husband close and marveled with him over the babe, as Julian and I did now. He would not lay Marina in the cradle but held her, so I fancied, in such a way that I, too, could see her face.

"I wish I could call her by name," the Prince said in a low voice. "Already she is so much herself and no one else."

"But why should you not?" I asked, startled.

"She has no name yet. The Princess has not chosen. She would not decide all while she waited. My father did not like it, of course, but she has a way with him such as I've never seen. As for me, I would do anything to make her happy—anything."

I averted my gaze, distressed by the lovesickness, so plain in his face, as some people are sickened by the sight of an open wound. Also, I had to hide my alarm at this evidence of fresh treachery. Did Aurelie mean to break every promise?

"I did think she would know the name when she saw the babe," he continued. "She said she would. But now she has called for the Book of Names and for everyone in court to come and tell her all the names they know."

Then I understood. It was not the babe's name she sought to know but mine.

"It is strange," he sighed. "I feel that I know her name, but I dare not call her by it lest my Lady choose another."

"What would you call her?"

"Well, if you will tell no one else," he said softly, "I would call her Marina."

Within me pain held joy in a fierce embrace. "You do well to call her so, for that is her name."

Julian's face lit with surprise and delight.

"But how can you be sure?"

"Am I not a Wise Woman?"

I meant to speak lightly, but the weight of my words crushed me. No! No! I wanted to cry, I'm not! I'm just a girl, the girl you met in the Wood. Look at me! See me! But I said nothing, as I watched him take comfort from the Mother.

In the next instant, I was glad of any joy or comfort the Prince could find, whatever the cost to me, for the source of his suffering strode into the nursery, and I beheld, at last, the King.

He was, in truth, as handsome as I had heard, but where some beauty is generous, enhancing all who admire it; the King's good looks struck me as greedy. Indeed, though it might have been the effect of his gleaming hair and heavy crown, he seemed to draw all the light in the chamber to himself, leaving the rest of the room—and everyone in it—obscured. With his restless pacing, he occupied the space of ten men. He did not greet the Prince or so much as glance at the babe but abruptly began his abuse.

"Is there no nursery maid that you should sit the day long tending the child while affairs of state wait you? The banquet tables groan, and you are not yet dressed. What is more, when any child is born to the crown—even when it's but a female—there are papers to be drawn and signed, announcements and appearances to be made. It should not be necessary for me to instruct you in statecraft."

The Prince looked fearful and shamefaced as a child caught stealing from the jam pot. That he should be thus reduced and demeaned enraged me. I rose and took Marina from the Prince and, in a moment of rashness, made bold to rebuke majesty.

"His Highness is but admiring his firstborn, as is meet and right, for a more perfect child never saw light."

As you would see for yourself if you troubled to look, I added silently, not for fear of giving further offense but because I already regretted inviting his scrutiny of Marina. I could scarcely bear it or believe it that he was related by blood to my babe.

My words drew his glance not to the child but to myself. Without surprise, I noted that mixture of fear and loathing with which many greet the sight of insects or reptiles.

"Whence came this person?" the King demanded of his son, as if I were, in fact, not person enough to speak for myself.

"She is the Wise Woman of the Western Wood, the most skilled in midwife in all the land."

I was touched that the Prince had summoned courage enough to defend me, but the King's lip still curled, and I guessed I was not out of danger. Silently I cursed myself as a fool for attracting his notice. This man could stand between me and Marina.

"Aurelie would have her," the Prince added, and though I knew enough to doubt their truthfulness, his words were well chosen.

The King shrugged and turned his gaze from me.

"I suppose the woman cannot be blamed for the child's sex," he remarked, leaving us in no doubt upon whom he did cast the blame. "Hold the child up, Midwife."

Only my desire to be rid of him as soon as possible made me comply.

"Well, let us hope she'll resemble her mother" was his only remark. "Come," he commanded the Prince as he turned and made for the door. " At once."

Julian cast one glance of longing towards his daughter, then followed forthwith, a hound called to heel.

Once more alone with Marina, I held her close, seeking comfort from her tiny warmth. With Marina still in my arms, I lay down upon my cot, too weary to sustain disdain for the King, overcome, as I was, with sadness and doubt. When I took Marina home with me, as I still determined to do, I would be abandoning my Beloved to "those two," as I began to think of them. I had just witnessed how his father cowed him and held him in contempt. And I was certain that Aurelie felt no passion for her husband but regarded him as a child to be indulged or ignored according to her whim. How could I leave him to their mercy—or mercilessness?

I wished that I could gather my Prince as easily as Marina, hide them both under my cloak, and flee the Castle. We would not return to the cave in the Wood where those two would be sure to find us. No, we would journey beyond the Kingdom, all the way to the wide, wild sea. There we would find us a boat. We would slough off our images as a snake sheds old skin and be merely two merry pilgrims abroad with our babe.

Taking false comfort in this foolish fancy, I followed Marina into sleep.

Neither of us woke until dawn.

CHAPTER ELEVEN

WHEN I BROUGHT MARINA TO AURELIE to be nursed, I found her chamber crowded with folk reciting names, her bed awash with books and parchments. I relinquished Marina, refusing to meet Aurelie's eyes, and made to leave the room at once.

"Stay, Midwife!" Aurelie called after me. "I want you to hear the names I have gathered, wise woman that you are. I will trust you to tell me if any of these names is the One."

Her tone was both commanding and pleading; there was no mistaking her meaning. I answered by turning towards the bed and bowing my head, to indicate consent but also to avoid the sight of Marina's avid nursing.

Aurelie bade each person recite in turn the names he knew. And so began a seemingly endless procession of names, of which I now recall only a few.

Edwina

Delphina

Natalia

Roxanne

Xanthippe

Clothilda

Alfreda

Justine

After a time I did not distinguish one voice from another. It was as if each name pronounced itself as it marched past my inner eye. For I could see the names, not just the letters, though they were clear, but also the shadowy female shape that bore each name, carrying it aloft that I might look. On and on came the names.

Alethea

Gwendolyn

Flavia

Rose

Hedwig

Euphemia

Sigrid

Brunhilde

The intoning of the names acted on me like a dream potion. I lost all sense of time and place; or rather I entered a different time and place. A time before time's beginning or after time's end, a place as close to nothingness as the mind can conceive: a vast and aweful emptiness where everyone assembles, yet each of us stands alone. Here I heard and beheld the names.

Hildegarde

    Vivian

        Magdalen

          Nell

              Phoebe

                  Cassandra

                  Diana

                      Undine

Then the voice changed in some subtle way, no longer one voice merging with another, nor the voices of the names themselves. Not any voice I knew or had ever known, yet it was a voice that made me tremble. How I longed to hide in the nothing that surrounded me, to become nothing. But there was no oblivion in that void, and no mercy. I remained painfully present, worse, no longer a bystander but part of that solemn, that dreadful procession.

                              Hippolyta

                      Leah

                Sophronia

            Mab

        Kezia

      Benedicta

    Theodosia

Aline

I waited with a longing equal to my despair for that voice to sound my name, the voice of my judge. For when my name was called aloud, I would stand naked before Heaven and Earth. Surely, surely I would die of shame. I would lose Marina. I would lose the image that oppressed and protected me. I would lose everything. But then, oh then, the one who knew her name might be saved.

Silence.

At first I did not understand what had happened. I only knew that all the others had gone, and I stood alone in that nothing, unnamed, unborn, as if some great womb had drawn me inside, back into deep unknowing.

"Mother! Mother!"

The trance broke, and nothing dissolved into form. I gazed about me at the faces of the courtiers, still standing at uneasy attention.

"The Name, Mother. Did you hear it? Tell me the name. Which one? Tell me!"

At last I looked at Aurelie. Marina, long since sated, slept, her head resting on that plenteous breast. I made myself look, though to look was pain far worse than any I had ever known, pain made and mixed of all the passions at their most furious pitch. It was a wonder I could contain such raging force and not shatter. Indeed, I believe it was the other way round. I did not contain the pain, pain held me, held me still and made me see. Though I fought the knowledge with the full strength of my hatred, knowledge won. I looked at Aurelie and knew her pain.

"The name." She spoke again, her voice breaking.

I shook my head, then turned and fled.

"There is still time," she shouted after me. "There is still time. More names," she cried to her attendants. "Get me more names! I must have more names."

Her voice followed me back to the empty nursery and echoed there. I gathered my few belongings into the sack, as swiftly as I could, knowing that if I delayed a moment too long I would lose my resolve.

It was near the hour for the midday meal. The noble folk were primping and the common folk toiling. The halls and courtyard were empty, the Watch indifferent. I went my way unseen, a shadow strayed from the flesh, lost in the light of noon.

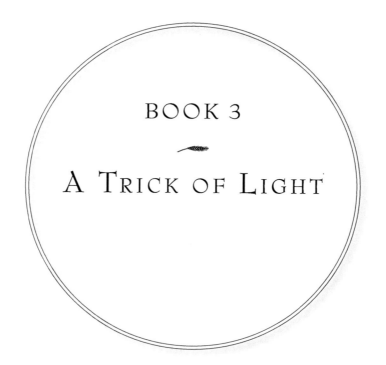

BOOK 3

A TRICK OF LIGHT

CHAPTER ONE

ACCOUNTS OF CRUEL PROMISES exacted for magical services and desperate guessing games in which the beautiful princess triumphs at last make for a more thrilling hearth tale. Few have ears for the truth; fewer still will remember it, and of those few, who will trouble themselves to proclaim it. Yet I must persist with my story, even if silence alone receives my words.

Know then, all you who hear me, just as I made no bargain with Aurelie before I spun the gold, so with no bargain, either broken or fulfilled, I yielded the child of my own will.

But wait! I am no self-abjuring saint. I refuse to bear yet another image.

Listen, and I will tell you how it was with me in those days of living death. The priests say that when the body dies, the soul lives on in torment or in bliss. For me it was the reverse. My soul was dead, and my stupid body had not the sense to follow suit.

I know now that I needed to grieve. Then I did not know how. The tears that might have eased me were frozen within as soon all the world without was frozen. The Winter that followed Marina's birth was one of the bitterest I remember, air so cold it hurt to breathe. On the morning of the killing frost, I made a bonfire of the cradle and all the tiny clothes and coverlets. Even that flame failed to sear the cold at the heart of me.

Sometimes when I woke in the night to tend the fire, I felt the stirrings of unbearable pain, like the pain of frozen limbs when the feeling returns. Except during those midnight hours, I renounced all thought, all feeling, all knowledge of pain. If pain had given me power, then I had squandered it. I had held life in my arms, and I had put it from me. Life would not offer itself again. And so I must live as one dead for the rest of my days.

Of course, I still had my work to do and since my body insisted on staying alive, I let my body perform whatever tasks were necessary to that end. With such a harsh Winter, there was much sickness, though folk did not brave the cold to seek my aid, save in the direst need. Indeed, for a time I blamed the severity of the season for the unusual number of deaths among those I visited. Though I endeavored to ignore it, truth dogged me like a pesky cur, undeterred by kicks and curses.

To be sure, I was still a living store of herb lore. I could recite all the ingredients of myriad potions and remedies as readily as ever. But I could no longer look at a person or feel of his body and know what was wrong. I had lost my healer's sense and sense it was, something between sight and second sight.

My touch had gone blind. Worse, I did not care. Before, I had made Death my enemy in an intimate war. Now, it seemed, the war was done, and Death had dominion over me.

When at last, I acknowledged the truth, I wondered if I ought to refuse the help I could not give or even disappear from the Wood. Or better, demand of Death that it complete its task with me. But I found I had not the strength of will even to choose my own end. And certainly, I thought, the people will not long suffer my existence, now that I am of no use to them. They will rise up and call me Witch. They will drag me to the Market-place to be stoned or hanged. I had only to wait.

So passed the Winter. Then, one night when the stars proclaimed Spring in spite of cold as deep as ever, I woke, as I often did, to tend the fire, and there before the hearth sat the Mother, my Mother, carding wool as if she had never gone away. Do not ask if I dreamed. I do not know, nor does it matter. However she appeared, whether by magic or by special dispensation from Heaven or through the workings of my own mind, she was there, facing my pallet, though not looking at me. She was simply there, waiting, not waiting. There.

And she was alive, aglow with life. I fancied I could feel the warmth of her across the cave. Of the two, if ghost there were, then I was the ghost. It was I who lacked substance. And I felt ashamed, so full of shame I lacked room for joy and wonder. She had come to reproach me, I knew. Why else, after all this time, would she appear? Sorely as I had missed her, I felt powerless to greet her. So I remained, a miserable child who longs for comfort but cannot receive it.

"Daughter," the Mother called, still carding wool, sparing me her gaze.

"Come." She spoke my name. Its sound made me want to weep. My name was so beautiful, and I was so hideous. "Sit with me. Warm yourself."

"I must get more wood," I mumbled.

Then, glancing at the hearth where there should have been only coal and ash, I saw a merry blaze. How like the Mother, returned from the dead, to tend the fire before all else.

I pulled up my stool and sat at an angle, like the Mother, so that unless we turned our faces towards one another our eyes would not meet. Silence. The crackle and hiss of burning wood, the rhythmic dragging of comb through wool. I could hardly bear it that we sat thus again, as if nothing had changed when everything had changed.

"How is it you have come?" The words burst from me.

"I came because you did not call."

I almost laughed. Death had not altered the Mother. Her rare answers were as cryptic as ever. Then remorse overtook me, and I began to accuse myself.

"Mother, I have failed you. You served Life, and I have become the servant of Death. I cannot heal. People die at my hands. I am cursed. You were mistaken in me. I am not the chosen one. I cannot bear the image. It is killing me."

The Mother's silence spoke, and in it, I heard the sound of my own lies. Then the Mother uttered my name again, her voice unbearably tender.

"Why do you suffer?"

"Marina." A sob rent my heart, and all the pain I had refused rushed in.

"Marina, Marina!" I called her name again and again, flooded with grief like a spring river when the ice flows. I let the current take me, for I knew I would not drown. The Mother was with me, and I was safe.

I woke the next morning on my pallet, my face stiff with what could only be dried tears. The fire burned low; the Mother was gone. Though I could not swear it had not been there before, next to the spinning wheel lay a pile of clean carded wool.

I had not much time to ponder this miracle. I had scarcely finished milking when I was called to tend a woman burning with childbed fever. Moments after I reached her side, I found the lump in her breast where the milk had clogged. A leech man had wrongly told her that her milk had gone bad and would harm the babe. Brandishing my authority, I put the babe to her breast. Then I gave her a medicine made of wheat mold, that I carried with me on such cases, applied compresses, and flooded her with tea infused with Balm of Gilead to bring down the fever and make her pass water.

By nightfall the fever had turned, and the lump and the pain were gone. I returned to the cave wearied with nursing. I still had the goats and the other animals to tend. Only as I sank into sleep did it dawn on me: my skill had returned.

Spring came at last. Sap rose in the trees; the earth softened and yielded to the plough. And I was alive, wholly alive, though weak as one new-recovered from long illness. Or maybe it was not weakness I felt but a tranquility previously unknown to me. For the first time, I found myself choosing the life that had mysteriously chosen me. Before now I had not prized it. I was too intent on all I had missed, all I hungered to possess. I had always been waiting: for the Prince to find me, for Marina to be born. Now I had done with waiting. Not that it was easy to dwell simply in each passing moment. Often I sorrowed, but my sorrow had lost much of its bitterness, except when I thought of Aurelie, which I earnestly endeavored not to do. When I pictured Marina, I placed her in her father's arms.

Since, with the Mother's help, I had known my grief, I found myself more and more able to enjoy the small pleasures my life afforded me: the warmth of fresh milk and fresh bread, the affection of the animals. I found new satisfaction in seeking plants and preserving them in useful forms.

Of course, I had always delighted in my weaver's art. Congress with human beings was never so simple or satisfying as the tasks performed alone, but I began to rejoice in the healing of body or spirit accomplished through me. Though I could never deliver a babe without pain to rival joy, I no longer rebelled against the pain nor hated anyone because of it—save, in an unprobed corner of my soul, Aurelie.

Apart from that hatred, a small canker I did my best to ignore, I believed myself healed. The gap between who and what I was appeared to narrow. On the rare occasions when I glimpsed myself in a pool or puddle, I fancied I was coming to resemble the one who had been Mother before me. There no longer seemed so great a difference between us. I imagined my life as a stream flowing unimpeded towards a great river that she had already joined.

Yet, as the time for the May revels approached, though my supplies were scanty, I found myself reluctant to make a journey to the village. I did not want to disturb my peace nor put its strength to any test. In truth, I knew my peace to be exceedingly delicate, as in need of a nest as a new laid egg. Whenever I went abroad in the world, the image waxed in weight, like the body emerging from water. I did not feel strong enough to bear it for a whole day in the crowded streets. Let me remain alone in the Wood where I wore the image lightly, as a shawl, easily slipped on or off as the need arose.

CHAPTER TWO

I OBSERVED THE RITES OF MAY in a solitary fashion, rising with the sun and gathering blossoms of hawthorn and wild plum with which I festooned the cave. I plaited myself a crown of periwinkle and wore one of my gayest garments as if I were myself a bloom of Spring. I spent the fine, mild day in my herb garden, thinking that for once I would have the luxury of laboring undisturbed. Folk were too busy frolicking to have any need of the Mother.

Therefore, I was startled when, just as the light was fading and I was beginning to think of getting my evening meal, I heard a snapping of twigs and a rustling of leaves that betokened the approach of some creature larger than a squirrel, a rabbit, or a badger. The sound seemed too purposeful to be made by anything but human footsteps. It came steadily closer but no one called a greeting. I was frightened neither of bear nor wolf. But the human animal was another matter. Could May madness have so emboldened some ruffians that they thought to make sport with the Witch? The noise ceased all of a sudden. I could not distinguish figures among the trees, but that extra sense that comes into play when other senses fail told me that someone's eye was trained on me.

"Who seeks the Mother?" I challenged the twilit gloom.

After a moment, someone called in a harsh whisper, "Mother, are you alone?"

"Save for goats and chickens, rabbits, snakes, and toads, I am."

Then crept into the clearing two figures, one tall, one slight, and soon I found myself greeting Amelia and Gretal.

"You are just in time to sup with me." I made them welcome.

"Mother, we dare not stay long," said Amelia. "We've come with a warning. Then we must fly."

"All the more reason to refresh yourselves. Come. I've bread and ale and cheese. You may tell me what happened while you eat."

Inside, by the light of the fire, I got a better look at their faces. Both appeared to be frightened, but Amelia's fear took the form of a tense watchfulness, while Gretal's terror merely made her look even more bewildered than she usually was. I urged both of them to eat, but Amelia had scarcely swallowed a bite when she launched into her tale.

"It's like this, Mother," Amelia began glancing uneasily at Gretal. I sensed she wished she could speak with me alone but dared not let the child out of her sight. "You must know Gretal's habit of singing little songs to herself."

I nodded.

"Well, one day Rolf heard her crooning a tale of a beautiful lady locked in a tower who, to save her life, must spin straw to gold." She paused. "You know the rest of the story, Mother?"

"Yes, but how much did she tell?"

"She sang of a witch who came and spun the gold in exchange for the lady's first-born child."

Amelia did not look at me. I guessed she did not know what to believe. No doubt it troubled her to think that the one she called Mother could make so cruel a demand. I longed to defend myself, to tell her all my tale as I am telling it now, but there was no time for lengthy explanation.

"It did not happen quite that way." I allowed myself that much. "But Gretal could not know that," I admitted. "Go on."

"Rolf, of course, pounced on the tale like a cat on a mouse and at once set about making it into verse and fixing the wandering tune into a mournful melody. I argued with him to no avail. He could not comprehend my concern for an unknown witch or for Gretal. To him it was just a story, true or not, and he knew it for a crowd-drawer and a money-maker.

"But when I threatened to leave the group, taking Gretal with me, he sat down to bargain with me. At my insistence, he agreed to change the witch to a man. Then, in a fit of inspiration, Rolf decided to make it the Devil himself who spun the straw into gold. That pleased him mightily as he intended to sing the Devil's part."

It did not please me, however, that man or devil should take credit for my one great deed. But I hid my displeasure from Amelia. She had meant to protect me.

"And so," Amelia was saying, "he wrote the ballad of the lovely lady beguiled by the Devil. In the end, of course, the angels came to her aid. Rolf is a fine musician, but he has a most conventional turn of mind when it comes to narrative, but then that is what pleases the crowds, and pleasing the crowds is all Rolf's care.

"For a fortnight he rehearsed Gretal without mercy. He had the poor child all but singing the song in her sleep. Then he brought it before the people. Of course they went wild for it. All this Winter and Spring its fame has preceded it. Folk in every village have clamored to hear it again and again. With this great success, Rolf was stone deaf to the protest I continued to make; for I could not quell my uneasiness. Forgive me Mother, I should have heeded my doubts. I should have fled with Gretal in the dark of some night. I should have known."

"What happened?" I interrupted Amelia's self-recrimination.

"Today is May Day, as you doubtless know. We spend most of the year wending our way from village to village, and we found ourselves this morning at the gates of the chief market town nearest the Castle. I told Rolf that I believed the Princess had been a maiden here, and I pleaded with him not to make Gretal sing the ballad. He would have none of my fears and declared it would be a rare treat for the village folk to hear one of their own thus celebrated.

"So, right in the market square, we performed the ballad. The crowd soon formed itself around us. Gretal's sweet voice, the plaintive tune, the tale itself caused a hush, unnatural to such numbers, to pass from one to another as a whisper will. Soon the square itself was silent as if it were a church when the Host is transformed. Save, of course, for the music: Gretal's voice, the recorder making harmony with it, my lute, the others joining in the refrain.

"The song has always held an audience, but today, perhaps because the Lady, as Rolf remarked, was one of their own, the crowd was spellbound, as if by magic, in and beyond the words and music. Or else how could people fail to notice the approach of the royal carriage? True, the crowd had its back to the way the carriage approached, but not one turned towards the sound of hooves and wheels on cobblestone.

"We minstrels faced that direction, but Rolf was too intent on the performance to notice and, I doubt not, on calculating his take from the crowd. Gretal, when she sings, I swear sees nothing, or else she might have flung herself towards the Lady. For it was the Princess Aurelie who sat in that coach. I knew her even at a distance. Her hair vied with the sun for glory. She sat between two men, one, I surmised, was the Prince; the other I was certain was the King. By some power of their own, my fingers kept strumming the chords while my mind scrambled frantically, seeking a plan.

"The Royal Carriage drew ever nearer. Hope died that the interminable ballad would end before the royal party could hear it. Over and over came the thrice-cursed refrain of the ballad, strong and clear, so that everyone, including the three in the carriage, which had now come to a halt, must hear.

The price is set; the child is sold,
The Devil spins the straw to gold.

"I thought of seizing Gretal then and there, but I knew this for a fool-ish act. To cease in mid-song would serve as an alarm to all. As subtly as I could, I glanced about for a way to escape or a place to hide. I spied a side door to the church in an alley some few feet behind us. I made a hasty prayer to God and all the Saints that the door be unlocked. I had some vague notion of seeking sanctuary at the altar, for even a king cannot seize you at the foot of God.

"The song ended at last. I remained motionless in the moment's silence that followed, save to get an iron grip on Gretal's arm. Then, when the ap-plause broke, I dragged her with me into the alley to that side door, which, God be praised, received us. We were graced with some minutes before Rolf, the crowd, or the King took in what had happened.

"Thinking more swiftly than I can express in the recounting, I decided against a dash, for the streets of the town and any routes of escape were unknown to me and we would likely be cornered in no time. Nor did I fancy sanctuary, save as a last resort. It would serve us days at best. Then hunger and thirst would force us into the waiting arms of the guards the King would post at the doors.

"Surely there is a God and one that for some unfathomed reason took our side. I would never have given myself credit for so much mother wit. A plan came to me fully formed, and I hastily enacted it. Thrusting Gretal behind the priest's screen in the confessional, I headed for the baptismal font, taking care to scuff the floor with my muddy shoes. Then I climbed on top of the font and, God forgive me, raised my lute and bashed in a lovely rose window as neatly and thoroughly as I could, doing considerable damage to my poor instrument.

"Outside I could hear the roar of the crowd and above it shouts of 'Seize them, Seize them!' Saints be praised, fear made me nimble. I scampered to the confessional, where I stashed my battered lute, pulled my cloak over my head, yanked out the Rosary that I had retained from my former life of re-spectability, for reasons more sentimental than religious, and began mak-ing my confession to Gretal, whom, I later discovered, had fallen asleep.

"When the King's soldiers burst into the church, they found but a queru-lous widow at her prayers. One of them roughly grasped my shoulder and made to question me. With my long experience as a dutiful daughter, wife, and dowager, I am practiced in the art of anonymity, and it served me well.

The soldier did not connect the penitent widow with the lute player. Before he could even consider the possibility, I began a litany of complaint—how I had been disturbed in my devotions, how no one showed respect for the Holy Church anymore, what with wanton hussies running wild, and what was wrong with the King's command that soldiers should be molesting an upright widow instead of keeping peace in the streets—all in that whining tone of voice that drives men mad.

"Look you! Over here!' shouted one of the other soldiers. 'The window! That's how they got out.'

"My interrogator turned from me with obvious relief, and the soldiers were off, hounds hot on a false scent. As soon as they had quit the church, my knees, unused to the rigors of kneeling, and my nerves collapsed. I sank back on my heels shivering despite the warmth of the day and the heavy cloak that I dared not doff. We would have to wait in the church until the hue and cry died down and everyone had grown lax with drunkenness. I thought to ease myself into a still more comfortable position when someone entered the church, this time by the main door. Light spilled down the nave, then receded as the door closed again. I peered around the confessional and beheld the Princess.

"As she walked towards the center of the church, I lowered my eyes again and turned my face away lest she notice me and catch me watching her, but no sound or movement indicated that she had any awareness of my presence. At length I ventured another look at her. She was standing motionless, not facing the altar nor any shrine, as if she herself were some sacred statue. She had no intention, it seemed, of flinging herself on God's mercy or importuning any saint. She appeared to want nothing more than to be alone, still, silent.

"Then the door opened again, and there entered one I guessed to be the Prince, for though I had seen him before, his face had made on me no lasting impression. In his haste to reach the Princess, he did not close the heavy doors but rushed to her and threw himself at her feet, hugging her legs like a small child, as if it were he, not she, in need of comfort and protection. She patted his head absently without looking at him, a gesture of habit.

"Then the Prince, a trifle shamefaced so I fancied, recovered himself and stood before her. Putting his arms about her, he tried to draw her close, but she would not yield. So he moved to one side of her and began to speak softly into her ear, now and again raising a tentative hand to her shoulder or hair, once caressing her cheek. From the look on his face, tender, troubled, but adoring, I guessed he was attempting to reassure her that he believed not a word of the wretched ballad nor could anyone else. She was too good, too beautiful for such a tale to be true. Thus I imagined him to speak. But if his words had been water, they would have rolled from her back, leaving her dry as she was dry-eyed. She remained unmoved, unmoving, as if she were still alone.

"I saw only the shadow of the King, and yet I am certain it belonged to him. The shadow stretched from the open door towards the Princess, stopping just at her feet. The Prince, I could tell, did not mark it. He babbled on all unknowing. But the Princess knew; she raised her head ever so slightly and shifted her gaze towards the door. I could see her eyes, and, as if they were mirrors, I could see the King reflected in them. I don't mean that I could see his exact image, but in her eyes I saw his power.

"Never have I seen a woman look so stark, so undefended as she did in that wordless exchange. I felt the blood rush to my face, and, in my woman's parts, I knew a shame so deep it almost felt like pleasure. The Princess did not blush, though the fear and desire and knowledge in her face made her naked before him. My life, as you know, contains no such moments, but the look that passed between those two was of such force that I knew, as if I dwelt within that woman's skin: the man who so beheld her must kill her or claim her before there dawned another day."

CHAPTER THREE

ND I KNEW IT, TOO. I could see the scene Amelia conjured as clearly as if I had been there. I knew what she told me was true, and I knew it without surprise. No, I had not foreseen this turn of events. Yet, as so often, when fateful knowledge comes, dire or joyous, I felt as if I had always known.

"Then the King spoke," Amelia was saying, "though I could not distinguish the words, and the Prince whirled about, looking as if he had been caught dallying with some chamber maid instead of comforting his lawful wife. In the presence of his father, he seems to lose what small dignity he possesses."

"Go on," I hurried her, pained for Julian.

"There is little more to tell. The Prince and Princess followed the King out of the church, and that is the last I saw of the royal three.

"I waited perhaps an hour more, until it seemed that all the world had returned to its bustle. Then I arranged my lute to look like a disfiguring hump on my back. I did what I could to alter Gretal's appearance by braiding her hair in a different fashion. Then, slipping out the same side door by which we had entered, we kept to the alleys and found our way at last to the postern gate where, Heaven be thanked, the only guard was enjoying a snooze in the last of the light.

"I had but the vaguest of notions how to find my way to you, Mother, but Gretal here is a marvel in that respect. If she has been any place once, she can find it again no matter how different the approach. Once she understood where we were bound, she never faltered a step, even in the thickest part of the Wood."

At last Amelia rested from her tale and, sensible woman that she was, fell upon her food. And yet what a wonder she was! Once a prisoner to fear of all that had never befallen her, here she was in the midst of disaster, at large in the world without roof, bed, or even such dubious protection as Rolf had provided, a fugitive with a simple-minded wench in tow. And if she was not utterly calm, she was, to say the least, in supreme command of her wits. More, for she thought not only of her own survival but had paused in her flight to warn me of danger.

My conscience smote me a harsh and well-deserved blow. But for me, Amelia would have remained safe, if wretched, on her son's manor. But for my foisting Gretal upon her, her scanty living as a minstrel might yet be secure.

"Oh, Amelia!" I wailed, my guilt seeking ease in expressions. "What have I done to you?"

Amelia looked at me with honest bewilderment. "You, Mother? What can you mean?"

"Don't you see? One way or another, it's all my doing. I have brought you to this dreadful pass."

I expected her to protest politely, well-bred lady that she was. Instead she appeared both amused and annoyed as she chided me.

"Am I to receive no honor then for my gallant conduct? Had I no power to choose? Come, come, Mother."

"But I counseled you to leave your home," I persisted.

"And never told me I would not meet danger."

"I gave you charge over Gretal—"

"Yes, and I took it. Now, hush. I am fond of the child. Don't make such a fuss. If I am such a dupe as you would have me, then I am the dupe of life itself. I know you for a wise woman, but in truth, Mother, are you the author of life? Does your hand turn Fortune's Wheel?"

Amelia's words humbled me. I saw as never before the arrogance, the greed in claiming all the guilt. It was a way of hoarding power—or rather the illusion of power.

"And so what will you do?"

I would no longer play the wise woman to Amelia. Any wisdom I had offered she had made her own.

"Truly, I do not know, but we must not tarry here. Nor should you, Mother. It's what I came to tell you. Who knows what Rolf might have told the King? Or, indeed, what the Princess will say to him? Come with us, Mother. We could be in the border mountains by daybreak."

"No," I said, surprised by my utter certainty. "My place is here. If the King plans to seize me, let him come. It will avail him nothing. I doubt I could spin gold for him to save my life. And if I could, I would not. But listen to me, if the King's men come for me, then you are safe enough. I will go out to meet them. Rest here and make your plans. I'll wager no one will venture here before daybreak. Even King's men fear this Wood by night."

"There is reason in what you say," Amelia agreed. "And we are weary. Look, Gretal sleeps at my knee."

"Come, let me put you both to bed."

Amelia and Gretal slept soundly on my pallet and the Mother's. Myself, I stayed awake all night, doing what I could to mend Amelia's lute and sewing what coin I had into Amelia's cloak. Then I checked my stores and packed a sack with enough cheese and flat bread to last them weeks if they were frugal.

In the morning, Amelia told me she was resolved to set forth with Gretal. The whole of Summer with its bounty was before them. If I could show them the way, they would walk through the Wood, emerging on the side farthest from the King's Castle and lands, then they would head for the mountains and, beyond the mountains, the sea and a thriving port Amelia had toured with Rolf's band. If life proved dangerous for two women alone, they would endeavor to join with another band. If need be, Amelia assured me, they could shelter for the Winter at a convent Amelia knew.

Inland bred like me, Amelia had fallen in love with the sea on sight and was eager to be near it again. Her descriptions of its sound, its scent, its everchanging changelessness, of the strange and wonderful life with which it teemed filled me with longing both for the sea and the child I had named for its vast mystery. I was sorely tempted to leave the Wood and wander with Amelia, but the temptation was not so strong as my growing sense that my life, my death, my fate were rooted here as surely as the trees.

I walked with Amelia and Gretal some miles, a basket in hand, for I intended to gather monkshood as well as any spring mushrooms I might find on the way back. Not until we had made our parting remarks and exchanged embraces did I tell Amelia of the modest fortune hidden in her cloak, for I feared she might refuse it. But she did not protest or even exclaim overmuch. She had shed the overbred nicety of a rich woman, but she had lived too much of her life in easy comfort to have the perilous pride of the poor. In short, she was practical and accepted my aid as freely as she had given hers in coming to warn me of danger.

Now it was time for us to part once more, maybe forever. It came to me, as I stood facing Amelia in that ancient Wood made young with Spring, that here, at last, was one I might call friend. If I had been to her the Mother, then she had grown up, outgrown her need of the image. We had canceled each other's debts. Neither had a claim on the other, but our past services had forged a bond between us, though we might never meet again. Here, then, was one to whom I could give my name. Indeed, it was right she should know me by name as I knew her.

I opened my mouth. I summoned from the depths of my being the name I had never pronounced. Before my voice responded to my will, I found myself distracted by Gretal's presence. Though she was nearly a grown woman now, she fidgeted, kicking at the old leaves underfoot like any impatient child waiting for her elders to finish their incomprehensible business. I closed my mouth. I was too miserly to let Gretal hear my name, even if she was not listening. Thus I lost a chance to tell my name that likely would not come again.

Amelia and I embraced once more. I gave an awkward pat to Gretal's shoulder, which she scarcely acknowledged, and they turned to go. I watched until they were out of sight. Before they disappeared among the trees, I saw Gretal take Amelia's arm. Envy, always a light sleeper, wakened in me. However burdensome a charge Gretal might be, at least she recompensed Amelia with affection.

I had no one, no child, not even an apprentice, to receive my teachings as I had received the Mother's. Would there one day come an heir to my arts? I had no premonition of such an event, unlike the Mother, who claimed to have waited for me, who had been mysteriously present at the time and place of my readiness. But then, as I have noted, I have known only rare flashes of that other sight. And the Mother was possessed of wisdom to which I will never attain.

CHAPTER FOUR

THERE WAS ANOTHER POSSIBILITY, and all that Summer I entertained it as if it were some diverting guest come to relieve the tedium of my long, though industrious, days: Perhaps I would die before I could instruct another in my arts. Daily, no, hourly, I expected an envoy from the King. Of course, should soldiers approach, I could easily hide. I knew the forest better than anyone alive, and I had learned the art of stillness from the Mother, who had learned it first from the wild creatures.

But I had fully resolved not to resist arrest. How could I forego the pleasure of confronting the King, thwarting outright his goldlust? Moreover, I would delight to astonish him with a most unflattering view of himself, for I had no doubt he surrounded himself with sycophants and hypocrites. Even dearer to my heart was the prospect of making Aurelie squirm with fear.

In spite of my recent contentment with what I thought of as my fate, evil still tempted me. Accepting as I might appear to be, there dwelt within me an unrepentant rebel. When that rebel held sway, I grew restless, heedless of what havoc I might wreak upon myself and others. So I reckoned myself willing to die for the brief malicious pleasure of venting my long-pent venom.

Nothing happened.

No one came to seek me, much less seize me, except, as always, those who had need of my skills. Nothing continued to happen until that very eventlessness chastened me. As the leaves began to change, I began to accept that my life would not. A violent death full of the high drama of bitter last words was not to be mine. It seemed there was no reprieve from a sentence long since passed. I was condemned to live.

Then one fine brisk morning, when I was out in my yard skutching some flax, I looked up and saw two men leading their horses into the clearing. Horses are a rare sight in the depths of the Wood, for the paths are narrow and, of course, peasants do not own them. Therefore, I knew at once, before I spotted the insignia, that these were the King's men come for me at last. Because of the din the skutching had made, I'd had no warning of their approach. Now I could not hide, even if I wanted to, which, to my dismay, I found I did. In none of my imaginings of this moment had my palms sweat or my fingers trembled. Nor had I anticipated the heat in my belly, as if I had swallowed a live coal, while my limbs were like ice. Yet it was not altogether a disagreeable fright, but perhaps akin to what a bride feels at the dawn of her wedding day. I only wished I'd had time to ready myself.

"Good day to you," one of the men hailed me. An odd greeting, I thought, to one you have come to take prisoner. Or had the King, awed by my reputed powers, instructed them to proceed with all due caution and respect? I noted, however, that the man seemed not to know the proper manner in which to address me. A gross oversight.

"You seek the Mother," I stated, providing a hint regarding my title.

"No, Mother." The same man spoke again with a deferent nod. "But since we are so fortunate as to have found you, perhaps you may be of help to us."

"In what regard?" I felt confused; this was not how the story was to unfold.

"We are hunting a small, misshapen man of evil countenance. His name is said to be Rumplestiltskin, though he may go under the guise of other names. Have you seen anyone of that description loitering in the Wood, Mother?"

"I have not."

Nor, added to myself, would I tell you if I had. The mention of deformity and this soldier's assumption that there was evil in a face that was likely only ugly had roused my pity for this Rumplestiltskin, some sort of outlaw, I supposed.

"Nor have I seen anyone since Lady Day save sick folk and breeding women. One poor lass bleeding like a stuck pig and her in her fifth month. One with a breach babe it took me all day to turn. A man with boils the size of love apples on his privy parts .... "

The effect of my talk was as I desired. The men took me for a babbling crone and would not disbelieve or question me further. Like so many men who will face the blood bath of battle without a qualm, they turned green at the mention of childbearing or illness. Moreover, so great was their relief when I changed the subject, they made no objection to my questioning.

"What has this man done?"

"That we don't know, Mother, but we reckon he is a dangerous criminal, for he is wanted by the King himself and a fat reward will go to the one who brings him in. Are you alone here, Mother? Well, a word of advice. Bar your door well at night. And if you should see anything of such a man, report it to the Castle at once."

"Oh, indeed," I lied. "I will not sleep sound until I hear of this knave's capture. But come," I added, "won't you have a tankard of ale or a bite to eat to hearten you on your way?"

Perhaps if I sat them down and plied them with drink, I might pry from them some word of what had befallen Aurelie. The charge of bargaining with the Devil, even if it was made only in song, was a serious one and must be answered. Then, too, devil or no devil, she had deceived the King. But plainly the men were restless and eager to be off. Doubtless they feared that if they lingered, some laboring creature would arrive and drop a monstrous birth at their feet. So I paid for my fun, for they would not bide.

"Remember the name," they called as they left the clearing, "Rumplestiltskin!"

It was an odd name and I found it hard to hold in my mind, not that I made any effort to do so. My first shock of fear and the confusion that followed had now turned to a consuming curiosity about what tale Aurelie could have told the King. The Harvest Festival was but a few days away. It was more than a year since I had gone to market. I had lived off the bounty of the earth all Summer, but all I had in reserve I had given to Amelia and Gretal. So I must make the journey to the village, and there, amidst the holiday throng, I might glean a good supply of gossip.

On the appointed day, I took my place in the alley, restoring myself from time to time with whiffs from a satchel of rosemary, mint, and camphor. It was one of those days in Autumn when Summer fleetingly returns, tantalizing folk with fond remembrance before Winter begins its stem reign. I studied my customers—no more or less in number than usual- for some change in manner towards me: a further degree of awe or fear, a new toadying, some sign that the truth of who it was spun straw to gold had made its way to the marketplace. But after a morning of surpassing dullness, I had to admit there was no difference in the wary deference folk had always displayed towards me.

But there was a difference, so it seemed to me as I later walked abroad on my round of errands, in the village itself or rather in the crowd, so thick I often felt like a fly mired in a honey pot. I could find no exact name for a restlessness I sensed among the people. I noted more idlers, more strangers, more entertainers of all kinds than was customary even on a festival day. Folk paid desultory attention to anything or anyone that afforded amusement, but there was no center of interest, no heart beating life into the crowd.

Not until I passed the village green where the Harvest Queen held court did it come to me what might be wrong. She was a pretty wench, to be sure, enthroned amidst the sheaves of wheat and rye and oat. She giggled and blushed most winningly and, I wagered, would be a wife or anyway a mother before another harvest. Yet she remained what she was: a simple lass, childishly pleased and plainly ill at ease with the queenly image she bore for the day.

I remembered only too well another village maiden who had reigned as Queen of all the seasons. Now and again, to prevent ill will, others had taken a turn with the crown. Aurelie never minded. Why should she? The image was hers. Others might try it on, but it fitted them like a borrowed gown. No one had Aurelie's stature.

As I gazed upon this silly girl playing queen, I understood that the people, knowing or not, wanted Aurelie: the miller's daughter who had married the Prince, who might one day be their Queen in truth. She was the one with the power to transform their drab lives, if only for the instant they beheld her, into a tale of magic and beauty. Did she guess their need or did it answer some need in her? For until now it had been her custom to return on festival days to her native place. Whatever her dealings with the Prince of Darkness, the people worshipped her. Nothing but her presence would suffice them.

I confess I craved to see her, too. I fancied a glimpse of her face would tell me all I longed to know: the truth of what had passed between her and the King, whether she had betrayed the Prince, and how well she loved Marina now that she was no longer a tiny, coveted babe. I knew her face better than I knew my own. I would detect the tiniest change. Yes, I wanted to look on her face and judge.

My goods sold, my cart piled high with bags of millet and meal, kegs of ale, new-shorn fleeces, I still lingered in the Village, waiting with all the rest until it was nearly dusk. Just as the torches were being lit, I gave up, called my goats, and went to fetch my cart from the alley. Crossing the market square on my way to the gate, I noticed a larger gathering than any I had seen that day, and I thought I heard strains of music. Curious, I told my goats to wait, and I joined the throng, rudely elbowing my way to the fore.

As I had suspected, the attraction was a band of minstrels. They were playing a lively pipe and drum piece that stirred some folk to dance. The leader, I swear, answered Amelia's description of Rolf; there was something of the wolf about him, a lean and hungry look. Even in the torch-lit dusk,

I could see the scar on his cheek that Amelia had described. When I observed that the band lacked a lute player, I decided I was right. So somehow Rolf had escaped the King's wrath alive.

When the tune came to an end, Rolf passed the hat. Then he stepped forward flanked by a younger man and a maid. The three, accompanied by recorder and tambourine, began singing as one.

> *Come gather round and we shall sing,*
> *How chose a great and mighty King,*
> *A miller's lass to be the one,*
> *To wed his true and only son.*

I gasped and had to stay my hand from clutching the nearest arm. How could the King allow Rolf, not only to go free, but also to keep singing this damning song? Did that mean he had believed the tale and condemned Aurelie? But I must listen to the song. Now the lad sang alone, his voice weak but true.

> *The King had heard a claim most bold,*
> *How she from straw could spin pure gold.*
> *He locked her in a tower high.*
> *She must spin gold from straw or die.*

That much was true enough.

> *The Lady took the straw in hand,*
> *But even at the King's command,*
> *No gold could spin nor even thread.*
> *She'd die a maiden never wed.*

> *Then from the midst of nowhere came,*
> *An unknown man who gave no name.*
> *She turned to him in her despair.*
> *She ne'er bethought her to beware.*

Now I began to understand. The Devil had departed the song, in his place merely" an unknown man."

"Whoever you be lend me your aid,
For I am young and sore afraid,
This mass of straw surrounding me,
Must on the morrow pure gold be. "

The wench sang at the same pitch as the young man, her voice low and as coarse as her appearance, both wrong for the part of Aurelie. Truly, Rolf had reason to regret the loss of Gretal.

"I'll take the straw, pure gold I'll spin,
Nor count it wrong, nor call it sin,
For you shall promise all I ask,
When I have done for you your task."

Rolf sang in response. His voice made me think of sludge from the river bottom, but at least he was well cast as the "unknown man." I could almost forget my intimate knowledge of the truth and picture Rolf instead of myself appearing to Aurelie.

The Lady slept and as foretold,
She wakened in the midst of gold.
The unknown man was standing near.
His countenance filled her with fear.

"And now you must your promise keep,
Though you may mourn, though you may weep,
Though you may swear you were beguiled,
Yet will I claim your first-born Child."

Into a swoon the Lady fell,
And woke to hear the wedding bell.
She shook from her the evil dream,
For who would harm the one-day Queen?

I could not reconcile this hapless maiden, whose innocence bordered on idiocy, with Aurelie and her arrogant laughter as she assured me she would bear only sons. But then, I reckoned, that was the purpose of this ballad:

to remove any blemish from Aurelie's image, however bland a complexion remained.

> *Forgetting all her troubles sore,*
> *A lovely babe the Lady bore,*
> *Then at her side the man appeared,*
> *And she remembered all she feared.*

> *"Take not my babe, be not so cruel,*
> *Oh, fate has made of me a fool,*
> *I wish the gold had ne'er been spun.*
> *Now is my joy, my life undone."*

> *"Some pity on you will I take,*
> *and grant you guesses three to make.*
> *My name to none on earth is known,*
> *Find out, else is the babe my own."*

At these words I nearly swooned myself, and this time I did grab the arm of a neighboring man, who turned to look on me with mingled concern and fear and had the great courtesy not to snatch his arm away. I recovered myself quickly and relinquished my hold. I must not miss a word.

> *Then came an angel of the Lord,*
> *Who parted with his fiery sword,*
> *The mists of distant space and time.*
> *She saw the man; she heard his rhyme.*

> *"Despised, misshapen though I be,*
> *There's no one knows my name save me.*
> *I'll take the child, I cannot fail.*
> *Yea, Rumplestiltskin will prevail. "*

Rumplestiltskin! My mind reeled in confusion. But that was the outlaw, the misshapen man of evil countenance hunted by the King's men. How came he into this tale?

Then I understood.

Despised. Misshapen.

When he returned secure in guile,
The Lady frowned to hide a smile.
He answered with a wicked grin,
"The time has come. Make haste. Begin."

"My first guess Solomon shall be,
For you are near as wise as he.
Your wisdom heeding evil's voice,
Makes Lucifer my second choice."

"Your first two guesses now are cast —
"Do not rejoice, I've yet the last.
You may be wise in Satan's game,
But Rumplestiltskin is your name."

"No!" I cried aloud. "No!"

No one noticed me, enthralled as everyone was by the tale. Accompanied by Rolf's exaggerated pantomime, the lad sang the last verse.

He howled and cursed and rent his hair,
Then vanished wholly into air.
So unto God all glory be,
Who gave the Lady victory.

Amid the cheers and clapping, whistling and foot stomping that followed, I could not hear my own voice.

But I felt it, struggling to break free from my throat, to rise above the roar of the crowd, as a bird with a broken wing struggles to fly.

CHAPTER FIVE

I BEGAN TO WRITE MY TALE that very night on a few pieces of parchment I managed to find, with a goose quill pen dipped into a bowl of makeshift ink, mostly berry juice. Deep into the night I wrote by the light of the fire, but the fire that lit my labor was nothing compared to the conflagration within.

If it was possible to hate Aurelie more than I had before, then that night I did.

I blamed her entirely for the spurious account being sounded abroad by Rolf's band, for so, I surmised, Rolf had secured his liberty. He was under sentence to sing Aurelie's innocence in every market square, in the highways and byways, until everyone had heard the approved version and accepted it as the truth. It was plain the King had authorized this ballad, but its author, I had no doubt, was Aurelie. I ascribed to her only the basest of motives. She had sought not simply to clear her name of ignominy—that was to be expected—but in doing so, she had taken revenge on me, who had never, in fact, succeeded in harming her.

The cleverness of her cruelty both astonished and infuriated me. I was neither revealed in this official tale nor excluded from it but merely disguised, grotesquely, as this Rumplestiltskin. Rumplestiltskin! I still cringe at the name. I forever repudiate it.

Yet I wonder now if, underlying my rage and revulsion, was not some unacknowledged dread that the detested name suited me better than my own precious, untold name.

I have been writing this tale for many years now. I write on odd nights when all my tasks are done, and I am not so tired that I have strength only to crawl onto my pallet. The writing has proved a lengthy procedure, often halted. Parchment is costly and difficult to procure. More than once I have run out of ink. Though I have refined my recipe, berries are still the base, and I can harvest them only once a year.

Since the night I began my story, many things have come to pass, which I must record if I am to remain true to the task I have set myself—though its purpose, I confess, becomes less clear to me the older I grow. Often I lack faith in my power to vindicate myself before the world. Now and then I even doubt my right to vindication. I have discovered that words rendered in ink on parchment where I, if no one else, must see them in all their starkness, compel an honesty I have never before demanded of myself. Perhaps this reckoning with the truth is reason enough to write the rest.

After a Winter bereft of event, the following Spring brought tidings that ought not to have surprised me so when I chanced to hear them. I was at the cottage of a freeman who had his own small flock of sheep. I had in the past purchased from him fleece of high quality. I respected his skill and he, mine, for I had saved his wife from almost certain death during the perilous delivery of their first child. Though the births of their next three children, all girls like the first, one set of twins, were simple, neither he nor his wife would have any other midwife. They were secure enough in their modest wealth and position to ignore those who looked on my presence askance. So on a fine Spring night, the air fragrant with the scent of blossoms, I received into my hands their fifth child and first son.

When I called Tom, the freeman, into the room to behold his newborn man-child, he beamed on me as if neither his wife nor himself nor even God but I alone could take credit for the long-desired sex of the babe. As midwife, lo these many years, often and often have I beheld this abundant rejoicing at the birth of a boy. To be sure, most folk were glad enough to welcome any living child and doubly so if it did not claim the life of its mother in being born. But healthy girls were greeted with sighs of mingled relief and regret, while with every boy it was as if Christ himself were born again.

Tom, jubilant, begged me to stay and break fast with his family and promised me his finest fleece come shearing time. I felt it would be ungracious to refuse his hospitality, though I regretted staying when he sent forth his twins to bid all the neighbors come and drink with him. Soon the small cottage was crowded, and I was trapped in the corner to which I'd retreated. I never knew what to say to folk nor they to me on such occasions. No one took much notice of me, however, so great was everyone's excitement. At first I thought it was all for the lusty little lad sucking like a fierce wild piglet at his mother's breast. But as the din subsided and one voice distinguished itself from another, I discerned that the mood of celebration had more than one source.

"Ho, Tom," boomed one man. "So your first son is of an age to the hour with the next heir to the throne. Send your goodwife to be wetnurse and your laddie will suck alongside the little princeling. Sure we all know Emma's got enough milk in those jugs for two."

He winked and gestured towards the twins as mildly ribald laughter greeted his advice. Emma blushed. I might have bid them leave her alone and let her rest, but I was rendered speechless by the news. That Aurelie should have a son and I not even know she'd been with child! What would it mean for Marina that there was now a male heir?

"I heard the Princess suckled the first child herself, the little lass," said one woman.

"Yes, and the King liked it not. It's not fitting for royalty."

"But she comes from simple folk," another woman spoke, "as well we know, and she's not forgotten."

"She's a fine wench," declared a man. "Does us proud, she does. Still looks like a virgin, God be praised, though a mother twice."

"Hmph!" someone snorted; I could not tell whether it was a man or a woman.

"There's some say she's no better than she should be."

"Well, she's done her duty twice and that's sure," countered another stoutly.

"I'll warrant the King'll be pleased there's another male heir. They say there's no love lost between him and his son. The Prince has always been frail, poor lad, like his mother, God rest her."

"That's what comes of breeding with foreigners. That's why the King picked one of his own, however humble, to wed his son. And well he picked, too. Our finest flower. No doubt he'll dote on the young Prince."

"That's right," spoke the strange male-female voice. "As if the babe were his own, as there's some say he is."

"Enough of that," said Tom gruffly. "I'll not have such talk in this house. It's treason."

"It's common knowledge. And do you think the King cares for the talk of the likes of you and me? Why he doesn't know the difference between poor folk and the dirt beneath his feet. He's the King, I tell you. And if he wants to bed his son's wife, who's to stop him?"

"Did you not hear me?" Tom's face resembled one of the red onions strung over the hearth. "I'll not have such talk!"

No one spoke for the space of a few moments, constrained by Tom's anger or perhaps even more by the suspicion that the unpleasant voice had uttered an even unpleasanter truth.

Then a man I recognized as a tanner proposed a toast to Tom and Emma's new son, and the laughter and talk commenced again. I moved from my place to have another look at the mother and child before taking my leave as quietly as I could.

I needed to be alone to meet the onslaught of passion unleashed by this revelation. I had been warned by Amelia of Aurelie's likely infidelity, but the birth of this son, whose sinful parentage I did not doubt despite Tom's protest, brought it home to me with breathtaking force. I was, of course, outraged at the wicked pair's double betrayal of the Prince. Then, too, I was fearful for Marina. But I know now that my strongest feeling was one of grim satisfaction at this confirmation of Aurelie's iniquity, this crowning justification for my judgment on her. Yes, I confess I rejoiced that Aurelie might be unmasked before the multitudes, that her faithlessness would become, in the words of that insinuating voice, common knowledge.

All that Spring and Summer whenever I went abroad to childbirth or sick bed or to market—which I did more often than had been my custom or was needful—I strained my ears for rumors concerning the Royal household, and my attention was often rewarded. There were some good folk, like Tom, who resisted the temptation to indulge in what had, indeed, become common talk. Some even continued to refute the rumors and rebuke those who spread them long after the behavior of the King and Aurelie had become so flagrant that only the most doggedly loyal could credit their innocence. Yet, in the stubborn goodness of these faithful folk, I sensed a sorrow, as if they, like the Prince, were betrayed lovers.

Then there were those who reveled in moral outrage, some honestly offended, others merely taking malicious delight in the growing evidence that their betters were as bad—or worse!—than they were themselves. Among these, no meal was complete without a morsel of gossip. "Did you know that they were seen riding out alone together?" "Pah, that's nothing. Ursine, whose daughter is a serving wench, says they sit together at the high table and eat from the same plate, even drink the loving cup, like any bride and groom." Without fail someone would predict for these high living sinners certain damnation. "Let them drink long and deep, for the fires of Hell are hot, and they'll have an eternity to thirst."

Indeed, these self-styled righteous ones had little recourse but to anticipate God's punishment of the pair, for the Almighty's representatives on earth kept silent or were silenced. The wise among them found their coffers lined and the foolish, who would rant of sin and repentance, found themselves tried on trumped up charges and like as not defrocked or exiled or even condemned to death for heresy.

Among some few, mostly men, Aurelie's image and the King's remained untarnished, even enhanced. These made bold to mock the Prince. "They say he skulks in the nursery and changes the swaddling! No true man would behave so. No wonder our Princess prefers the King's bed. She's a lusty wench, I'll warrant. They do make a fine pair. It's a wonder and a pity the King didn't wed her himself in the first place." I was determined to draw no attention to myself, lest folk cease their chatter, but when I heard anyone speak thus, I had to bite my tongue to keep it from lashing.

I returned from these forays into the world and worldliness exhausted both in body and spirit. Yet I could find no rest in the Wood. My hard-won peace, the joy in work that had begun to recompense me for all I lacked became a dim memory, a dream of health in the midst of sickness. Truly, I was feverish with agitation, my nights as restless as my days, both filled with wild fancies of rescue and retribution.

Over and over in my mind, I would save Marina and my Prince while utterly destroying Aurelie and the King. At first I recognized the madness of my schemes, but as the Summer wore on, I lost the capacity to distinguish between what was possible and what was not. In my imaginings I was all powerful, capable of unleashing upon my enemies all the destructive forces of the heavens and the earth. My drastic action was delayed only by my need to refine endlessly the details of their doom, such as: should they perish by fire or flood; would a sudden violent end be best, leaving them no time to repent and possibly save their souls, or, since I was not certain they had any souls to save or lose, should I indulge myself by inflicting a death of excruciating lengthiness?

Though I paid the matter scant attention, my healing skills began to slip again. Whereas before I was frozen, now I was molten within, my brain aboil. I could not concentrate; I would find myself in the midst of some task, unable to remember what it was I'd begun or how to complete it. It was at just such a moment the Mother, my Mother, came to me again.

I was presiding over a birth in the home of a wool merchant. I had just delivered a fine, fat baby girl, almost by rote. True, the child had been breach, which was why I had been summoned, but I was so accustomed to such complications that my hands did my work for me while my mind strayed. The child, red-faced and squalling, one of those infants that seem born in a rage, had been washed and oiled and swaddled by her grandmother while I absently attended to the afterbirth.

There is always a considerable flow of blood; at first I noticed nothing amiss but went on with my task of cleaning the mother as a sleepwalker might. Then, all at once, as if some warning bell had sounded, I wakened fully to the present moment. There were my hands, floundering vainly in a growing pool of blood. The woman, half-conscious, whimpered with exhaustion and fright. In horror I stared at my blood-soaked hands. I was acutely conscious of every sound and sensation—the baby wailing, the alarmed cries of the grandmother, the woman moaning, the hiss of the kettle, the smoke from the fire, the hot stench of blood contrasting with the fragrance of fresh herbs and rushes underfoot—but I could scarcely remember how I came to be there. I could not comprehend what had happened or what I must do. My skill had abandoned me utterly, leaving me awash and aghast in the dying woman's blood.

It was then—praise God or whatever power gave her leave from the land of the dead to come to my aid—that I heard the Mother's voice clear and commanding: Knead the womb! Knead the womb! I hastened to obey, and sweat broke out on my brow as much from shame and relief as from the exertion. The woman had almost died, but thanks be to the Mother, she was saved and so was I.

The Mother stayed with me as I journeyed home at sunset. No, this time I could not see her, but I knew she was there. She held my hand and led me, for I was faint with weariness, not only from my labors that day but from the whole frantic summer. The evening air felt blessedly cool; so did the Mother's hand. For weeks I had paid scant attention to my bodily needs. Now calmed by the Mother's presence, I discovered my hunger and thirst to be profound. Under her influence, I ate a light but nourishing meal and drank deeply of spring water. My last memory of that day is of the Mother's hands laying a compress of mint and comfrey on my brow as I sank into a healing sleep.

CHAPTER SIX

WHEN I WOKE I WAS ALONE AGAIN. The Mother had gone, and so had all my sick fancies. Mistake me not: my loves and hates remained unchanged, but now I recognized the bounds of my power to act on them, and that, perhaps, is the beginning of wisdom. Thus, I resolved to store my passions, like the weavings in the chest or the potions on the shelf, deep within me. I only troubled to take them out and examine them on those occasions when I labored over the tale of my life. And when a night's writing was done, I sternly bade myself put them away again.

All the rest of my waking life, with renewed gratitude towards the Mother and a desire to prove myself worthy of the name she had bestowed upon me, I endeavored to give myself wholly unto each day, to the matter, great or small, at hand. I doubt I will ever master absolutely the art of enjoyment that transforms the most tedious task into an act of grace. Of that art the Mother was high priestess; I remain at best a handmaiden. But my life took on a pleasant orderliness. With that I tried to be content.

Then, one afternoon so mild, for all that it was almost Yuletide, that it might have been the beginning of Spring instead of Winter, I was out in my yard in a lather of sweat as I stirred a cauldron in which I was washing new-spun yarn. If rapture did not transport me as I performed this necessary labor, at least my attention was fully engaged, and I was so startled when a riderless horse thundered into my clearing that I jumped and narrowly missed upsetting the cauldron.

The poor animal was far more exercised than I, its flanks and mouth afoam, its eyes wild, and its coat much bloodied with scratches. It stood panting before me, doubtless relieved to be out of the thick of the Wood. Speaking in the most soothing tones I could summon and moving ever so slowly, I approached the frightened creature, taking note of its torn and muddied reins, the braids of its tail and mane coming undone, its costly saddle. I reckoned the horse had borne some noble rider in a royal hunting party, for until deep snow made wood and field impassable, it was the season for such sport, though the hunt seldom ventured this far into the Wood.

The horse, his strength spent, gladly suffered my ministrations. I walked him—I had observed he was a stallion—round the clearing until his breathing slowed. Then I tied him to a tree, rubbed him down, put a blanket over

his back, and fetched a bucket of water for him to drink. When I was satis-
fied of the beast's comfort, I left him in the company of my goats and went
to seek his rider.

Why, you may wonder, did I not leave the horse to recover himself and
go at once in search of a fellow human being? Had my ancient grievance
against mankind eroded all compassion? Judge me as you will. My task here
is neither to defend or condemn myself but to tell my tale as truly as I may.
At the time, I believe, I merely resented the intrusion of a hunting party so
deep in the Wood, and I blamed human folly—or cruelty—for the frenzy
that had driven the creature into my clearing.

I had no difficulty tracing the course of the horse's frantic flight. Broken branches and trampled brush abounded. I followed the trail for more
than a mile, hurrying, but not unduly. No premonition warned me of what
I would find, nor could I guess that I neared the end of a path that had
its beginning not in my clearing but in another part of the Wood, and in
another time.

And so when I came upon his still form, my own heart died for an
instant, and the world went black. But for me, it seems, there is to be no
escape into the comforting darkness. Before I could collapse, I came to
myself again and knew that Hooked upon my own Julian.

At first I thought him already dead. From the angle of his head I could
tell that his neck was broken. I detected also, from blood staining newly
disturbed leaves, that he had made an attempt to move himself. Ah, dear
God, if God there be, had I more swiftly come to him, might I have saved
his life? I will never know if the fall alone would have killed him or if I
could have healed that broken neck had I arrived in time to keep him still.

He lay still now as I sank to my knees beside him, and he would not
move again. I bent over him, hoping without hope to feel his breath, and—
O wonder—he opened his eyes, the beautiful eyes the color of that long ago
Summer wood. He looked at me, and, I will swear before all the hosts of
heaven, he knew me before he died: not as the Wise Woman of the Western
Wood but as the Girl with the Silver Eye.

For a long time after I had closed his eyes forever, I sat beside him, holding his hands that were warm at first with the life that had just left them
but slowly turned colder and colder, like the evening air bereft of light. I
fancied that my own hands received this warmth. I could not bear to think
of his life all lost, dispersed in the wide world. You may chide me, who hear
this tale, and instruct me on the journey and salvation of the soul, the bliss

that awaits it when it has been made pure in the purgatory fires. But if soul there be that lives beyond the body, all I could feel then was its loneliness.

When I had grown nearly as cold as my Beloved, I roused myself to go fetch my goats and cart, for I was not strong enough to bear his weight all that way alone. Night had fallen by the time I brought the Prince's body to my clearing. With much struggle I lifted him, carried him into the cave, and laid him on my pallet. There I undressed him and washed him clean of all the dirt and sweat and blood. His body was still smooth and slender as a boy's, all but hairless. I covered him with my finest weaving—a glossy magnificence of purple, scarlet, and gold—while I mended his garments, then washed them, and hung them to dry before the fire. Though I wanted no food, I made myself eat and drink. I would need strength for the journey to the Castle the next day. In the meantime, I lit candles and sat beside Julian's body all night, as if I were indeed the wife I had yearned to be.

For all my sorrow I was strangely calm. You will marvel, who have come to know me through these reams of parchment, that I was not frantic with self reproach or consumed with fantasies of what might have been if he had lived, and I had nursed him back to health and joy, healing both broken body and spirit. You may wonder even more that I was not wild with suspicion that the King or Aurelie had played a part in his death, either by causing the horse to run mad or by driving the Prince to end his life himself.

Yet when the vision of happy-ever-after knocked at any heart, I gently shook my head and bade it depart forever. As for fixing blame, I could never know whether it belonged to one more than another. And if blame there be, then a portion of it is my own.

Seduced neither by rage nor vain regret, I simply mourned for Julian— or for my dreams of him. It dawned on me with painful force as I gazed on the body I had so often imagined, that in all my life I had spent no more than a few hours in his company. Had I loved him or only the form he gave to my longings? I could not know, nor did the quandary stay my weeping. And it did not matter whether I grieved for myself or for him and his brief unhappy life or for Marina—for I did not forget the babe and the look of adoration with which her father had greeted her. There are moments, no doubt in every life, when grief is so great it does not belong to one person or to one cause. It breaks the bounds of the single soul and becomes one with the sorrow of the world.

Such was my grief that night.

When day dawned, I dried my tears and washed away all trace of them.

After I had done my chores and broken fast, I dressed the Prince in his own clothes and laid him, as decorously as I could, in the cart, which I had lined with boughs of evergreen and branches of bittersweet. To my distress, the cart was not quite long enough to accommodate his full length, and his feet had to hang over the edge, making him look faintly ridiculous instead of as dignified as I could have wished. I tried to remedy the matter by draping him with the weaving that had covered him in the night. That improved his appearance somewhat. Lamentably, the horse was far too large to harness to my cart, and so I had to call upon my goats. There was no help for it.

Breaking with my custom of going abroad cloaked only in the drabbest of grey or brown, I donned my richest robe, a shimmering many-colored weave that came close to matching the color of my silver eye. I brushed my long straight hair, more striking now that grey streaked the brown, and wore it flowing loose over my shoulders and down my back. Without consulting the pool that served me as a mirror, I knew I made an astonishing sight. Never before had I allowed myself to be so visible.

Leading the horse, the goats behind me pulling the Prince on his make-shift bier, I set off for the Castle, with no notion of what I would do or say when I arrived. For once I was content—and determined—to let the drama direct itself.

CHAPTER SEVEN

I APPROACHED THE CASTLE GATES about midmorning, I believe, though the sky was overcast and the sun's course obscured. It was that close, breathless sort of day that makes the very air seem soiled. I was covered with a film of sweat and dust but trusted that from a distance my appearance was daunting. The guard in the tower I recognized as the same man who had sneered at me before. Now there was no trace of mockery in his face, just a gaping hole where his mouth hung open. I stifled a silly remark about frogs waiting for flies. My errand was grave, and I must conduct myself accordingly.

"Ho! Guard! Open at once. I come bearing the body of the Prince of the realm."

Without delay he complied, and I crossed the drawbridge and entered the open gate.

"His Majesty has been out with a search party since dawn," blithered the guard, glancing with evident fright at the body. "Nor has he returned."

"Then fetch his Lady," I commanded.

It occurred to me that 'his' could mean either the Prince's or the King's. The ambiguity was fitting.

"I will wait with the body, and I charge you: if you value your life or your children's, tell the Princess only that I am come, the Wise Woman of the Western Wood. Nothing more than that. Do you understand me, Man?"

The fear in his eyes assured me that I would be obeyed.

Some who hear this tale may think me cruel for withholding warning from Aurelie. You will say that I took this occasion to get some form of revenge. I will not deny that I have hated Aurelie and have often wished to see her suffer, but truly I believe it was not the desire to punish that made me give that order. It was that I did not want Aurelie to have a chance to compose herself, to don her image, to select the proper sentiments to voice. The time had come for truth. I wanted it naked.

Soon Aurelie entered the courtyard from the opposite side. She could see me and my goats, but not the cart or its burden, for I deliberately stood in front of it and obscured her view. As for the Prince's horse, which might have alerted her, he had been led away by a stable hand. Aurelie's steps, as she approached me, were neither swift nor slow but measured, deliberate, her expression guarded. For she knew well enough that she entered the presence of her enemy. She was still beautiful, but her beauty had lost its supple grace and grown hard, fixed like that of a wax figure. Neither of us spoke as she neared me, but our eyes locked, fiercely, intimately, as our limbs might have in mortal combat, hand to hand.

Then I stepped aside and gestured towards the cart. An unexpected delicacy made me turn my face away. I heard her gasp and call on God's name. When I looked again she was kneeling beside the cart, her head bent. I could not discern whether she wept or not. She made no sound after that first indrawn breath. She scarcely seemed to breathe at all.

I stood and waited. I knew no words to say, either to comfort or accuse, nor sought any. I cannot say how long we remained thus in silence, in stillness. Time has no measure for such moments. At last she raised her face.

And I saw a woman: neither beautiful nor plain, neither good nor evil, neither courageous nor craven. A woman.

I do not think I had ever seen her before.

She rose, and we faced one another across the cart, across the body of the Prince.

"He is dead." Her tone wavered between question and statement.

I nodded. "Something caused his horse to run wild in the Western Wood."

I carefully did not say "someone" but no doubt Aurelie could hear the unspoken word. "I traced the horse's path and found your wedded Lord. His neck was broken. He died soon after I reached him."

I did not confess my delay in seeking him but watched her shudder as she looked once more on him she had called husband. When she lifted her eyes to mine again, it was my turn to tremble. Cool and grey in color though they were, her eyes burned. I could feel the heat.

"And so you have come to lay his death at my feet."

"Where else should I bring him but to his wife and to his Castle?" I demanded, deliberately misunderstanding her.

"Yes, but you have come to judge me, as you have always judged me."

"I loved him!"

I blurted the words; all at once I wanted her to know. I could not bear to be the cold, inhuman judge she saw.

"Ah," she said, her gaze suddenly quizzical. "Of course. I see that now. You loved him, and so you hated me, because I scorned him you so desired."

I felt my whole face ignite. Was it so simple as that? Was I so base?

"Well and I admit it," she went on. "I will play the hypocrite no more. I scorned him, and I betrayed him, and likely my contempt and treachery killed him. See? I accuse myself. God no doubt will punish me. Is that not enough for you?"

Her voice shook with fury and fear, and with the tears that would follow as surely as rain follows a driving wind.

"No!" I stretched out my hand towards her, but I was no Christ to bid this storm be still.

"No?" she repeated, mistaking my anguished cry for an answer. "Well then, listen, you who would judge me, and hear it all. You think it is only he who suffered, an innocent lamb among the wolves. Well, I have suffered, too, suffered his blind, unceasing adoration. You rail against being despised. Do you know what it is to be worshipped? I did not throw him from his horse, but there were times when I would have rejoiced to destroy him with my bare hands. Even when I betrayed him, he worshipped me. How could I bear it?

"But truly, he did not worship me. I scarcely existed for him. I scarcely existed for myself. Until the King saw me for what I am—a simple woman who would lie like any other to save her skin—and loved me all the same. But him you call my wedded Lord loved only the beauty he mistook for me. Yes, just as you did once. Deny it not. And when you found I was not as perfect as my cursed beauty, you sought to destroy me."

"What do you mean I sought to destroy you!" I protested.

Surely, I had desired her destruction, but I had renounced whatever power I had to bring it upon her. Truly, for all I had sickened with hatred of her, I had done nothing.

"You threatened to take my child."

"But I did not take her!" Hurt and anger welled within me from a bitter spring.

"No, you were too crafty for that."

"What! Are you mad?" I gasped. "Do you think I gave up the child of my heart, yielded her to my enemy—yes, I confess I hated you—as some twisted form of revenge?"

"What else was I to think, pray? You disappeared without a word, leaving your mark upon her and leaving me in constant terror of your return."

"My mark?" I repeated in utter bewilderment. "What mark?" For the first time she seemed to hesitate.

"Why the same mark you bear upon your cheek. Surely by your magic powers you made its imprint upon Marina. As soon as you had gone, the mark appeared. To this day, the child bears it upon her own cheek. None of the King's physicians has been able to remove it."

I looked directly into her eyes. "I swear by the Mother before me, I know nothing of this mark" I willed her to believe me. "And whatever suffering I indeed meant to cause you by leaving you in doubt, I have matched with my own."

The anger that had flamed in her eyes died away, and I felt the fire go out of me as well. Between us lay death, within us ashes.

Then Aurelie began to weep.

I wonder still: would I have gone to her? Could I have touched her? Might I even have told her my name? I will never know.

At that moment there came a clattering of hooves across the drawbridge. We both turned towards the commotion. The King sprang from his horse and strode towards the cart where he stopped, his face working with a passion I could not name as he gazed first on the body of the Prince, then on Aurelie, and finally on me, his eyes beseeching as if I alone could tell him what it all meant.

"Here is your son," spoke the Wise Woman of the Western Wood.

And I turned my face from his, wise enough at last to know that I can tell no story but my own.

CHAPTER EIGHT

YEARS HAVE PASSED since the ink with which I wrote those words dried on the parchment. I thought my tale had ended with my strife, and so I stored away the manuscript in the depths of the great chest nestled among my weavings. Nor is there anything to say of those years, save that they were years of peaceful toil. I endured loneliness when it oppressed me, and I took delight in every passing pleasure. To my relief, I remained unmoved by what soon became common knowledge: that the King and Aurelie lived openly together, since the Church refused to sanction their marriage, the King acknowledging every one of Aurelie's sons, now numbering four, as his own. If bond there had been between Aurelie and me, then that bond was loosed. I was free of her as she of me.

I did keep count of Marina's birthdays and felt concern for her welfare, the legitimate daughter amidst that brood of bastard brothers—or uncles. I pondered also the mystery of the mark upon her cheek. When I went-abroad in the world, my ears were always alert for news of her, but I heard no rumors of abuse or neglect, and truth to tell, I did not have much time to brood.

For a wise woman living alone in the Wood, I see a great deal of humanity.

I often wonder, when I consider my earlier life, how I ever found the time or strength to war so ceaselessly with myself. Perhaps I have been busier these last years. Strangely, my reputation for wisdom is on the rise, and as many or more come for counsel as to be cured of bodily ills. Nor do I know why they come in such numbers, for it seems to me I seldom tell them anything.

Tonight I am compelled to take up my tale again, though I forfeit my sleep and write until the rise of the morning star when the rooster will crow and the goats—generations removed from Delilah and Marguerite—bleat their summons. For I have received, whether of chance or the gods, a wondrous gift.

I had gone to the Harvest Festival at the village. For a number of years after the Prince's death, the King and Aurelie kept away from such gatherings. They knew that the common folk looked askance on their sinful alliance and furthermore suspected foul play in the death of the Prince. The pair feared, with some reason, that their appearance together would occasion riots and rebellion. As the years passed, with Aurelie proving her

fertility again and again and the wicked lovers resembling more and more
a staid married couple, folk grew weary of the outraged mutterings of the
righteous and merely shrugged, accepting the moral vagary of royalty.

On the day in question, to the excitement of the holiday crowd, the
King and Aurelie deigned to be present at the festival with three of their
sons, supposedly in the charge of an army of ineffectual nurses. The fourth
was in arms, not left behind, as Aurelie persisted in the practice of nursing
all her babes herself. I caught a glimpse of Aurelie, as I gazed out at the
market square from my alley, and noted with amusement and perhaps a
touch of malice, that after her fifth lying-in, the perennial Harvest Queen
was looking decidedly overripe. But the sight of Aurelie no longer had the
power to rouse in me passionate love or hatred. It was the thought of Marina's nearness that stirred me.

All day my eyes raked the crowd for her. Though I could identify the
royal nurses, Marina was too old to be clinging to their skirts, and when one
of them made a dash, a naughty boy was the inevitable object of her chase.
I wondered if Marina had been denied the treat of a trip to the village, and
I indulged in some indignation on her behalf. Then it occurred to me that
she might dread crowds because of the unsightly mark upon her cheek. It
grieved me to think that my sole legacy to the child, unknowingly and unwillingly bestowed, should be deformity.

The day passed without event, and I left the village at dusk. The harvest
moon rose and shone on the frozen motion of fields ploughed under for
Winter or new sown with Wmter rye. With hard-won ease, I relinquished
my vain fretting over Marina and gave myself to enjoyment of the evening. The night promised to be fine and frosty, but my pace was brisk and I
trusted hot broth simmered over live coals in my hearth. As for the goats, I
had already tended them in my alley and sold their milk fresh and warm. I
had nothing to do but bask in the coziness of my cave, spinning or weaving
as it pleased me.

The moon-flooded fields were marvelous, but the Wood was my own
place; I loved the weaving of light and shadow. I walked the familiar way,
every dip and rise, every root and rock intimately known to my feet, pondering how I might devise a pattern of this moonlit night to stretch upon
my loom. We were almost home when all at once my goats, who knew the
path as well as I, came to a halt. I stumbled against the cart. Then I saw.

Before us stood what appeared to be a child. Had I been a peasant, daring enough to venture into the Wood at night, I might have turned and

fled, for the Wood was reputed to be haunted. Though I myself had never encountered an apparition, I did not dismiss the possibility that the form might be ghostly. It stood so very still, and the light of the full moon lent translucence to the solidest of objects. Then from the figure came a ragged sigh followed by a distinctly human sniffle.

"My dear child," I spoke at once in the most reassuring tone I could summon, "have you lost your way?"

There was no answer, and I guessed the child was struggling against giving way to sobs.

"Come along, then, with me and my goats. My home is scarcely a stone's throw from here. You shall rest and drink and eat and tell me whence you came."

I went forward and took the child's small, cold hand in mine. The goats followed us to the clearing. There I swiftly unharnessed them, leaving the unloading of the cart for later. Gathering an armload of kindling and logs, I led the way inside. The coals on the hearth did not provide much light, and I sensed my small guest's uncertainty. Setting down my load, I led the child to a stool.

"Rest there. We'll soon have a merry blaze."

I was as good as my word. Flames sprang into being, and light licked the walls of the cave. I turned to the child who gazed about her—I could see now she wore the dress of a girl—with more curiosity than fear.

"Why you live in a cave!" she marveled. "Just like a bear!"

She turned a wondering gaze on me. Then it was my turn to wonder. Eyes the color of a sun-dappled wood stared into mine, such gentle eyes, balanced by a determined chin. Brown curls framed her face, and on her left cheek she bore a mark, near as dark as her hair, in the shape of a crescent moon.

"Marina! "

She smiled ever so slightly in acknowledgment of her name, still young enough, just nine years by my reckoning, not to be surprised that I should know her name. She regarded me with frank and friendly interest.

"You have a mark on your cheek, same as mine," she observed. "I thought I was the only one."

To my astonishment, she seemed disappointed rather than relieved to discover that she was not alone in what I considered an unfortunate distinction. Then it dawned on me that the mark did not mar her face. She was a lovely child, not beautiful in the way her mother had been—there was little of her mother in her face, save for that strong jaw line that made me remember Aurelie as she had labored, proud and silent, to give birth to this very child. Marina's beauty was of a different sort. Unbidden the words came to mind: "a strange beauty, like a twisted tree or a speckled rock." Words her father had spoken of me, though I had never believed them. Nor did Marina resemble me, save for the mark. But her beauty did have an unusual quality, elfin, mysterious. And she bore the mark not as a misfortune but as if it were some mystical sign.

"Oh!" she cried with a quickened interest, for she had been studying me as I studied her. "Your eyes are different colors! I like that one best," she pointed to the silver eye. "It looks like a wishing well. How do you make it look like that?"

"Child," I laughed aloud, "I was born with this eye. I didn't do anything to make it this way."

"Oh."

Again she sounded disappointed, and again I marveled that she admired what I had always considered an affliction.

"Now tell me, Marina," I spoke briskly as I busied myself with readying some food. "How came you to be so deep in the Wood?"

"I ran away." Her voice trembled a little.

Before I could stop them, images of the cruelty she fled sprang to me mind. "I only wanted to run away for the day," she added.

Sternly I banished my fancies.

"I wanted to find, I wanted to .... " She hesitated, then began again. "People say the King is my father, but I don't believe it. All my brothers have fair hair and blue or grey eyes like the King and my mother, while I am brown as a nut, folk say. And besides," she said in a whisper, "I remember my father."

There was an urgency in her tone, as if she had waited all her life to speak those words. Perhaps the strangeness of her surroundings or of my presence, instead of making her cautious, had released her from constraint.

"I was scarcely more than a babe when he went away, but I do remember. He used to come to the nursery and sing and tell stories. There was a book he'd let me look at with beautiful pictures of flowers and birds and strange beasts. The other day I found it stored away in a chest. It made me more certain than ever that I really did have that father that I remember.

"Also," she continued, "the servants talk, even though they're not supposed to. And I have a way of being very quiet and hard to see when I want to. I heard Cook telling about a Prince who died in the Wood. And I thought maybe that was my father and that's why my mother and the King won't ride in the Wood, and they grow angry with me if I even ask to come here. Then I thought, perhaps my father really isn't dead, and I could find him if I searched.

"So when we all went to the Festival, I sneaked away. It was easy. No one was watching me. I left the Village and ran across the fields as fast as I could. I played in the Wood all day. I liked it in the daytime. I made believe my father was there with me, and we were playing hide and seek. Then it got dark, and my father wasn't there, and my mother wasn't there, and I didn't know how to get back." Her voice got smaller and disappeared.

I had a great longing to fold the child in my arms and hold her again as I had held her years ago, but I did not want to frighten her or offend her dignity. She was a great girl now, and a brave one, and, after all, she did not know me—or did not know that she knew me. Still, if I could not comfort her, at least I could relieve her doubt and help her lay her father's ghost.

"Marina," I addressed her gently and solemnly, "you are indeed right: the King is not your father. Your father was the King's son, the late Prince of the realm."

I wondered, as I spoke, whether I had the right to tell her this truth. Better her mother had told her, but perhaps that lady's vision was too clouded with her own guilt to allow her to see her daughter's need to know.

"Long ago," I went on with the tale I had begun, "I met your father at the edge of this Wood. He was as kindly and gentle a man as ever lived. Later I was present at your birth. My hands received you from your mother's womb. As I watched by your cradle, mere hours after you were born, I saw your father lift you and look at you for the first time. He loved you as he loved no other. Of that be certain. Two years later, your father fell from his horse, not far from here, and, indeed, he died in this Wood. I found him and brought him to your mother."

Marina remained silent for a time, gazing at the fire, as if the story I'd told her took form in the flames.

"Have you ever seen his ghost?" she asked at length. Again I sensed that curiosity held an edge over fear.

"No," I answered firmly. "He has no cause to linger here. His soul is at rest," I stated with more authority and certainty than I possessed. "And now, Child, it's time for you and me to have our supper."

And in truth it was, but I confess I also hoped to forestall any awkward questions that my revelations might occasion, such as the nature and origin of her mother's liaison with the King, who, if Marina cared to reason it out, was her grandfather. But Marina, it seemed, neither knew nor cared enough for convention to crave precise definitions of relations she took for granted. After all, I reminded myself, she had hardly known any other arrangement.

I ladled steaming broth into bowls and cut Marina a thick slab of black bread on which I spread soft goat's cheese. I was pleased to see that she did not disdain this simple fare but ate with good appetite—using her left hand, I noted. The warm food and the comfort of having been found combined to make the child sleepy. With her face relaxed, her eyelids drooping, she looked much younger than she was, and I caught a glimpse of my precious babe. This time I did not resist the impulse to gather her in my arms, for she was falling asleep where she sat.

"Now, Sweeting," I said, suddenly fluent in a language of tenderness I had never before spoken. "I'm going to tuck you into bed. Tomorrow, first thing, I will take you home to your mother," I assured her, wanting to allay any fears she might have. I also deemed it wise to bind myself with that promise.

As I laid her on my pallet, her arms tightened around me in an embrace that moved me to tears.

"How should I call you?" she murmured as I covered her with my warmest blankets.

I hesitated; care I utter my name at last? But no, I thought, as I looked on the child's face, her square chin softened as she yielded to dreams, she is so young. A gift untimely can be a burden.

"Most people call me the Mother," I told her. "Goodnight, Mother," she whispered. "Goodnight, Daughter. Goodnight, Marina."

Worn out with adventure, Marina slept deeply, scarcely stirring a limb. I know, because I watched her all night long, sleepless with joy.

CHAPTER NINE

THE NEXT MORNING WE DID NOT LEAVE first thing, as I had promised Marina. If her curiosity was still alive the night before amidst all her weariness and fright, then after a long sleep and a hearty breakfast of hot, thick porridge with honey and milk, it was unbounded. Marina inspected what she called my den with thorough delight. The loom attracted her interest, and she insisted on learning how it worked. Then, too, she wanted to know the names of the herbs that hung drying and to smell all my bottled powders and potions.

There were also the animals to tend. She was in a rapture over the goats and begged to be allowed to milk. I thought her small princess' hands would not be strong enough, but the strength of her will more than made up for any weakness. Then she gathered eggs with me and crowed so whenever she found one, you would have thought the eggs were made of gold and she herself had laid them. Without my asking her, she helped unload the cart.

The chores done, I packed some bread and cheese and a flask of wine for our journey, thinking at last we would start on our way, when a woman arrived at the clearing with a small boy who suffered from an abscessed sore on his foot, doubtless the result of a cut that had not healed properly. The sore was a hideous sight, and a foul smell issued from it. Marina, however, showed no sign of disgust but rather watched intently as I lanced the wound, cleansed it with wood spirit, and bound it with clean cloth. Nor did she seem bored as I gave the mother detailed instructions on how to care for the sore, bidding her return if it showed no sign of improvement in three days.

Shortly after they had gone, we ventured forth, taking a different path from the mother and child. For a time Marina was silent, a silence I'd come to recognize as a deceptive calm before a storm of questions.

"Why were that woman and boy so ragged and thin?" she asked. "Why did they wear no shoes?"

"Because they are poor folk," I answered. I reckoned in her life at the Castle poverty was something she might never have encountered face to face.

"Why are they poor?" she persisted. "What makes people poor?"

I considered several answers: some people are just born that way. It's the way of the world. We all have our station in life. Confronted with the stark sincerity of the child's question, I discarded these too-ready answers and

found myself explaining the conditions suffered by the villains and peasants, save for a few freemen, serfs all and bound to the land, land which
belonged to the King, land they must work, giving over most of its bounty
to the King for the keeping of his Castle and army.

Marina listened gravely, and when I had done, declared the arrangement
unjust. I did not know whether to applaud or reprove the child's precocity.
It occurred to me that I had never given the matter of justice much thought,
perhaps because I came of the lowly and landless myself and took poverty
for granted, or, more likely, because I had always been taken up with my
grievance against my own peculiar fate. To be sure, I had listened to grum-
blings against the rich all my life. But most common folk looked on the
nobility as a natural and inevitable force, inexplicably cruel or benevolent
like the weather.

I was still pondering the swift and incisive judgment of this young princess—who put me in mind of nothing so much as the boy Christ instruct-
ing his elders in the Temple—when Marina, her lively mind sprinting
ahead, beset me with another flurry of questions. Indeed, her questions
outnumbered the trees in the Wood—whose names she must know, likewise the names of all the creatures that dwelt in the Wood and their ways.
And whence the stream came and where it was going. And at least another
score of questions about the folk who sought me and what sorts of sick-
nesses did they have and how did I know which medicines to use and how
did I make them and could I teach her? Her questions massed themselves
in veritable constellations, like the starry host, which, fortunately, were not
visible during the day.

Though I loved her more every moment, I began to feel quite worn out
with her unflagging interest. I was unused to the rigors of such eager conversation. I wondered if my questions had likewise amused and fatigued the
Mother when I first came to learn from her. But I am sure I never asked so
many; nor were my questions so happy or innocent. I had been too angry
with what I will call life, for lack of a better word. Marina was plainly in
love with it, passionately.

To give myself respite, I questioned her from time to time. If some small,
mean part of me had hoped to hear that Marina was unhappy in her family,
it was given no encouragement. By her own account, Marina appeared to
be fond of her little brothers, and she took her mother's love so for granted
there was no cause for comment.

The King, I sensed, she did not like so well, largely because he had definite ideas of what young Princesses did and did not do, and these did not concur with Marina's. No one could prevent her learning to read and write, for she taught herself, but though she begged to be allowed to take lessons with the priest, who tutored her brothers in Latin and History, the King thought it unseemly. Nor was she trained in martial arts or statecraft. The latter omission surprised me, as she, the only legitimate issue, was to succeed to the throne. Apparently, while failing to gain the succession for his bastard sons, the King had established a condition for Marina's succeeding: that she marry a man of his choice to act as regent over her. I sensed, however, that marriage and monarchy had little meaning for Marina as yet.

Though she chafed at the restrictions placed on her, she managed to lead a merry life, evading, whenever possible, her mother and the other ladies, slipping away to the kitchen, where she enjoyed making puddings and cakes, or to the stables, where she assisted with the care and grooming of the horses. She was allowed to ride, though never alone and never far enough to suit her. I asked her what her mother did when she Marina shirked her needlepoint to consort with grooms and cooks, and she admitted that her mother would scold. Yet I gathered that Aurelie found it difficult to be angry with her daughter and inclined towards indulgence. She even, it seemed, conspired to keep the child's escapades from the King, protecting them both from his displeasure. Since I had abandoned my petty hope of finding fault with Aurelie, I was pleased to learn that she had spirit enough to defy the King's wishes, however covertly.

With all our chatter, the journey passed swiftly, and all at once, long before I was ready, we found ourselves nearing the edge of the Wood, near where I had first met the Prince. There was yet the river to cross. It could be forded here, but sensible grown person that I was, I would have suggested that we look for a shallower place where there were stepping stones. Before I could speak, Marina doffed her shoes and stockings with squeals of delight. There was nothing for it but to follow Marina's lead, though I did not relish the prospect of wading above my knees through frigid waters.

Once across, we sat upon some sun drenched rocks where I dried my legs with my skirts and swiftly donned my footgear. Marina preferred extending her bare legs in the breeze and wriggling her toes. Though we had less than an hour's walk to reach the Castle, I suggested we rest and eat, more out of desire to prolong the journey than because of hunger.

Marina readily agreed, and we ate and drank in surprising silence. Whether she was intent on her food or pondering what punishment might await her at home, I could not tell, but I was pleased to find her capable of quiet.

Myself, I made use of the silence to drink in Marina's presence, and the strong noonday light, the slope of the land, the curve of the rocks, the patterns that the bare trees made against the sky, the song of the Winter birds, the rush of the stream: all that surrounded us and held us together in this time, this place. Here, now, without a word, I greeted Marina and bade her farewell. I held her fast and let her go.

Marina continued to eat long after I had slaked my small appetite. At last there were only crumbs left, and not many of those. Marina made no move to rise. She, too, gazed about her, as if she understood the power of fine detail to call forth the fullness of memory.

"I will live in this Wood one day," she announced.

My heart leaped for joy, but a sterner part of me commanded it down, as if it were some foolish hound frantic to bestow slobbery kisses.

"A queen must live in her castle and reign over her people," I made myself reply.

Marina frowned for a moment, then brightened.

"But surely when I am queen I may do as I like. Although my mother does not," she considered, looking worried again. "I think she feels dull at times. You know she used to work in my grandfather's mill. I don't know why she wanted to come to the Castle when she could have lived in the village and run the mill. It must have been so much more interesting."

I remembered Aurelie weighing grain and flour on market day, her proud determination to claim her inheritance, and I had to agree with Marina.

"But then," added Marina, "my mother isn't really a queen, just a Consort."

That was the polite word for it, I thought to myself.

"And I will be a real queen." She paused. I wondered if she was brooding over the required husband. "Anyway, someday I shall do as I like, and I like being in the Wood. There are so many things to know about."

Marina's stated desire, though I reminded myself she was a child and changeable, was even my own. But there was no possibility of its ever being fulfilled.

"You know you may visit whenever you like, Marina." The words spoke themselves. Then, remembering how willful and independent she had proved herself to be, I felt compelled to add, "but please don't run away again. I am sure your mother is beside herself with grief and terror."

"Why, yes," said Marina with mild surprise, sweetly self-centered as only a well-loved child may be. "I suppose she is. Poor Mama."

With that we both rose to go. Soon we reached the fields that spread out from the Castle. Marina turned to bid the Wood farewell and would have embraced every tree in sight had I allowed her to. The prospect of the Castle subdued Marina to some degree, and, as we drew nearer, she looked as pensive as one could with such a lively face.

"I reckon I shall be beaten," she sighed with resignation and a trace of apprehension.

"As you richly deserve," I pointed out.

She did not argue, but a moment later her face brightened, and she turned to me.

"I still will have seen the Wood and you and your cave and the goats and how you popped that boy's sore. So it doesn't really matter if I'm beaten. I did what I wanted, and no one can make my adventure unhappen."

I did not know whether to reprove her utter lack of repentance or to applaud her astonishing grasp both simple and profound, of the very essence of freedom. Before I could decide, laughter overtook me. I shook with it all the rest of the way. Though I doubt she understood the cause of my mirth, Marina laughed, too. We arrived at the gate a mad and merry pair.

"Ho, Guard!" I shouted for the third time in my life, returning the very child I had once come to claim. The same man appeared, his insolent good looks had surrendered to time and doubtless drink. "Open at once for her Highness, the Princess Marina."

Immediately the gate opened, and Marina clutched my hand.

"Quickly, Daughter," I said, kneeling beside her. "We must say farewell. May we meet again one day."

Marina flung herself at me and gave me the warmest embrace I have ever known.

"Please, please, just come through the gate with me," she whispered. "Child, I have no place here—" I began, but I could not resist her plea or her surprising strength as she dragged me along after her. As we entered the courtyard, I saw Aurelie emerging from a doorway on the other side.

"Marina!"

There was no mistaking either the anguish or the joy in Aurelie's cry. Swiftly as a girl, she ran towards her daughter. Marina, dropping my hand as if it were a bunch of wildflowers she'd plucked then forgotten, sped to meet her mother.

You have no place here, I reminded myself, and yet I remained where I stood. Even as she reached Marina and clasped the child to her breast, Aurelie looked up at me. Our eyes met and held. Then, displaying the wisdom reputed to me, I turned and went my way.

As I walked across the fields, I wondered at my lightness of step. For had I not left a beloved child in the arms of a woman I had once despised? Yet this lightness. Nor was it lightness of foot alone. It dwelled in the very quick of me, and I grew great with light, as if I carried within the clean emptiness of sky.

I neared the edge of the Wood as the sun neared the edge of the world. The valley where the river ran was already in shadow. I crossed in a shallower place than we had earlier, stones and a fallen tree granting me dry passage. Here might I have crossed with the Mother long ago, though I could not be sure of the place in that waning light and with the changes time works even in the Wood.

As I climbed the gentler slope on the stream's other side, I felt the power of the Wood to transform time. Or maybe it was not the Wood: not the ancient or the new-sprung trees, neither the rocks nor their mute witness, not the generation and regeneration of wild creatures, but something within me, some imp that seized the one loose thread and tugged until time unraveled, the painstaking pattern, so tightly woven, reduced to a riot of loose wool. Nor were the colors fast, as all the moments of my life ran together, and the daughter and the mother, the lover and the hater met and mingled. And I was all of them at once and none of them at all as I walked the way each had come.

I crested the hill, and sun smote me with unclouded force. Instinctively I turned, and then I saw. O, Mother, is all magic but a trick of light? For light, I knew, had touched the trees and crowned the ridge with gold. And yet the magic seemed no less for being light. I stood carried by vision back across the valley, where golden branches stretched against the sky. I gazed until gold was all I knew.

Then memory, deep buried, rose. I heard once more the whir of the wheel.

In my left hand, the prickle of straw and, between the fingers of my right, the rough fibers twisted and turned to the strange, smooth warmth and cold of spun gold. Round and round spun the wheel, and its rhythm held the Mother's rhyme.

> *Take the dung and make it flower,*
> *Take the pain and make it power,*
> *Let your own fear make you bold,*
> *Take the straw and spin, spin, spin the gold.*

How many times had I heard that cursed, blessed rhyme and refused its meaning—save for moments, bright, brief as the fall of a star? Of late years I had ceased to ponder it, had all but forgotten it. Now here was the rhyme again: joyous, insistent. Transfixed, transformed in the heart of gold, I laughed, yes, laughed aloud at the grim tale I have told.

Light left the trees grey, then black against sudden stars. But the vision still illumined me as I made my way through the dusky Wood, wondering at the power, released at last through my open hands.

CHAPTER TEN

H AD I WAITED ONE MORE SEASON to take up once more this twice concluded tale, then there might have been no beginning. Mice, it seems, find parchment to their liking. Yet for this story to serve as the lining of nests for baby mice is a purpose not ignoble and perhaps more beneficial than the one I now contemplate. As to the wisdom of that purpose, I am of several minds. So let me begin at the beginning and write until my several minds are one.

I calculate some seven years have come and gone since the night I stayed awake to write a second ending to my tale. Do I now embark upon a third? No, I have grown wary of prophecy. Stories end, and so do lives, but if I would make of my life a story, I cannot hope to have the last word. Enough:

I am a wise woman, not a philosopher.

Suffice it to say these seven years have been peaceful enough for me and have even held some delightful surprises—such as when Gretal appeared, great with child and accompanied by a doting, if somewhat elderly, husband. Amelia, before what Gretal described as a peaceful death—so far as I can gather, her heart simply failed, and she died in her sleep—arranged a marriage for her with a prosperous widower, a spice merchant, offering the cloak, all the coins I had sewn into it untouched, as a dowry. Her last request of Gretal was that she seek my services as a midwife should she bear a child.

Gretal was old to bring forth a first-born, well past five and twenty. Yet she retained her childlike qualities, though I found her more given to talk than before, and I gladly listened to tales of her travels with Amelia while we awaited the birth. In due season, I had the pleasure of receiving into the world another Amelia; for so Gretal had named the sweet girl-child while she was yet in the womb, never doubting her sex. If Gretal's husband had wished for a son, I never knew it. The three of us vied with one another to hold the babe during the joyous interlude of Gretal's recovery. I felt so close to Gretal after delivering her child, I truly believe that had she asked my name, I would have told her. But she did not, and silence is the hardest habit to break.

As I have been about the business of birthing and healing, the King has seen fit to go to war again. Perhaps it is for that reason that Aurelie has borne no children after the last two, also boys, making six the number of her sons. Or maybe the change of life is upon her, even as it is upon me. The poor folk who seek my services know little of the war, except that it takes bread from their mouths and men from their fields. I have seen some starvation and much sickness and weakness. Because the mothers are so ill fed, many more babes than usual hardly live before they die. I do what I can. As I grow older, I need less food to sustain me, and so I always bring a cheese or a loaf or fresh eggs whenever I go to a birth or a sickbed. I have tried to teach folk what wild foods are good to eat. Times are hard.

As if food were not scarce enough, what with the peasants forced to feed the King's army, more than once a foreign army has passed through our land, ravishing the crops and emptying the granaries like a plague of locusts or rats. For the wars are to the South, and all the Kings of Christendom have ceased, for the moment, to war with one another that they might make war upon what they call the Infidel. Myself, I cannot believe that God makes such petty distinctions between mortal folk. I believe only a handful of priests pay more than lip service to the holiness of the cause.

As for our King, he has never been a pious man. He turns to war as another man might to a youthful mistress. He lusts to prove his waning prowess. He wars with his own mortality. Then, too, he presides over the rite of passage of his sons. A girl becomes a woman when her womb bleeds. Boys, too, it seems, must shed blood in order to become men. Or so their elders believe.

I have even found it in my heart to pity Aurelie. Her three oldest sons marched away with their father. Only two came back with him. For he has recently returned with spoils and riches from faraway lands hoping—vainly considering his impoverished kingdom—to refurbish his ragged army and to arrange the marriage of Aurelie's only true-born child with a wealthy monarch, once an enemy, from the kingdom over the mountains.

Save that unbeknownst to the King, Marina is with me, deep asleep on what was once the Mother's pallet, while I, no longer needing much sleep, pass yet another night writing by firelight. But I have gotten ahead of my story. First I must tell how she comes to be here.

She fled by night, as all respectable runaways do, using the very dungeon door that opens onto the moat by which I must have entered when I went with Gretal to answer Aurelie's summons. On the pretext of picking water lilies, she had paddled about the moat the day before, making fast a small boat to the iron ring. When on the night of her escape, she safely gained the other shore, she left the vessel hidden among the reeds and sped across the fields to the Wood. Very sensibly, she chose a moonless night, and the Watch did not spot her.

She spent the remainder of the night wandering uncertainly in the Wood—I must teach her how to navigate by the stars—only snatching a little sleep before dawn when she deemed she was deep enough in the Wood to be safe, for a time, from the earliest search parties. These, she reckoned, if all went well, should not even go abroad until after noontide. By midmorning she found me, having discovered and followed up current the brook that runs near my cave and, after a winding course, joins the river at the edge of the Wood.

I was just returning from gathering Dyer's Broom, it being late Summer, when Marina entered the clearing. I knew her at once, not only by the mark on her cheek but because she was no stranger to me. Though she had never, until now, returned to the Wood, she had visited me from time to time in my alley on festival days. Thus her radiant young womanhood, undimmed by the rigors of a sleepless night, was not such a shock as it might have been had I seen her last as a child. Yet for all the womanliness of her figure, her face was still elfin, even impish, as that of any naughty girl. She stood grinning at me from the other side of the clearing.

"Welcome, Daughter," I said, trying to imitate the Mother before me who always seemed to expect the unexpected.

Marina laughed, not in the least deceived, delighted with having surprised me. Then she bounded towards me, like a young deer, and fairly lifted me off my feet with her embrace. She had grown taller than I and very strong. When she had greeted as effusively all the animals and had inspected the den to make sure it was as she remembered—it was, save smaller, she remarked—I succeeded in getting her to sit down beside me with some food and drink, and I begged her, more abruptly than I intended, to state her purpose.

"It's very simple, Mother," she said after downing her ale all at once. "If you will have me, I mean to live with you and learn all you can teach me."

I was dumbfounded and managed no more than to open my mouth. Marina, mistaking my lack of response for lack of understanding, endeavored to make herself clearer.

"I want to learn about plants and animals. I want to learn the arts of dyeing and weaving. Most of all I want to learn about the sick people and how to heal them. And I want to know all about their lives when they're not sick, too."

She fell silent, plainly waiting for an answer from me. I remembered all the times I had waited in vain for answers from the Mother, and all the times she had answered my questions with questions. Well, a little silence, as I gathered my thoughts, would do Marina no harm. If she meant to live with me, she must grow accustomed to silence, for, to my surprise, silence had become my natural element. Yet I must find words now.

As I waited for them to form, I pondered on the Mother, on Marina, on myself. The Mother and I had served the same people, borne the same image. Most folk had made little or no distinction between us. For the image of the Mother was immortal. Yet the untold differences were telling. The Mother's first love had been the animals and the plants, tending them. My chief delight had always been the making of fabric; spinning, dying, weaving. Only in these pursuits do I lose the discomfiting sense of not being what I appear to be, for then my being and doing form a unity. Now here was Marina, wanting most of all to know the people I have always dreaded, even as I served them and, in some instances, have come to admire or care for them.

Then, suddenly, I stopped my thoughts in their tracks, horrified to find myself casting Marina as my successor. I must not presume. Image-bearers are chosen, the Mother had told me—but not by their predecessors. Nor would I even wish to impose on Marina an image I had so often found confining. But perhaps, I considered, images are not immortal. Maybe they, too, must die—or be transformed. How could I tell? I only knew that more than anything, I desired Marina to be wholly free.

"What makes you long for this learning, Daughter? What will you do with it if you make it yours?"

I was pleased to see that she took time to think before she answered.

"As for why I want to learn, since I can remember I have always wanted to know about everything. I don't know why. I just have."

I smiled in recollection of the child Marina's unnumbered questions.

"For the rest, I cannot honestly say what I will do with the learning, save that I will try to use it for good. I've never forgotten about that boy and his mother, watching you lance his wound. That was the first time I ever thought about there being people who didn't live in the Castle.

"When the wars came, I wanted desperately to go with my brothers. Of course, I was forbidden. It's not that I wanted to fight. I've not been trained, and I don't fancy killing anyone, even Infidel. But I wanted to see the world, and I thought maybe I could help care for the wounded, though, to be sure,

I've no training for that either. Indeed, I reckon I would have been useless, and I don't want to be useless.

"But, in truth, beyond seeking you, I have no plan, I don't know what will become of me. I guess I had better tell you: I've run away again."

"Yes, I think you had better."

CHAPTER ELEVEN

MARINA BEGAN BY TELLING ME of the king to whom her grandfather meant to marry her.

"He's old! Older than my mother, though not so old as the King. He is said to be handsome, for an old man, but there's something about his eyes. They make me think of the moat when it's all overgrown with slime. I suppose they might have wed me to his son, but his only son was killed when they fought that war before I was born. Since then he's had three wives, the last one dead but a year, and they've brought him only daughters. There are plans to wed my brothers to some of them. With all those marriages, the kingdoms would be well-knit, and I am told that would be for the good. I know, too, that it is my duty to think of the good. I reckon I am very wicked and selfish.

"But I cannot bear the thought of what my life would be. I would be, in name, the Queen of one realm and heir to another, but I would have only as much power as I could win from my husband with my womanly wiles. I don't even know if I have wiles. You would think I'd have learned by now from watching my mother with the King. She pouts or seduces, wears him down one way or another, and it's true she's kept him in love with her; he's never looked at another woman, let alone taken a mistress. But what my mother usually wants is a banquet or some fine cloth or a new jewel. What I would want would be to lower the grain tax, to make treaties instead of wars—what would be called meddling in affairs of state."

Marina rested a moment from her impassioned speech.

"And what of your mother, Marina? Does she know where you've gone?" Marina looked up at me and smiled a smile that could keep the wide world warm in deep Winter. Then she told, what was to me, the most wondrous part of her tale.

"You know I love my mother. I truly do. You mustn't think that I don't, even though I don't believe I could ever be like her. Let me tell you what transpired between my mother and me.

"It was after the banquet—such as it was; even Castle fare is scanty in these times—at which I was first presented to King Harold. At last the long evening was over. I was alone in my small chamber, having sent away Sally—she is my maid, and she is supposed to help undress me, but mostly we just chatter away like any two friends. Only that night I felt too angry and despairing to speak.

"I sank down on the window seat and looked out into the night but could find no comfort there. It was foggy. I could see nothing, not one star, only now and again a blur of light when the Watch went past. It struck me then that I was looking at my own life, and I could not see myself or anything else in it. Not if I submitted to the King's arrangements. I felt I would just sputter and then be utterly extinguished, like a flame drowned in wax.

"I don't know if Sally spoke to my mother or if she just knew. Suddenly she was there. Her hand was on my hair—so lightly—not like a breeze, more like sunlight. Only my mother has that touch.

"'Go away and leave me alone,' I snarled.

"I often do that, get angry with her for what the King does, angry with her for loving him. Of course she didn't go away. That's another thing about my mother. She knows exactly how much I mean and how much I don't mean what I say. It's lovely to have someone know that, but it turns me into a baby again, and I don't want to be a baby anymore.

"'I will not marry King Harold, Mother,' I said, trying to sound calm, so she would not treat me as a spoiled and petulant child.

"She sat down beside me on the window seat and spoke just as calmly. 'My darling girl, I fear you must. The King wishes it. It's all arranged.'

"'No, Mother. I have not given my consent. Nor will I. If no one listens to me before then, I will refuse at the very altar of God. Wilt thou have this man to be thy wedded husband? No, I will not. Neither the powers of Heaven nor Hell can make me.'

"I turned to look at her, willing her to believe me, not to seek to persuade or placate me. She looked back at me and sighed.

"'You were always a wild and willful child, Marina, and I fear it's my own fault. So the King often tells me. I could never bring myself to be strict with you. In my heart I rejoiced in your free ways. But it was wrong of me, Marina, grievously wrong. It's not a free world, not for women.'"

For a moment, listening to these words of Aurelie's, I felt indignant. No one had had a more indulgent parent or been freer or more willful than Aurelie as a child. But then, I reminded myself, it was her father's excessive fondness and pride that finally trapped her.

"'Do not think I have no sympathy for you, dearest child,' my mother added, 'But you must not defy the King. God help me, I love him, too, and I know him. He will destroy you if you oppose him openly. Listen, Daughter, women's power lies not in defiance or challenge. We are not the warriors. We are not the hunters. We are like the wild creatures, the prey. Our defense is in disguise. You must pretend you have no desire but your Lord's. You must seem to submit. Let him be convinced that he is in command. Then he will cease to keep watch, and you can go about your own affairs. In time you can go about his affairs, too, if that's what you want. You will see, Marina. You're a clever girl—'

"'No!'

"'Marina!'

"'No, Mother. To even seem to submit would be death to me.'

"'Marina, be sensible. All girls are afraid of marriage. Almost no one marries for love. You are making too much of this.'

"'No, Mother. I swear it. If I marry King Harold, I will die inside. I will not exist anymore. Do you understand? I will not exist! I would rather the King kill me outright.'

"'I'm still not sure what it was I said that touched her, but when she spoke again her manner was changed.

"'If you would not marry, Marina, what is it you would do?'

"'I did not answer my mother right away, for I knew what I said might determine my fate; nor did I know at once. I gazed out the window again, and then, before my eyes, the darkness lightened and took shape. I saw the dance of flame on the walls of your cave and you bending over the fire to stir a pot. Then I saw the goats and the chickens and the deep Wood surrounding the clearing and the plants waiting to yield their secrets and the people braving the Wood to seek healing. At last I saw myself, sitting on a low stool at your feet.

"'I turned to my mother.

"'I would go to the Wise Woman of the Western Wood. I would learn Wisdom.'

"'My mother did not say anything for a long time, not with words, but her whole face was speaking, if only I could have understood. There is something between the two of you, I'll swear it, but she won't tell me what it is, and I'll wager you won't either. No two women could be more different than you and my mother—save in the way you keep your secrets. Finally, after what seemed an age, she spoke.

"'Daughter.' She sounded so solemn, almost like you. 'If this is your heart's true desire, then I will help you.'

"'All at once I felt frightened. She was letting me go, not just allowing me to go to you in the Wood, but letting-me-go. I wanted to bury myself in her arms and be her baby girl again, but somehow I held myself in check.

She began speaking in a low tone, telling me about a dungeon door that gave unto the moat. I wondered how she knew about it but did not think to ask. Soon our plans were laid. We stared at one another in awe of ourselves until, at the same moment, we burst into tears and sobbed in one another's arms.

"But, Mother,' I asked at last, 'what will you do if the King finds out your part in this plot?'

"Then she smiled, and I could not tell if her smile was sad or tender.

"If we are clever enough, he will not find out. And I confess I am no stranger to the art of deception. If he does ...' She shrugged. 'Well, the King has long known and loved me for a liar. I will have to trust that he will love me a little longer.'

I did not know precisely what she meant by that, nor was she disposed to explain.

"What will you tell him if he presses you?'

"That you ran away to the Holy Land. It's common knowledge you were hot to see the wars.'

"But won't he suspect where I really am? Surely he knows of the Wise Woman?'

"I would guess that he knows less of her than the least of his subjects. As for me, I have told him nothing. Nothing.'

"Then she smiled another of those mysterious smiles.

And so," Marina ended her tale, "here I am. With my mother's blessing. I lack only yours. Oh, say you will let me—But, Mother, why do you weep? Is anything wrong?"

"No, Daughter. No, nothing is wrong. It's the rightness has undone me."

Marina sighed. "I don't suppose you will tell me what you mean by that."

Already she was learning.

"No, I don't suppose I shall, but with all my heart I welcome you, Marina, and I will gladly teach you all I know that can be taught."

"Which means there is more can't be. Ah, but, Mother, that is what I want most to learn. That quality in you. Sometimes I call it peace. Sometimes I call it power—the thing that lives in your silence. But I doubt I'll ever learn it. It's not in my nature. I'm too wild and restless. No doubt it is something you are born with or not. I'll wager you were always this way."

I could not keep myself from bursting into laughter, merry laughter, and in it I heard the echoes of the Mother's laughter at my younger self. But where the younger me had sulked, Marina had the grace at least to smile in her perplexity.

"Well-a-day, my girl, forgive a cackling old witch. Up then, and you will begin your quest for wisdom with the brewing of green dye."

We spent the rest of the day in such mundane pursuits. At first I feared Marina might be disappointed, as I had been as a girl, in the homely nature of these lessons. But Marina's curiosity proved to be much livelier than mine had ever been, and she was thus more easily intrigued.

I wondered, as the day wore on, could I choose to be a less mysterious tutor than the Mother? Might I share with Marina the story of my life? Marina's remarks about my peaceful nature had so startled me, they made me consider the Mother in a new light. Like Marina, I had been certain that the Mother was born at peace. Would it have helped me to hear her story? The Mother's voice sounded within me: "I have known all passions in their season." Had I believed her? Even now I could scarcely imagine that the Mother's life might have been as full of strife as mine.

What to do with this tale I have told? That is the question I set forth to answer this night. I think I shall put it away for a time and let the mice decide its fate.

One thing only do I know: soon, very soon, I shall tell my name, at last, to Marina. For in my name is the story gathered and complete, beautiful beyond my deserving.

CPSIA information can be obtained at www.ICGtesting.com
Printed in the USA
LVOW082003130612

285920LV00002B/100/P